He went into the dining room, seated himself and absently picked up the morning paper, which was folded beside his plate. He opened it and then sat as though frozen. Under his eyes ran the heavy black letters.

BEAUTIFUL YOUNG SOCIALITE MURDERED. Mrs. Paula Ruston, former wife of Fred Ruston, famous polo player, found dead in her apartment by her maid shortly after midnight. Death apparently due to strangulation. Police are working already upon certain clues . . .

For a minute he could not speak but sat staring unbelievingly at the page before him. Then, "My God! My God!" he kept repeating in an anguished voice. "Paula! Murdered! Why, it can't be! I was there myself until nearly midnight!"

Fawcett Crest Books
by Agnes Sligh Turnbull:

THE WEDDING BARGAIN
MANY A GREEN ISLE
WHISTLE, AND I'LL COME TO YOU
THE FLOWERING

AGNES SLIGH TURNBULL

THE
WEDDING
BARGAIN

A FAWCETT CREST BOOK

Fawcett Publications, Inc., Greenwich, Conn.

For Roxane O'Hearn

THE
WEDDING
BARGAIN

CHAPTER I

It was the breaking of the cup which caused her final decision. The delicate bit of Sevres that fell upon the kitchen tile with a light tinkling crash was precious, though certainly not irreplaceable. It was Eliza Hanford's unsteady hand after a night, wakeful with emotional stress, which caused her to say now, "That settles it. I'll tell him this morning." She spoke aloud, although no one else was in the apartment, then she stood looking down at the frail white pieces of china on the floor as though they were parts of a heart, drained of all blood, and broken.

She brushed up the fragments, got another cup and poured herself some coffee. The toast was hard to swallow, but she managed a little, watching the clock as she did every morning since punctuality was an absolute and not a relative quality in the eyes of Daniel Morgan, her employer. Before her bureau glass she carefully put the last touches to her toilette: the very faintest color on her lips, making them look not painted but merely healthy; a tiny extra hairpin in the tendril that always persisted in straying free from the severity of the coiled braids around her head. Mr. Morgan did not like make-up and what he termed "mussy hair-dos." Her tailored dark suit and white blouse had become a sort of office uniform over the years. *The years!*

She stopped, staring at the calendar on the wall. It portrayed a familiar Vermont scene which Aunt Sarah had sent down to her to keep her from getting homesick in New York, she had said. There were the towering green crested mountains, rock-ribbed and ancient as the sun; there was the gentle, meandering stream that ran under the covered bridge; there was the white church steeple nestling among the trees just beyond—all with an affectionate childhood familiarity to

Eliza. But at this moment her eyes were not upon the features of the landscape, they were fixed instead with something like horror upon the black figures above them. *Nineteen thirty-five,* they read with unmistakable clarity. The years, she repeated to herself. There had been eight of them.

It was when she was twenty-two, fresh from college where she had been wise enough to perfect her typing and learn shorthand on the side, since she knew she must earn her living and thought she would prefer the business world to teaching, she had heard of a position. It was the older sister of her roommate who was giving it up to be married and gladly supplied details.

"It's worth going after, Liza. He's the hardest block of granite outside the state of Vermont or maybe I should say lump of coal out of Pennsylvania, since that's his business. He hardly ever smiles, he works you hard as the devil but he's unfailingly decent and he pays top salary. You have to dress like a nun, no curls, no make-up. He's odd but if you can stand him, and if it's money you're interested in . . ."

It was. Eliza had dressed for the part and gone for an interview. It was still vivid in her memory. Mr. Morgan had looked at her gravely, consideringly, from behind his big desk while he held his chin cupped in one hand.

"Your appearance is satisfactory," he pronounced at last.

Liza smiled faintly. She was too frightened to speak.

"I don't like any fuss or feathers at work," he added. "Also there is no familiarity in this office. I do not approve of the modern use of first names between employer and employees. I treat my secretary with respect and wish to receive the same. So, you're a college graduate?" He glanced down at her application.

"Yes, as of this June."

"Your major?"

"English."

"Ah! I've been wanting someone who has a secure grip on the English tongue. How's your shorthand?"

"I'm fairly good, I think, but I know I could improve with daily practice."

"Uhm'm. Take a test letter." He pushed a tablet and pencil toward her and began. He spoke fast but distinctly, and while her fingers felt stiff she kept up with him. At several points he paused saying, "Just complete that sentence in the conventional way."

When she read it back to him, he nodded. "Not bad. Would you like to try the job for a month? If at the end of that time either of us is not satisfied we'll call it quits and you will have an extra month's salary. Agreed?" He named the figure.

"I'm agreed," she said, a little breathlessly.

"Can you start tomorrow?"

"Yes, I can."

"Be here at a quarter to nine." He raised a finger. "And I mean *exactly* that. By the way, your first name, Eliza, pleases me. God knows I've had enough Shirleys and Adeles and Maralyns applying. Eliza sounds sensible."

He gave her a curt nod of dismissal and picked up the phone. Eliza, somewhat dazed, left, passing interested glances from those in the next office as she went. She even overheard one whispered comment. "Well, he didn't take this one either, from her expression."

But they were wrong. He had not only taken her, he had kept her for eight years. Now she was on her way to announcing to him that she could work for him no longer. And not for all the tea in China could she tell anyone, least of all him, why she was leaving.

She glanced now around the small domain which she had made into a pleasant nest for herself, wondering if it would ever seem the same to her after this day. Once out on the sidewalk she found her legs as unsteady as her hands, so hailed a taxi and was soon going through the revolving door of the familiar building, going up in the elevator, passing through the outer offices with the usual greetings to those already there, pausing before the door marked *Private* until her watch showed the exact quarter of the hour and then, with a fast-beating heart, going inside.

Mr. Morgan did a strange thing. He rose as she entered, looking at her with a peculiar expression. Could he, she wondered, by some telepathic exchange of thought have divined what was in her mind? He said good morning also, which he did not always do. Very often in answer to her greeting he said merely, "We have a busy morning ahead, Miss Hanford.

Let's get to work." Now he crossed to the door, opened it and spoke to Miss Ross who sat just outside.

"Please don't put any calls through to me, no matter what they are. I don't want to be interrupted for any reason *whatever,* until I tell you."

"Very good, Mr. Morgan."

He closed the door and came back to his desk. Eliza started to speak but he silenced her with a wave of his hand.

"I want to talk to you first, Miss Hanford, if you don't mind, on a very personal matter. I hardly know how to begin, but at least you already know one of the big problems of my life. Women. You've handled a lot of social stuff for me, gotten me out of corners a good many times, but the trouble persists. I certainly am not vain enough to think I'm being pursued for *myself,* but a single man with money is fair game for designing mothers and a certain type of girl, and the widows—oh Lord, they're the worst! Well, I'm sick of the whole business. I have an unlisted phone and still they get to me. I've been edged into a few unpleasant situations and I'm not going to put up with it any longer. It's been borne in upon me lately that the only real cure for me is to get married."

Eliza's heart turned over. "So," she thought. "I'm now to find him a wife. Well, that is one thing I *will not do!*"

"You see," he was going on, "the situation is this. I do want to marry for the reason I've given, but I'm not in love with anyone. Don't believe I could be. All the romance was knocked out of me long ago. I may have told you I started working in the mines when I was twelve. To get to be an operator and make a fortune was all I thought of. Hard work and a lot of luck helped. Now it seems as though all I have to offer a woman is the money, and one that was merely mercenary, you see, I wouldn't want. So, well, what I'm leading up to, Miss Hanford, is this. Would *you* consider marrying me?"

Eliza sat as still as death while she felt her face grow scarlet and then drain of color.

"Don't say anything yet," he went on. An unnecessary admonition, as she couldn't have spoken if she had tried. "There is more I have to say in order to be honest. You see, I don't like the idea of giving up my freedom. I've been a lone

wolf too long. I would expect, of course, to have a very nice
home outside the city as most of the people I know do, but
I'd also expect to keep my own apartment here and stay in it
whenever I wanted, for a few days, a week, whatever, and
have no questions, no reproaches, no *comments* even from a
wife. And no tears. I've heard women cry a lot to gain their
points. Good heavens, I couldn't stand that!"

He paused for a moment while Eliza studied his face. The
marks of his long struggle were on it: deep lines on either
side of his mouth; a sharpness in his shrewd gray eyes; an
intensity in the strong features; a dash of white here and
there in the thick dark hair and a faint overall suggestion of
age beyond his forty-five years.

"I've got Dunmore trained pretty well, now. I can once in
a while take some pleasure in my own way. So, if I decided
to go off to shoot lions in Africa, I would expect no domestic
restraint whatsoever. To sum the whole thing up I would
want the advantages of being married, as I mentioned at the
beginning, without giving up anything myself."

For a few seconds they sat, looking at each other and then,
almost roughly, he said, "Miss Hanford, I had thought this
over, of course, but I didn't realize how it would all sound
until I spoke those last words. I think the proposition I just
made you is actually insulting and I hope you'll excuse me. It
was an impulsive thing to do and I'm ashamed of it. So, just
forget it and let's get on now with the morning's work."

He was pulling a sheaf of letters toward him when Eliza
found her voice.

"Mr. Morgan, I would like a little time to think over your
offer."

He leaned across the desk, his face one mask of amazement.

"You mean you will really *consider* it?"

"Yes. Tomorrow morning I'll give you my answer."

"*Tomorrow morning!* Surely you'll want to wait longer
than that before you decide."

Eliza smiled faintly. "That will be long enough. You've
made your points very clearly. One thing, though, you didn't
mention. Since this would be a marriage of convenience, did
you mean it would also be what I believe is called a 'marriage in name only?' "

He looked off over her head. "Well, no," he said slowly, "I didn't mean that, I guess. It might not be fair to either of us. Perhaps the blood doesn't run as hotly through my veins as that of many men, but I'm still a perfectly normal human being, if that answers your question?"

"Yes. Thank you. I do have a favor to ask. Could Miss Ross take over now if I go home for the day? I felt a bit queer this morning and now after this conversation . . ."

"I don't wonder. I must have startled you. You do look white round the gills. Can you make it back all right alone?"

"Oh, yes. I'll take a taxi."

"I'll have one called." He got up and walked toward the door with her. "There is this that I should have added for what it is worth, in regard to my feelings. I *respect* you," he said, "very deeply."

She didn't answer, only held out her hand. He looked as though surprised at the gesture but took the small palm in his own large one and held it for a moment, then opened the door.

"Miss Ross!" His voice was crisp as usual. "Will you come in here at once, please. I'll need you today. Miss Hanford isn't well. And see that someone calls a cab for her."

Eliza went through the outer office as quickly as she could. The girls were all concerned about her.

"Liza! You look as though you'd seen a ghost."

"I've got some aspirin. Hadn't you better sit down . . ."

"For *you* to get sick is unheard of. Hadn't one of us better go along home with you?"

She got away and into the waiting taxi. When she reached her apartment she sank down in a chair and relaxed all control. The tears came, not a gentle flow but a flood, and sobs with them. The tension of years was broken and not even till now had she realized how great this had been. To sit across from him day after day, watching every lineament of his face, every movement of his hands, hearing every changing tone of his voice while loving him as she did, while feeding her starving heart on crumbs: the rare smile, the occasional, "Very good, Miss Hanford"—this had demanded a self-control like steel. And now there was no more need for it. She could give way completely while her brain repeated the incredible fact, that she was to be *his wife!* For of course there was nothing to consider. She had specified a night to think it over to save her pride. She could have answered as soon as he finished speaking, "Yes, yes, I will marry you on any terms whatsoever!"

When at last the tears eased a little she stumbled into the bedroom, kicked off her pumps, flung herself, still dressed, upon the bed and was almost instantly asleep. It was dark when she woke, and for a few moments she was confused. Why waken in darkness? Why in bed fully clothed? What was the strange news she had heard? And then quickly and clearly it all came back. And with the realization a warmth, new and delicious, ran through her veins. She got up at last and slowly, smiling all the while, prepared some dinner. She ate ravenously, a thing she had not done for months, then with paper and pencil sat down in deep concentration. Once in a while she would stretch her arms above her head, her lips parted as if in an inner rapture, then, picking up the pencil, go on making notes.

The next morning as she passed through the next-to-inner office the girls already there fell upon her.

"Liza Hanford, you've got a *dress* on!"

"We had bet you didn't own anything but black suits. Girls, she's blushing!"

"I see it all now," said Miss Ross, pontifically. "I'll bet you came in yesterday to resign. Right?"

"Right," said Liza.

"And he raised the devil and you left, white as a sheet and now you're going back, tail up, to tell him you're going *to get married anyway*. Right?"

"Right," said Eliza laughing. "That is, for the most part."

She opened the door marked *Private* and went in, leaving the girls chattering. Mr. Morgan rose behind the desk and watched her gravely. He must be noticing her smart green dress, the pearl beads, the added lipstick, she thought. Her long relaxed sleep had given her cheeks warm color and she knew that she not only looked well, but different from other days.

"Good morning, Miss Hanford."

"Good morning, Mr. Morgan."

They both sat down and then Liza smiled directly into his eyes. "I have thought it over carefully and I've decided to accept your offer of marriage," she said.

"You have! Of course I *hoped,* but I hardly thought it was possible you would. Well, that's very good. We can call it settled then."

"Not quite yet," she said. "I have some conditions, too."

His eyes narrowed. "Conditions?" he asked, a faint displeasure in his tone.

"*You* gave a number, you know," she said steadily.

"That's true. I did. Well, let's hear yours."

Liza drew a piece of paper from her bag and began.

"First of all, I would like a really beautiful engagement ring."

To her amazement he threw back his head and laughed as she had never heard him before. When he could speak he said, "So you thought you had to ask me for *that?*"

"Well," Liza returned, "if this had been a normal proposal I certainly would not have mentioned a ring at all. But as it is . . ."

"All right," he said. "First condition accepted. You can scratch that one out."

"Then I would like you to bring the ring to my own apartment."

"That would be proper. Agreed."

"And I would want some little time for the engagement. A girl likes to collect her clothes. Also I have quite a few college friends, married and otherwise, living around here. There will be some luncheons and girls' parties, I'm sure. This may seem very trivial to you, but I don't want to miss all this."

He was grave as he studied her. "No," he said, "you shouldn't. How long a time would you want?"

"Oh, a few weeks . . . whatever you would feel was best."

"Three, four, five?"

"Four would be enough."

"Agreed," he said again.

"Now perhaps the last conditions are the hardest. I would want to be married in a church."

He drew his brows ominously.

"All the big churches have small chapels," she hurried on.

"One of these would be perfect. I would like to invite a few friends and surely you would. Everything very simple, but correct."

"I had certainly not thought of any religious ceremony," he said slowly. "I imagined under the circumstances, we'd just go to a magistrate . . . You feel strongly about this church business?"

"Very."

"Well, I suppose I can go along with that. Any more?"

"Just two. I'm almost afraid to speak of the next one, and you mustn't take it too seriously. But I've never been abroad and I'd love to go for a trip after our marriage. It wouldn't need to be long. Just a glimpse of Paris and a little of England . . . Would this be *possible?*" Her voice was pleading.

"That's no way to state a *condition,*" he smiled. "But yes. This is about the easiest of all for I always have business to do over there. I'll get a sailing arranged right away after we set the date. Anything more on your list?"

Liza folded her paper and put it back in her bag. "Yes," she said. "I want to have my hair cut."

"You *what?*"

"Just that. I've been thinking about it for quite a while. You know most of the girls now are having their hair bobbed. Matt Harvey has hers done and looks lovely. But with me it's not just style. My hair is very heavy and just brushing it at night is a chore. I would be *so* much more comfortable with it short. I know you spoke once quite bitterly about women cutting off their 'crowning glory' but I'd really like to do it."

"But I like it the way you wear it!"

Liza made no reply and he sat with his underlip drawn over his upper, as he had a habit of doing when thinking.

"Would you be willing to compromise on this last 'condition'?" he asked.

"I . . . I suppose so."

"Wait for two months before you have it cut, then do as you please."

"Very well," she answered slowly, her disappointment visible. "I'll try to put up with it that much longer."

"About the ring. Will you take time to go up to Tiffany's soon and ask for this man." He scribbled a name on a piece of paper and slid it over to her. "I know him. He'll measure your finger and I'll have the ring by Saturday evening. Oh, let me have your address, by the way. And phone number too."

She gave them and then he sat pondering. "This ought to be announced. Have you any family?"

"Just the aunt who brought me up. She's a great-aunt, really."

"Could we use her name?"

"Of course. I'll call her up tonight. She's Miss Sarah Hanford, of Waverly, Vermont."

He wrote the words carefully. "I'll have it put in next Saturday's papers. Well, I think we've covered a good deal of ground. Now, let's get to work."

"How much longer do you want me to come back?"

He groaned. "That's what's worrying me. I'm paying a big price for getting married. I'll be losing my right hand here in the office."

"You can still change your mind," she said gravely.

He gave her a sharp look as though to detect levity, but there was none.

"I don't change my mind easily," he said. "Could you finish out this week? Then I'll use Miss Ross. She's pretty good, but . . ." He left the sentence hanging.

At the end of the day—and it was a hard one—Liza rose to go. He did not offer to walk her to the door as he had done the afternoon before. She paused now.

"This is certainly not a *condition,* Mr. Morgan, but I was thinking that during our engagement if we could go out occasionally, to dinner, the theater, anything, we might have a chance to get to know each other better."

"You think we don't know each other now?" He sounded amazed.

"Just the *office* side of each of us."

"Well, I'll call for you at quarter to seven then Saturday evening, for dinner, and I'll pick up some tickets for a show. But Miss Hanford!" He raised a finger and his face looked stern. "There is one thing I must emphasize again. You are quite a bit younger than I am. Most girls, I'm sure, want *romance* in a marriage. I've tried to make it plain that I can't give you that. I don't want you to be disappointed. You must look this whole thing squarely in the face and back out now, if you want to. I'll certainly not hold it against you."

Liza looked at him steadily. "I don't change my mind easily, either, Mr. Morgan," she said, and turned toward the door.

When she had almost reached it he got up hastily and overtook her.

"About your hair," he said. "If you've disliked it so much this way, why didn't you have it cut before?"

She smiled. "I didn't want to jeopardize my job. I've liked working for you and I've tried hard to please you."

"But you're not going to try to any longer?"

"Of course I am! Surely you know that. But I felt your ideas on hairdressing applied to your secretary especially. You as much as said so. I thought perhaps as your . . . as your . . ."

She didn't say the word and neither did he. "I thought later, you might not mind."

"And if I do?" he persisted.

"Are we going to leave the *obey* in the marriage service?" she said with a twinkle.

"I don't care."

"Neither do I. Well, I'll wait the two months anyway. Good-night, Mr. Morgan."

"Good-night, Miss Hanford."

When she reached her apartment Liza was not as relaxed as she had been the night before nor, it must be admitted, quite as radiantly happy. Not that she had the slightest idea of changing her mind as he had suggested. Deep within her was her passionate love of him. But she realized now, with cool appraisal, how strange her married life might be. He had meant exactly what he had said. He did not love her; he did not want either his emotions or his routine of years to be disturbed seriously. In the fine house he would buy for her, she would probably be often alone, and she could never resent this, for with a brutal honesty he had pointed out that he expected to take what he needed from their relationship and give as little as possible, *except the money*. And she could not tell him how little she cared for that nor how much she cared for him.

All during the evening as she tried to concentrate only
upon the pleasures in store: telling the news to her friends,
being feted as a bride-to-be, buying clothes, going abroad—
the disturbing thoughts crept in. What, for example, did she
know of his private life up to this time? What of those bitter
years of his youth when his ambition had driven him so mer-
cilessly? She knew nothing, she had to admit, nothing. And
his knowledge of her was as scanty. Have you any family? he
had asked. Imagine a man of his age marrying a girl to
whom he could put such a question! Over all the eight years,
in spite of their daily proximity, they had each maintained a
dignified and personal reserve.

She knew that the elderly Mrs. Francis Moreland, who had
inherited coal interests, had taken him up when he had first
come to New York and introduced him to her own social
group. "I owe a great deal to her," he had said once, briefly.
"She rubbed the rough edges off me." It had been through
this connection that he had met the mothers, the daughters,
the young widows or divorcees who had marked him for
their own.

She suddenly went to the telephone and put in a call to
Aunt Sarah, her lips relaxing in a little smile as she did so.
She waited eagerly for a voice. When it came it was that of
the housekeeper, Mrs. Phinney.

"Oh, it's you, Liza. Miss Hanford will be pleased. Just a
minute."

Then Aunt Sarah's voice, firm and decided in spite of her
seventy-six years.

"Well, Liza, what have *you* been up to?"

"You'd never guess. I've gotten myself engaged."

"It's about time. Who's the man?"

"My employer, Daniel Morgan."

"Highty-tighty! Not that millionaire?"

"I guess he's that and more."

"Well, is he a steady, decent fellow? With all that money
. . . He's not *wild?*"

Liza laughed. "Far from it. I would say he's quite conservative. We're using your name in the papers if it's all right
with you. *Miss Sarah Hanford announces* et cetera. You
don't mind?"

"Well, how can I tell when I haven't met him? I trust your

judgment, though, and you're old enough to have some sense. You're not marrying him for his money, are you?"

"No, I am not. Can you keep a secret?"

"I've kept a few in my time."

"Well, I've been in love with him for years."

"So? And he's just now got around to asking you? I'd say he is conservative. When will you bring him up?"

"I hope for a weekend fairly soon. We plan to be married in about a month here in New York. A very small wedding in a church chapel . . . we haven't settled the details."

"Well, small or large, I'm coming to it. Child, are you happy?"

"Very."

"Well, that's all that matters. Let me know before you come, and blessings on you. I know I won't sleep a wink tonight. Good-bye. This telephone bill will be big enough by now."

"Good-bye, Aunt Sarah. You'll hear from me soon."

By six o'clock Saturday evening Liza was ready. She had run out in the late afternoon to get a few flowers. None had come as she had been rather hoping they might. She surveyed her living room critically. There was the rose satin sofa and chair, redone from Aunt Sarah's attic; there were other antiques of charm she had picked up in the city over the years, the desk, the highboy, the clock—these all with her books and minor adornments made an inviting setting. She had studied herself even more critically earlier. Her mirror had given her back a rather serious-looking young woman with good coloring, eyes that matched the sapphire blue dress she was wearing, brownish blond hair in braided coils as usual but farther back now on her head, leaving a softness to frame the face, and a cleft chin which added a piquant touch to the other features.

"I'm pretty," she had announced aloud in spite of Aunt Sarah's Spartan New England upbringing. "I am really, and I'd be an awful fool not to admit it."

She needed no rouge but she applied lipstick with generous care as she always did when not in the office, laid out her squirrel jacket, thinking as she did so, that probably, *incredibly,* she would later on be clad in mink—and finally sat down to await the bell. When it rang she rose to greet her guest with a heart that bade fair to jump out of her breast. She felt, she was thinking, just as Columbus must have done as he set forth upon an unknown and uncharted sea.

When she opened the door her eyes widened in surprise. At her suggestion they had dressed, since, as she said, it was an important occasion. He had not demurred so this was the first time she had seen him in dinner clothes and the effect was startling.

"Good evening," she said, adding impulsively, "You look very handsome, I must say."

He had been eying her. "So do you. I mean, very pretty. What have you done to yourself?"

"Oh, a little more lipstick, maybe. Have we time to sit down for a few minutes?"

"I'm afraid not if we're to get to the show on time." He glanced about. "This is a very attractive room you have here."

"I'm glad you like it. I've had fun over the years fixing it up. I'll get my jacket."

"Wait. I thought you would want to wear this tonight." He drew a small box from his inner pocket and placed it in her hand.

She opened it. An enormous solitaire diamond caught the light. She looked at it for the moment speechless. "It's . . . it's unbelievable!" she stammered at last. "I've never seen anything so beautiful. Oh, how can I ever thank you?"

"I'm glad it pleases you. After all I did have to live up to the *condition*, didn't I?"

Her face turned crimson.

"I'm so terribly ashamed of what I said. But don't you see how it was? I was afraid you would feel an engagement ring might be superfluous, too, too romantic, somehow. You do understand, don't you?"

"Of course. I was only joking. I can assure you that you didn't affect my selection in the least. And now I think we'd better start. You can never tell just how long dinner may take. I thought we'd go to the St. Regis where I always take my customers. They know me there."

In a half dream, like Cinderella at the ball, Liza went through the evening. If she tried to shed her office personality for her normally more animated one, Morgan also seemed to be trying to be a pleasant companion. But never, by look, word or action, anything more. When she leaned toward him once with a whispered comment about the play, she could feel his instinctive withdrawal.

Back at the apartment she asked him if he would stay to discuss some details she wished to have settled.

"That sofa," she said as he went toward it, "descended to me from ancestors who didn't believe in pampering themselves. Maybe you'd better try the wing chair for comfort."

"I think I'll stick to the sofa, if it doesn't mind my weight," he said. "I like the feel of firm things under me."

Liza told him about Aunt Sarah and her wish to meet him.

"I feel we ought to go. She is my whole family, for I was an orphan. She brought me up and put me through college at what I'm sure now was something of a sacrifice. I've tried to make it up but she's very proud about accepting anything. Pure New England, you know. I think you'll like her. She speaks Vermontese, and come to think of it, you do yourself, in a way."

"How is that?"

"Oh, no unnecessary verbiage. No emotion coming out in the words."

"I think we should go, of course. When had you thought of?"

"Oh, any weekend, and only for one night. If we left fairly early on a Saturday morning we'd have plenty of time to visit from say—four o'clock on that afternoon—and we could leave Sunday whenever you wished."

"That sounds easy enough. Would this next Saturday suit? It would be better for me than the following one."

"I'll call Aunt Sarah and let her know. There are a few other things I'd like to decide on now, if possible. How, for instance, shall we invite our guests? Just informally, by word of mouth?"

"I should think so."

"I want to tell Matt Harvey first. You remember her? She was the one who suggested the position to me. She's really my closest friend. It was her sister who was my roommate in college, but she and I were never as congenial, and besides she lives in California now. Matt's husband, Tom, is a lawyer,

and they live here in the city. I suppose you haven't told anyone yet of our . . . our plans?"

"Just Dunmore," he said.

She gave an involuntary start. "You've told *him,* already?"

"Why shouldn't I? He's my associate. In fact I'm thinking
of making him a vice president."

She did not answer, and he watched her with drawn brows.

"I don't understand your attitude toward Dunmore. I've
noticed it for a long time and I can't say that I like it. What's
the matter? Why do you freeze up whenever he's in the office?"

"Can't we just set it down to an irrational reaction? Please
don't press me."

"But I do. I want to *know*."

"Then don't be angry if I tell you. Remember, you insisted,
or I would never have spoken. The truth is I don't entirely
trust Dunmore somehow. I never have."

"What do you mean?" His voice was sharp.

"I really can't add to that. It's just a crazy woman's
'hunch.' Probably entirely wrong. Oh, do let's forget this and
go on with our arrangements. You aren't angry, are you?"

"No," he said slowly. "I couldn't very well be that. But I
don't like this feeling on your part. I'll try to show you later
how mistaken it is. Well, what's next on the agenda?"

When he stood up to leave they had settled on Liza's favorite chapel in The Little Church Around the Corner for the
service, on ten as the number of guests each would invite, on
an informal "reception" at the St. Regis after, on the fact
that they would have no attendants, and that Liza did not
like orchids but *would* like an old-fashioned bouquet of white
flowers to carry in her hand.

"I'll call up Mrs. Moreland tomorrow," Morgan said. "It's
due her to let her know at once. She'll probably want to have
us in to dinner to meet you."

"And Matt Harvey will be sure to invite us. What shall I
say?"

"Oh, just keep the social stuff down to a minimum as far
as I'm involved. You can go ahead with your girl parties all
you want."

She thanked him once more for the ring. "And I think at
this point we ought to first-name each other, don't you?"

"Of course. I hope I can remember. Eight years makes quite a habit."

She held out her hand for he had made no slightest gesture of a caress. "Well, good-night, Dan. Friends it is, isn't it?"

He clasped her hand warmly. "Good-night, Liza, friends it is! And you're the most sensible girl I've ever met!"

She locked the door after him automatically and sank down where he had been sitting. The evening had established the unusual quality of their relationship beyond all conjecture. Beyond all hope. What lay buried in his heart or in his past that had dried up all the normal streams of emotion in him she could not know. Perhaps would never know. But so it was, and she was committed to accept it. She stretched out her hands unconsciously as though to gather him to herself. She had never loved him so deeply as on this night when with their unaccustomed nearness they had been enclosed in a little circle of intimacy in spite of the hard inhibitions imposed. Friends! *Sensible,* was she? She had never felt less so in her life. All that word implied stung her to the quick. Was she not then desirable enough to arouse in him one spark of warmth? Evidently not. She got up and paced back and forth, her heart storming within her. Could she live up to the bargain he had made? *Could she?*

At last she grew quieter. She reminded herself that she was thirty years old. There had been young men along the way, some of them eager enough. One, David Colby from the office, had not given up yet though she had consistently refused him. Occasionally after an evening with him she had almost decided to say *yes.* Then the next day, sitting across from Dan she knew she couldn't do it. Impossible, for her at least, to marry one man while loving another. She looked down at the ring, glittering on her finger like a star. Dan's ring. And in a short time she would wear a gold band with it, also from him, with all that it implied. She drew a long breath. "I'll take my chances," she said aloud.

The following week was full enough of excitement to keep her from any self-analysis. Her spirits mounted as she told her news to her friends. Matt Harvey was delightfully incredulous.

"Liza Hanford! I don't believe it! *Engaged? To Dan Morgan?*"

"Yes ma'am. Very much so."

"Why, this is the biggest news since Lindbergh flew the Atlantic! Well, I tell you it justifies my faith in human nature that he's marrying *you*. I suppose you know he's been pretty hard run after."

"I gathered so."

"Ever hear of Paula Ruston?"

"Just the name."

"Well, she's been hot for Morgan for the last year. I just heard it all lately. He's the first thing she's ever wanted that she hasn't been able to get and it's about driving her crazy. She's divorced from Fred Ruston. You know. The pretty polo playing boy. Just watch out for her, Liza."

"What do you mean?"

"Oh, just see she doesn't murder you in your bed sometime. I wouldn't put anything past that lady. 'Hell hath no fury' et cetera, you know. Well, now when can you and Dan come to dinner?"

Liza explained that the next weeks were full for him, but Matt agreed that she and Tom would attend the wedding if it was the last thing they did on earth and meanwhile she'd plan a luncheon with the other girls.

"They'll all want to entertain you, Liza. You know this is . . . this is simply terrific!"

Mrs. Moreland called early in the week in a voice somewhat less than enthusiastic, and definitely condescending.

"Miss Hanford? This is Elizabeth Moreland. Dan has just given me the news. I must say it came as a surprise since I had not known he was seeing you socially. You are, I think, a *very* lucky girl."

Liza writhed inwardly. She had to be courteous but she also wanted to put the old lady in her place.

"Thank you," she said clearly, "for your good wishes."

She heard what sounded like a small gasp and then Mrs. Moreland recovered herself. "Of course. All my good wishes to you both. Dan thinks he will be free to come to dinner a week from Wednesday if that is agreeable to you."

"Entirely. I'll look forward to it. And of course we both want you to be at our wedding. It will be very small, very simple, but very important . . . to us."

At the end she felt she had scored a small triumph. At least she had not allowed herself to be trodden upon.

Between phone calls Liza shopped. She had lifted some of her savings set by with New England thrift, and now with an abandon she had never known before and with an assurance in her mien which the saleswomen noted and respected she made her deliberate selections in departments where she was not accustomed to find herself. Her most delicious moments were spent at the lingerie counters where she handled such beauty as she had never known existed, having before had no occasion to discover it.

On Saturday morning at exactly nine she stood ready in a new rose-colored suit and hat which she hoped might occasion a comment. Dan, however, looked her over carefully but said nothing. He was apparently morose as they drove through the city and finally onto the parkway. Liza tried to chat of this and that but his answers were brief. At last he unburdened himself.

"I'm in a spot," he said, "and I don't like it. When I told Dunmore I asked him to keep his mouth shut. Well, he spilled the beans somehow and the thing has gone all over the office. Everybody's agog and they're planning a party for us at five whatever afternoon suits. It's to be a surprise for you but they had to tell me so that I would see you got there. I've waited till I spoke to you, but I want the whole thing stopped."

"But *why?*"

"You ought to see why. I'm not going to be part of any such affair—playing the simpering bridegroom. I won't do it. This whole thing has got out of hand. Church wedding, guests, reception, and Lord knows what. We should have gone to a magistrate as I intended."

Liza sat very quiet, as the miles passed, with her hands too tightly clasped in her lap. She could see that once in a while he glanced at her, but she decided to wait until he spoke again. At last he did.

"I'm sorry. That wasn't a very nice thing to say. You certainly deserve something like a wedding. But I draw the line at this office party. What's the best way for me to stop it?"

"You shouldn't. If you do they will all be very much disappointed and they may be even a little resentful. They're planning this out of kindness. You're a good employer. I've always been friendly with them all. Don't you see they'll have a good time doing this for us? I think it's got to go on. But I do . . . have . . . an . . . idea . . ."

"Let's hear it then, for heaven's sake."

"It's like this. Why don't we set the day. You tell them you've asked me to come to your office at five. *Then,* if you have a good friend at a little distance somewhere who will wire or phone you of an emergency meeting that night—you can always say it's union business—something that makes it necessary for you to leave right after lunch, it will be too late then to stop the party."

"But . . . but *you?*"

"I'll be there. All dressed up as if we were going out somewhere; I'll be overcome with surprise. I'll be delighted. That will be real. I'll show all of them my ring. I'll tell them how very sorry I am that you aren't there. That will be true, too. I'll be as gay as I can and terribly appreciative and it will be a good party, and nobody will be completely disappointed."

He thought it over for a moment. "You're a wonder," he said. "You've got me off the hook again. I know a man who would do this for me and I believe it might work. If they will all swallow it. I'm not sure about Dunmore."

"I'll manage somewhere along the line to mention that you're very shy about the whole thing. I think that will cover the doubters."

He laughed. "Whether you know it or not, that's the truth. Well, I couldn't be more relieved and I certainly thank you for the idea."

"There's one other thing I want to speak about before we get to Aunt Sarah's," Liza said. "She believes of course that our marriage is a real . . . I mean a true . . ."

"Love match?" he supplied.

"Yes. And I want to ask you not to disillusion her."

"What do you want me to do? Act a part?"

"Mercy no! They don't act parts in Vermont. Just evade answering any question, that's all, if there should be one."

"Otherwise behave as usual?"

"Absolutely."

"Well, good! I think I can settle now to enjoy the rest of

the trip with these things off my mind. It's a fine day and beautiful country and I feel like some fresh air. By the way can you drive?"

"I've kept my Vermont license and driven when I've been up there."

"That's fine. You must have a car of course. When we're back from the trip I'll see to that, and we'll have to begin right away to look for a house. I'll get in touch with a good real estate man and he can show you around. I'll go out too on Sundays."

"It may take a little while to find the right thing. And where will I . . . we stay while we're looking?"

She could see that he was puzzled as though this contingency had not before struck him.

"I think we'd better have a hotel suite," he said slowly. "My apartment isn't just suited . . . I mean you mightn't be as comfortable there. Hotel all right?"

"I'll like that very much. I haven't often stayed in a hotel."

When they finally reached the spacious white clapboard house with its green shutters standing in generous grounds on the edge of Waverly, Morgan whistled.

"This it? I'd somehow pictured a very little house in the middle of town. I thought that was the way spinsters always lived. Why, this is a nice place."

"Aunt Sarah's the fourth generation to live in it," Liza said. "Just leave the car here in the drive while we report ourselves."

Aunt Sarah herself opened the door for them. "I've been watching out for you. Well, Liza," she said as she allowed her niece to kiss her cheek, "so this is your young man, eh?"

"This is Dan Morgan, Aunt Sarah, and I do hope you'll like each other."

"Well," Aunt Sarah said calmly, "we'll see. Go on up to your rooms now. You can show him the spare one, Liza, then come down to the sitting room and we'll have a cup of tea."

When they were seated where she had designated, side by side on the small horsehair sofa, Miss Hanford opposite them poured tea into the thin china cups which Mrs. Phinney, properly introduced, passed.

"How will you have yours?" the old lady had asked Morgan.

"One lump, please, and a little milk, Miss Hanford."

"I'm pleased that you named me properly. One or two whipper snappers Liza's brought here from time to time have *Aunt Sarahed* me before their feet were rightly in the door. I believe in keeping your distance till you've got some call to change it. About the milk now, in your tea, are you country-born or Scotch?"

"Scotch," he said. "At least my parents were."

"Well," Aunt Sarah conceded, "they're a good breed, the Scotch. Some of them are a dour lot, though. My father used to say a Scotchman never told his wife he loved her till she was on her death bed." She gave Morgan a sharp glance. "I've an idea you can do a little better than that. What about your parents, are they living?"

"No," Morgan answered. "They've been gone for many years."

"I'm sorry. Where did you grow up?"

"In a coal mine," he said with a faint smile.

Aunt Sarah chuckled. "All right," she said. "That'll do for the moment. Well, Liza, tell me about the wedding business. Mrs. Phinney and I intend to go. Can you put us up?"

"I'll see to that, Miss Hanford. And I'll send a car up for you. Before you know it people are going to be flying."

"Not me!" said Aunt Sarah. "I think airplanes were a terrible invention. I'm afraid of them. The idea of trusting your life to a man at the front of one of those enormous contraptions . . ."

"You wouldn't fly with Lindbergh?" Morgan asked curiously.

"I wouldn't fly with the angel Gabriel," she said, then added tartly, "though I s'pose some day I might have to. Well, Liza, what are the plans?"

By the time things had been told and discussed, Mrs. Phinney announced dinner and they moved into the dining room. Liza could see Dan's eyes taking in the marble-topped sideboard, the table laid with the best damask, the heavy silver sugar and creamer, the Waterford glasses. There was certainly nothing to be ashamed of at Aunt Sarah's.

"This is a young Tom turkey," she announced as they ate.

"I got it from Jabez Hart up the road He can't farm to save his life but he has a way with fowls. I think he chews the corn himself before he gives it to them. He's that choice of them. Won't you have some more, Mr. Morgan?"

"I'm ashamed," he said, "but I will. I haven't tasted anything so good in years. This dressing!"

"It's a family recipe. Liza makes it just as well as we do. I s'pose you know she's a pretty good cook."

He looked at Liza for the first time during the meal. "You *are?*" he asked incredulously.

"Oh," she laughed, "I had to pass my cooking tests before Aunt Sarah would let me go away to college."

"She's never made a dinner for you, all these years?" Aunt Sarah said in surprise. "Well, after all, I've warned her plenty about inviting a man to her apartment . . ."

There was the suggestion of a twinkle in Dan's eyes. "As far as I'm concerned she's been very careful indeed about that."

"Glad to hear it. The things you read nowadays make my hair stand on end. I took two books back to the library last week and I said, 'Give me Jane Austen. I'll read her again. And if you keep *this* kind of stuff on your shelves I'll withdraw my subscription.' What about another piece of pie, Mr. Morgan?"

"Oh," he demurred, "I shouldn't, really."

"Of course you should and so should I. Apple's my favorite. This is a family recipe too. I'll tell you the secret. A little finely chopped candied ginger. It makes that difference in the flavor. *You* know that, Liza."

"Oh, yes."

"Well, see you make this for Mr. Morgan after you're married."

When dinner was over Aunt Sarah stood before them in the sitting room, tall and regal in her black dress, her thin face under the white hair showing an inner excitement.

"Now," she said, "I'm going to give you your wedding present. It was your great grandmother's, Liza, and it's *good*. I've kept it hid all these years so it would be a surprise to you if you ever got around to getting married. It's taken her a while, Mr. Morgan," she added, "but they say there's luck in leisure."

She brought from a side table a large black leather case, browned with age, and placed it on Liza's knee. "Open it!" she said.

Inside on their faded red velvet were rows and rows. of shining silver!

"It's the mischief to polish," Aunt Sarah went on, "so don't ever let it get ahead of you, Liza. Well, what do you think of it? Tut, tut, child, it's not worth *crying* over!"

"I'm so surprised," Liza said, "and so pleased! To think I never even knew it was in the house! Isn't it lovely, Dan?"

"Very beautiful," he said. "Thank you, Miss Hanford."

"Well," she said, "I hope you'll enjoy it and pass it on to them that come after you."

As the conversation went on Liza still held the silver, fingering it at intervals, until at nine o'clock Aunt Sarah rose.

"I'm going out to the kitchen and speak to Mrs. Phinney and you two can say good-night. Then Liza I want you to go on to bed and Mr. Morgan to stay here for a little. I want to talk to him."

"Oh, *no*, Aunt Sarah! I mean . . ." Liza amended lamely, "I think Dan is very tired. Please don't keep him up."

"I've an idea he's been up a few times as late as this," Miss Hanford said dryly. "You do as I say, now, and no nonsense. I'll not quote you to him or him to you but as your only family I want a word with him alone." And she left the room.

Liza turned to Dan, her face flushing. "I'm sorry about this. I hope you won't be embarrassed."

"She's a great old lady but I think I can hold my own with her, so you run along. Good-night."

"Good-night," she answered and left the room.

The next morning at breakfast both Aunt Sarah and Dan seemed unchanged by their private visit except that she apparently looked upon him with slightly more favor than before.

"Now, I always go to church at eleven," she announced. "Will you young people come along?"

"I'm afraid not," Dan answered. "We'll have to be leaving about then. I don't want to be late getting back."

"I see," she said. "Well, Liza, I hope you'll stand by your upbringing as time goes on."

"Oh, I will," she said.

"Eliza can always do as she pleases," Dan put in firmly.

"That's a help, anyway. Well, it's been nice having you here."

On the way back Liza questioned him gently about the conversation of the night before, but he divulged little.

"Oh, I told her about my finances, that I'd settled a rather large sum upon you when we became engaged so if anything would suddenly clip me you'd be provided for. And of course I've made a new will to operate after we are married. She seemed pleased. I like her very much," he added.

"And that was all?"

"Oh, pretty much. As I've told you before, I respect you, Liza. Now I respect your background, too." Half under his breath he added, "It's a lot better than my own." But Liza caught the words.

The next few weeks passed quickly with certain milestones punctuating them. At Mrs. Moreland's dinner, nominally in her honor, Liza had felt constraint. There was still a certain patronage in the older woman's attitude and Paula Ruston, another guest and quite apparently a favorite, was too beautiful, too almost possessive in her glances at Dan for Liza to regard her with comfort. She was tall, slim and certainly seductive in a form-fitting black dress, her dark bob sleekly parted and shining, her pearls gleaming on a perfect throat. It would be hard, Liza thought, for a man to resist her.

Having grown up in a small town Liza had had ample opportunity to study human nature at close range. She was naturally perceptive and people interested her. Now, her gaze dwelt often upon her hostess, handsome, assured, slightly arrogant but whose eyes melted as they looked at Paula Ruston. In her turn, Paula with her quick glances around the table and her sharp sallies of wit still managed often to address Mrs. Moreland in terms of endearment.

"Oh, *darling,* did I tell you . . . ?"

The older woman glowed visibly under the affection, but something in the situation did not ring true to Liza. Mrs. Moreland is lonely, she thought, for Dan had mentioned she had no family. She has taken Paula to her heart and for various reasons Paula finds it convenient to remain there. But her attitude, in Aunt Sarah's crisp phrase, was "too sweet to be wholesome." Then Liza was ashamed of the thought and tried to concentrate on the conversation.

The girl parties, as Dan called them, had been fun but while she enjoyed being at last the center of such scenes, Liza knew that through all the bright chatter something of normal happiness was lacking within her. Oddly enough the office party had been the most pleasurable of all. Everyone was filled with friendly, excited participation, for this that had taken place was within the business family. They accepted Dan's absence with many expressions of regret but, outwardly at least, without question; the girls were breathless over the ring; and the men presented the silver fruit bowl with evident pride and produced champagne! Only David Colby had been missing from the office force. There had been no jarring note except from Dunmore. The expression on his thin, dark face was inscrutable and when he edged her into a corner at one point the smile she disliked became more pronounced.

"Well, well," he said, "so you've actually landed him! Morgan, the eligible and determined celibate! Congratulations. On the feat, I mean. Of course he's the one who deserves felicitations. I feel he's doing pretty well for himself."

"Thank you."

"Do you read poetry?"

"I'm very fond of it."

"Well, though you mightn't guess it, so am I. There's a little couplet I think you should remember. I'll give it to you as a wedding gift.

> *Where the apple reddens*
> *Do not pry!"*

Then he turned on his heel and left her. She was angry for the moment at his insolence but was soon swept back into the laughing group and forgot the words. But that evening they came back to her. She repeated them slowly and the meaning became clear. Do not, like Eve, reach for the apple in order to learn more than you should know. *Do not pry.* How unspeakably rude he had been to offer her this advice, or was it a warning? All the questions she had buried deep within her, rose now to the surface. Was her love for this man she was soon to marry strong enough to carry her into the future with him, blindfold, as it were?

But before she went to bed, she had decided it once more. Her strong, dimpled chin was set. "I'll take my chances," she repeated again.

The wedding day itself was one of April's smiling ones. Even in the city there was the feel of a gentle quickening in the air, a movement, a subtle tremor of waking life, beneath a shining sun. Liza's flowers had arrived that morning, white lilacs and rosebuds, arranged by a master hand to form a round bouquet. As she dressed, she stopped often to draw in the fragrance with its breath of spring. She had finally settled upon a white wool suit for her wedding attire and a small white hat with just enough veil to suggest the bride. They had arranged to go to the church together and enter when the guests would already be seated. They had planned the timing carefully but she had begun to watch the clock now a bit anxiously when he finally came. In the car he was quiet and she thought he looked pale.

"Are you nervous, Dan?" she asked.

"A little."

"Well, if it's any comfort to you, so am I." But he did not join in her laugh.

They walked through the small courtyard which Liza had loved ever since she had been in the city and entered the church. The clergyman met them as had been arranged and led the way to the altar of the tiny chapel in the rear where the vows were spoken and the prayers offered and where after the final benediction Dan and Liza rose, as man and wife. The clergyman eyed them for a second, smiling, then whispered to Dan, "You may kiss her now." She turned and his lips lightly touched hers. I'm sure, Liza thought, no one here would believe that was the first kiss.

The reception at the hotel was an astonishing success. No expense had been spared on the appointments, the food or the vintage champagne, but in addition to this everyone was unusually gay. Perhaps the element of surprise at the marriage made them now enter more animatedly into the celebration of it. The two groups of friends seemed to coalesce freely

and Aunt Sarah without the slightest effort dominated the
scene. Liza, watching the encounter between her and Mrs.
Moreland, had hard work to cover her amusement.

"You live in Vermont, I hear," Mrs. Moreland said in a
tone that suggested this was the final outpost of provincial-
ism.

Aunt Sarah looked down from her considerable height.
"Yes, we Hanfords have been there for six generations. Gives
us pretty deep roots. New York now always seems to me a
transitory kind of place. You live here?"

"Aunt Sarah's having the time of her life," Liza whispered
to Dan at one of the few moments he was near her.

"Good! I thought she would take care of herself!"

When a call came for the groom to toast the bride, Liza's
heart beat fast. What would he say? Would he use the word
wife at last? He raised his glass and looked soberly at her.
"To Eliza," he said, and that was all.

There was a flutter of comment. "So unusual! So charming! So simple!"

When the last light laughter and hearty guffaws with their
accompanying good wishes had drifted from the room, Liza
took tender leave of Aunt Sarah.

"Now see you take care of this girl, Dan," the old lady
said, turning to him.

"I'll do my best."

"I don't hold much with these foreign places but I s'pose
you'll get on all right. It's been an elegant party. I had *two*
glasses of champagne and I feel it now in my legs. It's dis-
graceful if I can't drink that weak tastin' stuff. My forbears
did better with hard cider. Give me your arm, Dan, will you
to the elevator? I must say it was good though, as nice as it's
cracked up to be."

When she and Mrs. Phinney were gone to enjoy the comfortable arrangements that Dan had provided, he and Liza
went up to their own suite where their luggage had already
been placed. Liza looked over the large living room with the
two connecting bedrooms adjoining it and gave a small gasp.

"Mercy! You could house two or three families here! What
luxury! But we really didn't need all this space."

He only smiled and then said, "You know I like your outfit. I was scared for fear you'd wear something fluffy and fussy. This is simple but very smart and becoming."

"I'm awfully glad it pleases you." Then she went on in a lower voice, "Perhaps you'd care to know that my wedding white is an honest symbol. I gather that it sometimes is not in these days. Well, mine is."

He walked over to the window where he stood looking out for several seconds. When he turned there was an expression in his eyes she had never seen before.

"I would have assumed so," he said, "but thank you for telling me."

They had dinner sent up and through the meal they were both at pains to chat easily about the party, the guests and Aunt Sarah especially.

"I can't imagine," he said once, "where Dunmore was. He planned to come. I'll give him a ring in the morning before we leave. It's not like him to miss any kind of a wing-ding. He's a great party-boy even if he is a good business man."

They drew out the meal to its longest extent, lingering over their liqueurs. At eleven Liza rose. "I think I'll go to my room now," she said.

"Yes, yes," he agreed somewhat nervously. "Of course. It is getting late."

Once there she hung up the white suit with care. Since he liked it she would wear it often on their trip. At last she put on the filmiest and most beautiful of all her costly purchases and sat down to unbraid her hair. It fell over her shoulders like a little cape. She paused, suddenly, brush in hand. Could Dan's reason for asking her to wait before having it cut have been because he wanted to see it down? In any event she now tied a ribbon round her head, giving her the look of a little girl, and let her hair hang loose.

She sat up against the pillows, her bouquet in a glass of water on the bed-stand so she could still enjoy its fragrance, and waited.

It seemed a long time to her heart, though not by the clock, until she heard a light tap upon her door.

CHAPTER II

Eliza stared out of her room window in the elegant little Hôtel Vouillemont and then slowly and carefully began a letter.

DEAR AUNT SARAH:

Here I am, incredibly, in Paris! And it all looks as enchanting as I expected. Through the day while Dan is busy I try to see as many important sights as I can. We are quite near La Place de la Concorde, the most spacious and beautiful square in the city. Of course it is altogether peaceful now except for the traffic, with fountains playing at either end, but right in the middle, I've learned, was where the guillotine once stood which took its terrible toll of lives in the French Revolution.

Yesterday I got one of the *millions* of taxis here and asked the driver to go very slowly along the Champs-Élysées, which is supposed to be the most beautiful street in the world, and I for one will never challenge its reputation. It's as wide as three boulevards put side by side and bordered with the loveliest big horse chestnut trees *in bloom* and of course handsome buildings. I liked some of the more intimate features best. Nearly every window, it seems, has either a box of blooming geraniums or a little iron balcony. And here is something that will please you and Mrs. Phinney. In practically every doorway there is a *cat*. Most of them seemed to have a slightly rakish look as though they would say to an unsophisticated lady like myself, "My dear, what *I* could tell you about life."

I've been in several cathedrals. I suppose it's tourist heresy but the part of Notre Dame I like best is the *outside*. You can come toward it along

the Seine embankment and from there the flying
buttresses look exactly like lace made into stone!
But my favorite cathedral is the Madeleine, all
gold and white and somehow, I thought, suited to
the Magdalene herself. Then outside in the very
shadow of the church is the most wonderful
flower market! Simply masses of every kind of
bloom! You would love it!

Liza paused here and drew a long sigh.

Of course [she wrote on] in the evenings Dan
takes me to all sorts of interesting places for dinner, and once we sat a long time at the Café
Dôme—you've heard of these outdoor cafés
where you can sit all night if you wish. This one
is in the student quarter and artists were there
with their sketches. I bought one for you. There
had been a light rain and the street was glistening
with it. Flower girls strolled back and forth along
the sidewalk selling their nosegays. This place
touched me, somehow. It seemed like the Paris
we all have imagined.
 The most thrilling experience so far was going
to the Palace of Versailles to see the fountains
play. I'll have to wait until I see you to describe
that. Great plumes of spray rising from every
corner of the endless gardens! I pictured how it
must have been in the days of Louis XIV with
the courtiers and their ladies watching this
beauty under a summer moon. Perhaps in the
face of it, we might all have forgotten that the
people in Paris had no bread to eat.

She paused again and then finished rapidly.

I've bought some wonderful new clothes. Dan
is so generous. We are coming home sooner than
we expected for he is anxious to get back to the
office. I'll call you as soon as we land. I *loved* the
trip across of course! You will probably have my
letter now that I wrote you on ship-board. Do
hope you are well.

She read it over. She had included the little historical refer-
ences purposely, for Aunt Sarah had a penchant for past

events. When the envelope was sealed Liza sat very still as she took stock again of her heart. She was a two-week-old bride and she was in Paris! Paris in the spring! The place and time in all the world for romantic love, but for her this element was absent. Dan went on exactly as he had begun. He was friendly, generous, interested in the daily report of her sight-seeing, a pleasant enough companion in the evenings, but with never an endearing word, never a caress. The kiss at the altar had been the only one. When there had been love-mak-ing it was purely physical and mechanical. Like his meals, Liza thought bitterly, *and meaning no more to him*. Except for this, they could have been a sister and brother who got on well together.

Liza studied him daily with growing amazement. Here was a strong man, a man of power who had overcome almost in-superable obstacles as he wrought a fortune from the shining veins of black carbon below the western Pennsylvania hills. But emotionally he was restrained, inhibited, as cold, as hard as the unmined coal itself.

Liza tried earnestly now to make herself believe that in spite of her unsatisfied cravings she still was fortunate. She still had much. Indeed, she thought, there were probably mil-lions of husbands and wives across the world who would never dream of demanding more warmth. The man needed a woman to cook for him, bear his children, assuage his desire; the woman needed a man to protect her, keep a roof over her head and bread upon the table. And with this they would be content. Well, in her different sphere of life so would she try to be! She rose and gave her shoulders a little shake as she had been accustomed to shrug off childish disappointments.

It was late afternoon and she decided to wear for the eve-ning her most expensive couturière dress. The way in which Dan pressed money upon her was in itself a bitterness. He seemed to feel that it would make up for any other lack. When she had demurred once at his generosity he had looked mystified and almost hurt.

"I told you before we were married that this was the main thing I had to offer a woman. I thought you would enjoy it."

"But I do," she insisted eagerly. "It's wonderful! Only I don't need so much."

"Go ahead and use it," he said. "There's plenty." Then he had added, "You know with all these clothes you're wearing now, Liza, you get better looking every day."

"Why, thank you," she said. "And you know you're pretty handsome yourself."

"You think so?" He had sounded surprised and pleased.

As she dressed now she thought of Dunmore and his cryptic quotation given her at the office party. Perhaps his meaning had not been an insolent warning to her not to pry into Dan's past, but rather to avoid Eve's own mistake of wanting more than she already had; demanding the ultimate instead of being content with the immediate. Was it possible that Dunmore's sharp and perceptive eyes might have read the secret of the marriage? He knew Dan better, probably, than anyone else did, but she hoped there had been no shared confidence between them. That would be a death-blow to her pride.

She was starting to put on her dress when she heard Dan come in. He called out cheerfully.

"Hello! Sorry I'm late. I had a long tough session with a man but at the end I got what I wanted. It won't take me long to dress. Are you ready?"

"In a few minutes, but don't hurry."

She put on the gown. It had a slim sheath skirt of blue silk, with a soft, magically draped chiffon top of the same color. Over all went a blue evening coat trimmed with white fur. As she looked at herself in the mirror Liza's heart leaped with pleasure in spite of her. *Whether clothes make the man or not,* she was thinking, *they certainly do make the woman!* And as proof, when Dan came out to the sitting room where she was standing, he gave a low whistle.

"Whew!" he said. "That's the best-looking outfit yet!"

"It ought to be. It cost you plenty!"

"Well worth it, I'd say. You know I feel pretty darned proud taking you out!"

Liza laughed and her heart felt lighter than for days. Perhaps after all it was merely a question of time until . . . They were quite gay over dinner with Liza describing the Paris *cats* and Dan laughing in apparent pleasure at her wit. Suddenly, however, as he glanced over the dining room his

eyes narrowed and for a second his face hardened. Then he
became more animated than before. *What had he seen? Or
whom?* Liza wondered.

At last as they stood under the gay awning at the door
waiting for a taxi, Dan suddenly leaned close and spoke distinctly above the voices just behind them.

"Sweetheart, are you too tired for the Follies? Would you
rather we went right back to the hotel?"

Her startled answer was instinctive, immediate and from
her heart.

"Oh, *darling,* no! I'd love to go on."

"Good, we'll do that then. Here's a cab."

His arm was about her as he guided her into the car. She
sank back in it, with waves of something like rapture flooding
over her. It *had* only been a matter of time then! Perhaps it
was the dress and coat now that had suddenly caused . . .
Dan had finished his instructions to the driver and leaned
back beside her.

"Well," he said in a tone of satisfaction, "that couldn't
have worked better. Did you see her?"

"Who?" Liza asked tremulously.

"Why, Paula Ruston. I saw her sitting with some people
across the restaurant while we were eating. Luckily she was
looking the other way at the time. But I heard her voice behind us just now and I decided I'd put on an act. And you!"
He caught her hand and gave it a little squeeze. "You were
simply wonderful, the way you played up to me!"

As she made no answer he went on.

"That woman has given me no peace for over a year. She's
hounded me day and night. That was one of the main reasons
I wanted to get married. But I made one mistake I'm sorry
for. She was everlastingly begging me to love her or make
love to her or something, and once when I was at the end of
my string I told her I never expected to *love* anybody. It
wasn't in me. And that if I ever married it would be purely
for convenience. I shouldn't have said that. I'm sorry now,
but I was desperate at the time. You see, she probably re-
members it and took it into her head to follow us. At least it
looks that way. She's a thoroughly unscrupulous woman.
Well, we gave her something to think about tonight." He
drew another sigh of satisfaction.

"You know, Liza, you're really quite an actress!" he added.

When she spoke it was in a small voice. "Perhaps I am. Dan, would you be too disappointed if we didn't go to the Follies?"

"Me? Good Lord, no. I'm tired as a dog. It was only because I thought you would want to. Shall we go back to the hotel?"

"Please. In spite of what I said I believe I am a little tired."

He spoke to the driver and then looked at her white face. "You're overdoing this sight-seeing business," he pronounced, "and you must take it easier. You needn't try to see everything in Paris in ten days. You'll be back. Maybe it's a good thing we're not going on to England just now."

"Maybe so," Eliza said faintly and then said nothing more.

Once back at the hotel she went straight to her room and Dan went to his also, saying he was glad to catch up a bit on his sleep. Liza removed the beautiful coat and gown, hung them up with a tenderness like that accorded the dead, and prepared for the night. But once between the sheets she felt a strange trembling overtake her. The night was mild, the room was warm but the shaking persisted and not all her will power could affect it in the slightest. She had heard of a *nervous chill* after shock and apparently this was it. Certainly there had been reason for it. As it continued she grew uneasy and finally called out. Dan opened the door between them at once.

"What is it?" he asked anxiously. "Liza, are you sick?"

He came over to the bed. "N-no," she chattered. "It—it's just a n-nervous ch-chill. C-could you order a h-hot drink?"

"Of course. And I'll call a doctor."

"P-please d-don't. It's j-just nerves."

"I didn't know you had any," he said. "What would cause this?"

"T-too m-many n-new c-clothes, maybe."

Dan laughed with relief. "Well, I guess you can't be really sick if you make a joke like that. I'll be right back."

She heard him calling room service and then he appeared with a glass of brandy. When she couldn't hold it steady he slid an arm behind her pillow to support her and held the glass to her lips. When the pot of chocolate arrived he did the same with the cup, allowing her to sip it slowly. The warmth was soothing and little by little her body grew calmer, more relaxed.

"You're not shaking much now," he said, withdrawing his arm.

"No, I'm better, and thank you so much. Do you think you could find some aspirin for me? It's in the little cabinet."

He was back in a minute with the tablets and glass of water.

"Now, this settles it," he said. "You've got to let up on the sight-seeing. I hope you'll not have any more trouble tonight, but I'll leave the door open and if you need anything at all you're to call. *Promise,*" he said sternly.

"I promise."

"Scout's honor?"

She looked up at him and smiled. *"Wife's* honor," she whispered.

"Good! Well, good-night, then."

"Good-night."

The next morning Liza found herself surprisingly rested. Contrary to her expectations she had slept in a deep lethargic reaction from the chill, and now her first thought was of Dan's care and solicitude rather than of the bitter memory of what had happened earlier. She could hear him moving about in his own room so knew he had not left early as he usually did to get an American breakfast of bacon and eggs at a little restaurant he had discovered. When she came out to the sitting room she found him at the little table by the window munching a *croissant,* the coffee, too, already there.

"Oh, how nice!" she said. "But I'm afraid you'll miss your usual fare, won't you? You shouldn't have waited."

"Well, I had to be sure you were all right. How *are* you?"

"Perfectly well. I'm terribly ashamed I caused you all that bother last night. You were a very good nurse, by the way."

"I can't understand it," he went on. "A nervous chill! I never heard of such a thing. And you of all people! I worked with you for eight years and I would have sworn you hadn't a nerve in your body."

She poured his coffee and handed it to him with a smile.

"Women are full of surprises," she said. "That's what makes us so interesting."

"Well, don't surprise me like that again," he said, "even for the interest. You really scared the liver out of me. You know," he added reaching for another *croissant*, "These things aren't bad if you have enough of them."

"I'm afraid you'll still be hungry before noon."

"Would you care to lunch with me today? I had made plans with a man but I can put him off. The thing is I can't trust you this morning. You might decide to climb to the top of the Eiffel Tower!"

Liza laughed. "Oh, I think I'll stop one short of that. But I'd love to have lunch with you."

"O.K. I'll pick you up here about one and we'll go out to the *Bois*. That's the great park, you know, and there's one restaurant there I particularly like."

"Oh, I know about the *Bois*! My great-uncle, Aunt Sarah's brother, used to sing me a song about it when I was a little girl.

> *As I walk along the Bois de Bologne*
> *With an independent air,*
> *You can hear the girls declare*
> *'He must be a millionaire!'*

There! You see, that's you, Dan."

He was amused. "I never heard that one. Do you remember any more?"

> *"You can hear them sigh and wish to die,*
> *You can see them wink the other eye*
> *At the man who broke the bank at Monte Carlo!"*

"Well," he said, "that lets me out. I've never gambled. At least not that way. I've done plenty, I suppose, in my own business. I'm right in the midst of a deal now that's touch and go."

"Could you tell me about it?"

"Oh, it's export problems. There's a firm here who's been buying from the Blair Company, you know, down South. I think I've swung them over to me but unless I can make good on all my promises about time of delivery and so on, I'm out and a lot of money and coal lost. It's the transportation from Pittsburgh to the coast that's the problem. The

Blair Company has the edge on me there. Dunmore is against this. He thinks we have enough export business already, but I like to take a chance. And I'm going to take this one!"

"Good!"

"Why do you say that so strongly? Still don't like Dunmore?"

"Let's just put it that I'd trust your judgment before his."

"About that song," he said as he rose from the table. "Funny you remembered it all these years. It's not a child's ditty."

"That's what Aunt Sarah thought. There was so much discussion about it that it fixed the thing in my mind. You see Uncle Charley in a mild, Vermont sort of way, was considered rather *wild* and not a good influence on me."

"I can imagine that. You must have been a serious little thing. Well, Aunt Sarah did a good job bringing you up. I consider her one of the best *extra benefits* I got in marrying you. I like her."

"And even better still, if possible, she likes you. So, we have a date for lunch?"

She felt the color rising in her cheeks as she said it, and hoped he wouldn't notice.

"That's right. Why don't you just stay here this morning and rest up a little? Can't you write letters or something?"

"I think I will. Good luck with your problems and I'll be ready at one."

It was a pleasant drive to the *Bois,* but the great Park itself filled Liza with delight. They ate in the open air, surrounded by other tables of men and women of all ages but with a common denominator of fashion and gaiety.

"This is truly Paris," Liza said once, "and I love it!"

Before Dan could answer a voice spoke at his elbow. Three people had paused as they passed the table. One was Paula, in a red suit with a wide hat drooping over her lustrous black hair.

"Why, Dan!" Her tone was full of surprise. "How wonderful to see you here! This is Marge and Fred Dorsey with whom I'm staying. Dan Morgan, Marge."

Dan rose, bowed briefly and shook hands with Fred. Then

after waiting an appreciable second he turned. "My wife," he said.

"Of course," Paula replied. "How stupid of me! I did hear you two had been married. And how are you enjoying Paris, Eliza?"

She used the name as she might have done to a domestic.

Liza smiled and stared her in the eye. "I'm finding it the most perfect place in the world for a honeymoon!"

"You're right," Marge Dorsey echoed. "Fred and I spent ours here!"

"And what about you, Dan?" Paula broke in with a faintly sarcastic smile. "How are you enjoying it?"

"What a question to ask a man about his honeymoon!" Fred Dorsey laughed. "Paula's a little crazy, you know."

"I'm delighted to answer," Dan's tone was incisive. "I'm finding it marvelous!"

"There's the waiter signing to us," Dorsey said. "Tables are at a premium here even if they're reserved. We'd better go along."

The Dorseys moved on with goodbyes and good wishes floating behind them. Paula waited.

"It's no good, Dan," she said in a low tone but audible to Liza. "I understand the situation perfectly. You needn't think you'll get rid of me this easily." Then she sauntered gracefully off to join her friends.

Dan sat down with a groan. "I don't know whether to laugh or to swear," he said. "The insolence of her! And I can't figure her out. She's got plenty of money of her own. She's just stubborn, I guess."

"Did it never occur to you," Eliza tried to ask casually, "that a woman might care for you for *yourself?*"

"No," he said sharply, "it didn't. Well, now let's forget her. But thanks again for the way you handled it. You know, Liza, you're a very satisfactory person. I'll tell you something. Up to the very time of the ceremony I would have gotten out of the marriage if I could decently. I was scared to death. But somehow I believe it's going to work out. Our bargain, I mean. Don't you think so?"

"Oh, yes," she said quietly.

"Good! Well, let's eat our lunch now for I can't stay too

long. About dinner tonight." He drew his brows. "I wonder what place you would like."

"Why not have a leisurely one in our sitting room? We could go out later if we wish."

"That sounds fine to me if you're satisfied," he said, "and we might try the Follies after. You said once you'd like to go there, and there aren't too many chances left. And wear the outfit you had on last night, will you? I like that."

"Dan," she said, as they were leaving the *Bois,* "I'm afraid of that woman."

"Paula? Don't be ridiculous. Why would you be *afraid* of her? What harm could she do?" He looked at her keenly. "You certainly don't think she could ever make any time with me, I hope."

"Oh, no. I think you're impervious. But of course she might feed me a poisoned apple like the witch in the fairy tale."

He laughed heartily. "There you go again scaring me and then making a joke of it. I'll have to learn never to take you seriously. But as to the Ruston woman, when I get back I'm going to have a straight talk with Mrs. Moreland and tell her what's what. I like her and I owe her a great deal as I've told you. I can't understand why she keeps Paula under her wing, but she does. I know she tried to make a match between us, but I never let on to her that I saw through it. Now, I'll tell her I want this business stopped once and for all. I'm sure her words have weight."

"Could you drop me at the Louvre?" Liza asked. "I won't tire myself but I'd like to browse a little. I'll go back early."

When she reached the hotel again she picked up a letter from Aunt Sarah in the lobby and then ascended in the little glass elevator to their own floor. She turned the key and entered their living room, then stopped short. There was a faint but noticeable perfume in the room. Not her own. She had encountered this exotic and distinctive fragrance the night they had dined with Mrs. Moreland and she had first met Paula Ruston. Unconscious of it at the time she remembered later that it had been present at the restaurant door when Dan had "put on his act," and she had noticed it again today during the lunch conversation. *Could Paula have been in this room?* But why? And how had she managed to get in? Of course money and a plausible story coupled with undeniable beauty could probably overcome a French bellboy. But this unwarrantable invasion of their privacy! She felt herself go white with anger and also with that uneasiness to which she had jokingly referred to Dan. Should she tell him now, of this? She felt sure she was not mistaken and yet after a few minutes in the room, growing accustomed to the air, the scent was not so pronounced. Could she have had some kind of psychological reaction since her mind had been full of the woman?

There should be now, she thought with a wild giggle, according to all the mystery books, a half-smoked cigarette with lipsticked end on an ashtray. But there was none. Nothing was in the slightest way disturbed. She decided she would say nothing to Dan.

During the dinner in their sitting room that evening a pleasant relaxation seemed to fall upon them both. Dan was unusually talkative.

"Of course," he said, "I don't want to get too sure of myself. Funny things can happen to any market. We've had strikes and depressions, but certainly the coal business seems to be running pretty high right now. I'll always stick to coal for I grew up with it, but I've got another bee in my bonnet. I've been getting very interested in *steel,* as I guess you know from the correspondence you've handled. Someday I want to buy into a steel plant."

"That's a big purchase, Dan."

"Do you think I don't know it?"

"Any particular mill in mind?"

"The Premium. I've been watching it for a good while."

"Have you a chance?"

"There's always a chance," he grinned. "The trick is first to get your build-up and then grab when the time is right. What I want to begin with is a combine with the Hadley Coal Company. That would give us real power in the field. I know Hadley. I've met his wife, too. Nice people. Sometime later on I'd like to entertain them when they come on to New York. A little softening up process."

"Dan?"

"Yes."

"What about a house? Do you suppose we could look for one soon?"

"Of course. We can start when we get back if you want to. You don't fancy hotel life, then?"

"For a while it's delightful, but not for long. I would like to begin the house-hunting right away because it may take some time before we find what we want."

"And just what *do* you want?" he asked with interest.

"It's a little hard to describe," she said slowly. "Perhaps every woman has her dream house. But I'll try to tell you about mine. I would like a lovely, formal drawing room and a library *lined* with books as the years pass, with a big fireplace and deep comfortable chairs and sofas with sort of faded-looking flowery slipcovers. Then a quite impressive dining room! I think that ought to be the heart and soul of the house."

She leaned forward. "But I would have a huge bay window in it with a small table set there for breakfast and occasional cozy daytime meals. Evenings, however, I would want full candlelight, silver and crystal at the big table. The whole works!" she smiled.

"Do we dress for dinner?"

"Now, you're laughing at me."

"No," he said, "I'm following every word with the closest attention. What else have you planned?"

"Oh, a porch and a terrace, *and a garden!* You can't imagine the joy it will be to me to have money enough for a really beautiful garden." Her eyes were shining. "Do you suppose we could have a fountain? I believe I'd rather have that than anything else I know."

Dan watched her in silence for a moment, then rose, come round to her side of the table and placed a light kiss on her forehead.

"I'm establishing no precedent," he said sternly and with evident embarrassment. "That's just a gesture of respect for a woman who evidently prefers a garden with a fountain to a diamond necklace."

"But I *do*," she said, as casually as she could, realizing that the moment must contain no sentiment, "and thank you for the gesture." Then she went on. "Upstairs a conventional arrangement except that I thought you might like a sort of little office-den next to your dressing room. If you ever wanted to do a letter or two there would always be a secretary available," she laughed. "Do you like my ideas at all?"

"Surprisingly well. As a matter of fact I don't believe I could add to them and I should say they were very modest. The location may be the biggest problem."

"I know. Because of the commuting. Will you mind that very much?"

"I suppose I will, but if other men can do it so can I. When I have days that run too long I can stay in at my apartment. I told you I would probably spend some time there. But of course you mustn't be alone. We'll have to begin by finding a good couple, butler-cook combination. Scotch if we can get them. I like to hear the burr on a woman's tongue, especially."

"Dan, how long is it since your mother died?"

His face clouded darkly. "I don't like personal questions."

"It was surely an innocent one," Liza said gently, but began at once to speak of something else.

A small shadow, however, lay between them even as they set forth for the theater, and Liza felt again his instinctive withdrawal when she once leaned closer to make a remark. Sad, she thought, just after his touching dinner *gesture*.

As they stood waiting for a cab after the show, an unpleasantly familiar voice spoke. Paula, with a very young man as escort, came up to them.

"How delightful to see you twice on the same day!" she said. "Are you staying in Paris long, Dan?" As before she ignored Liza.

"My plans are unsettled," Dan returned crisply. "We're taking this taxi. Good evening."

"I'll be seeing you soon again, I'm sure," she said sweetly.

"Not if I can help it," Dan gritted as he got into the cab. "I don't think she was in the theater at all. She was just waiting there. That means she's put a tail on us. Well, two can play at that game. I will not be *hounded*."

He was morose as they rode back to their hotel. Once in their suite he said a hasty good-night and went to his own room. Liza lay for a long time, depressed and wakeful, in her own. In the morning, however, she found he had waited again to have breakfast with her.

"I've been thinking," he said, "that if you don't mind seriously, it might be nice for you to have a guide with you these next days. I can easily get a good one through Ronsard in our office. Would you object to that?"

"No," Liza said slowly, "I think I would enjoy it."

"I'm certainly not worrying about *poisoned apples*," he said with a short laugh, "but I don't want that bitch to corner you any time when you're out alone and embarrass you. I believe in this case a man would be best. As a matter of fact Ronsard's young brother has been helping me with the paper work to earn some money. He's a student at the Sorbonne. Nice chap. He might be glad to change jobs for a day or so."

"Can you manage without him?"

"Oh, yes. Things are pretty well lined up now. I have tickets for a sailing on Tuesday. Is that all right?"

"Of course. Whenever you wish. With a guide I can do a lot these next days. More than alone."

"Good. How about staying here then until young René turns up? If you hear nothing from me, be ready for him about eleven."

One thing in their strange relationship brought pleasure to Liza's heart. It was the feeling that she was being cared for, watched over. After the long years of looking out for yourself as a lonely career girl there was a deep satisfaction in feeling that from now on she had a protector.

When she met young Ronsard in the lobby at eleven she found him a handsome eager-eyed youth who smiled easily and with French finesse accorded her just the right glance of admiration. His English was excellent and from the first there was a quick rapport between them, which made their intimate conversation seem natural. As they moved out into the street and entered a taxi he asked her what she would most like to see. "We'll ride around a little until we decide on our direction," he said. She told him briefly what she had already done and then said impulsively, "I would like to go to some really romantic places. Surely there must be many here."

"Ah, yes. We like to think Paris is the city of romance. And we also like to believe that Frenchmen make more of an

art of love than do men of other nationalities. A bit of pride,
I suppose. Were you thinking of old-time romances perhaps?"

"Yes, I believe I was."

"What about Héloïse and Abelard?"

Her face lighted. "Oh, perfect!" she said. "I had actually
forgotten they ever lived here!"

"Not only lived here, Madame, but are buried here." He
gave a quick order to the driver. "Since they met and loved
in the shadow of Notre Dame, we'll go there first, and later
to the cemetery. I am glad you are interested, for my last
paper in an English course was about them. I think their love
story was probably the most beautiful and the most tragic in
the world. Such passion! Such constancy! I kept wondering as
I wrote whether their short blazing fire before the darkness
might have been more to be desired than long years of a
lesser light."

He stopped, embarrassed. "You must forgive me, Madame.
I am young and enjoy talking of love stories. Knowing Monsieur Morgan and now having met you I know how perfect
your own must be. But I mean only generalities when I say
that perhaps such a passion as that of Abelard and Héloïse
would rarely happen now."

"You think men and women have changed over the centuries?"

"Perhaps not so much in their essential natures as in the
milieu in which they live. This must affect them, no? All the
pressures from every side, the hundreds of new interests now,
the new discoveries, the new *dangers,* all of this might in
many cases cause love to take a minor place, to be a thing
apart from the major problems of living. To be less than the
completeness of union." He paused and then quoted thoughtfully:

> *"Never yet*
> *Hath he possessed her wholly, never yet*
> *Hath twain been one.*

I think it may be like that with many others, especially in this
age."

"Will you please say those lines again, René?"

He looked startled at the intensity of her voice, but re-

peated the words. "From Lucretius, I think," he added.
"Here we are at the Cathedral. Shall we dismiss the fiacre
and walk around for a little?"

"Oh, please. It's the *outside* I like best."

"So do I. You are perceptive, Madame. I have seen many
tourists go in with never a glance to left or right. Now, I
shall begin to be a real *guide,* as we move about. Here in the
year 1115 Peter Abelard became a Canon of the Cathedral
and at the same time was the greatest teacher of philosophy
in all France. An older Canon, Fulbert, had living with him
here in the Cathedral precincts his beautiful young niece,
Héloïse. She had a brilliant mind, so Fulbert asked Abelard to
live with them in return for tutoring Héloïse."

René paused with a side glance at Liza. "A somewhat dan-
gerous arrangement, n'est ce pas?"

She only smiled. "Go on with the story. I need to have my
memory refreshed."

"Abelard and Héloïse fell passionately, rapturously in love,
became lovers, had a child and were finally married, though
Héloïse unselfishly opposed this because it would wreck all
his preferment in the church, which it did. Fulbert never forgave Abelard and at last hired men to go at night to his room
and perform the greatest act of cruelty possible . . ."

"Yes," Liza said hastily. "I remember. Then Héloïse went
permanently into a convent, didn't she?"

"And Abelard as a monk wandered hopelessly from monastery to monastery over the years, taught for a time again
with his old brilliance, was persecuted for his beliefs and
finally died in despair. His body was then taken to Héloïse,
for all knew of their devotion even after the flaming fire had
been quenched. Can you feel the living story here where so
much of it took place?"

"Yes," Liza breathed, as they walked around the back of
the cathedral. "Oh, yes, I feel it *terribly.*"

"Just over there was once the building in which they lived.
While I was writing my paper I often used to come here at
night and stand, imagining they were leaning from a window,
listening to the Cathedral bell ringing for *Compline.* You are
not a Catholic, Madame?"

"No."

"Compline is the last service of the day. Just after Vespers, they would hear the voices singing the old prayer for a quiet night and a perfect end. For God's mercy on all who waked and His peace for those who slept and for Paris, commending it for another night to the keeping of God . . . I liked to think of them, hearing the beauty of these words through the darkness and then turning to their own transports . . . You have been kind, Madame, to listen to me. Forgive me. I have talked too much."

"It is you who have been kind," she said. "So heavenly kind to make all this live for me. Without you I would never have known it or felt it. And you say they are buried here in Paris?"

"Their bodies were finally brought back here after the death of Héloïse and they lie in one tomb. We'll see it later. Perhaps now we can walk about a little more until it will not seem like desecration to think of lunch!" He laughed easily, and Liza joined, though her heart was deeply stirred.

As they moved slowly along the street before the open bookstalls, Eliza said, "You have told this like a poet, René. What are you planning to do after the University?"

"Write. If I can. Your husband tells me there may be work in his office here. I will need to keep body and soul together somehow," he smiled, "while I'm becoming immortal. He is a wonderful man, your husband. A strong man. Always I kept thinking how fortunate his wife must be to be chosen by such a man. Now, since meeting you, Madame, I know that he is the one to be most congratulated."

"How gracefully you put it, René. Thank you!" Liza felt her cheeks coloring under his openly admiring gaze. "Women love pretty speeches," she added.

"This has the added grace of sincerity, if I may say so. Ah, Madame, what is it?" For Eliza had slowed her steps suddenly and the sudden color had left her face. "You are ill?" he asked anxiously.

"Not ill, just angry."

René looked sharply at the elegant figure which had alighted from a cab and was approaching them with smiling assurance.

"You do not wish to meet this woman?"

"No."

"Eh bien. We will turn here." He guided her quickly down a side street and into a small restaurant.

"Not quite what I had planned but I hope good enough."

He selected a table that would seat only two and had signaled the waiter just as Paula Ruston entered the restaurant and came up to them.

"Eliza! How interesting to see you again so soon—and your charming companion," she added.

"This is Monsieur Ronsard, Mrs. Ruston. My guide for the day."

René, having risen, bowed stiffly.

"How fortunate you are, Eliza. I have to go blundering about alone. Would you both care to join me as my guests for lunch and tell me what you've been doing? *Such* a kindness, if you will. I'll get a larger table."

She raised an imperious hand but René stopped her swiftly.

"If you will excuse us, Madame," he said coldly.

"Ah, so?" Paula's voice was full of meaning. "Of course. Have a pleasant time sight-seeing."

"How unutterably rude," René said as she moved away. "How *gauche*."

"I should explain perhaps. She was a great annoyance to my husband before we were married and now it seems as though she has suddenly taken a notion to follow us over here and embarrass us whenever she can, by following us about."

"Exactly. I think I recognize her type. Let us try to enjoy our lunch and forget her."

When they found themselves later at the Cemetery of Père Lachaise, Eliza's eyes swept the acres of winding streets with the noble sculpture and small mansions of the dead rising white from the green foliage.

"The beauty of it!" she cried. "Oh the sad beauty of it!"

René guided her to the place they sought, where beneath a stone canopy lay the ancient lovers.

"They are together now," he said. "This has been called 'the bridal bed of the tomb.' "

He spoke softly for they were not alone. A young couple,

hands clasped, stood opposite them, tears running down the girl's cheeks.

"So many lovers come here," René went on quietly. "I suppose they think they will receive some sort of blessing. They often kneel to pray."

Eliza's eyes rested long upon the grave. When she raised them they too were wet.

"I will never forget this," she said.

"There are many famous ones buried here. Would you care to pay your respects to some of the others as we walk about? Chopin, for instance, Sarah Bernhardt, perhaps, and so many more?"

Liza's look was pure amazement.

"Can this really be true!" she said breathlessly.

It was late afternoon when near exhaustion compelled her to end their pilgrimages to the resting places of what René described as "the royalty of heart and brain," and when they arrived again at the hotel Dan was waiting in the lobby.

"Well," he said, "you certainly have spent plenty of time."

René began to speak, but Liza forestalled him. "It was all my fault. This has been the most interesting day I've ever had and I couldn't bear to shorten it."

René looked a little anxiously at Dan. "It has been the greatest pleasure to escort Madame. Tomorrow I shall see that she does not become so tired. Thank you."

He kissed the hand gracefully which Liza extended, bowed and was gone. When she and Dan reached their sitting room, she dropped into a chair. "I'm afraid I'm too dead tired to go out to dinner. Would you mind just staying here again?"

"That would suit me perfectly."

"After we eat I'll tell you the wonderful story of my day. Did you ever hear of Abelard and Héloïse?"

"Not that I know of."

"Then it will all be new to you. I think I'll get into something more comfortable now. Won't you please order? I like anything, you know."

She put on a light blue peignoir which fell gracefully about her. Since her head ached she unbraided her hair, brushed it and tied it back with a ribbon as she had done on her bridal night. She studied herself in the mirror, wondering, hoping . . .

When she returned to the sitting room Dan looked at her with what seemed an approving eye.

"You're not still planning to have your hair cut, are you?"

Liza laughed. "That depends upon how much pressure is brought to bear on me."

"There might be a good deal," he said.

"Well, there's one thing sure. The cutting wouldn't be irrevocable. My hair grows fast."

During their dinner conversation it developed that Dan knew about this latest meeting with Paula for he had arranged a check upon her movements.

"I was glad René was with me," Liza said. "He handled her with the greatest ease. 'If you will excuse us, Madame,' he said in a voice like ice. There was nothing for her to do but move on. But what will happen when we get back to New York? I have a most uncomfortable feeling."

"Don't worry. I'm counting heavily on Mrs. Moreland to put a stop to the whole crazy business. If she doesn't, I'll find a way if I have to use my good right arm. As a matter of fact I could cheerfully choke the creature this minute. So you liked René?"

"Oh, very much. He's a darling, really, and more than that I think he's something of a poet. He wants to write, he told me."

Dan sniffed. "He might do better than that, but he'll probably get over it. Well, when am I going to hear this great story?"

"Right now," Liza said as they rose from the table and found comfortable chairs. "And please try to *feel* it, Dan, won't you? I wish I could tell it as well as René."

But she also told it well. Beautifully, in fact. Dan listened intently, lighting no new cigarette when the first burnt out, making no comment except a sharp, "Good God!" at one point.

At the end Liza said, "And René has an idea that there may now be no lovers like Abelard and Héloïse. Perhaps can't be because of the complexities of our modern life.

> *Never yet*
> *Hath he possessed her wholly, never yet*
> *Hath twain been one."*

She repeated the words slowly, softly. "He quoted this in support of his theory."

She waited but Dan said nothing so she told him briefly of the tomb and the rest of the Père Lachaise.

"René says that on All Saints and All Souls days they estimate that a hundred thousand people visit the cemetery."

"Good heavens! I can't think of anything more uninteresting!"

"But don't you feel it, Dan? Don't you *feel* the story, itself?"

"Well, I can't say that I do. But I think *you've* felt it a little too much for some reason. You look used up, to me. You'd better got to bed and got a good rest. And as I've told you, take the sight-seeing a little easier. What are you planning to do tomorrow?"

"I've left that with René."

"Well, just remember that Paris has been here for quite a few centuries and will likely be here when you come back, so leave something for the next time."

He smiled, but for once she didn't return it. She rose slowly and stood before him as though waiting. And then, "Good-night," she said at last.

"Good-night, Eliza. You told your story very well," he returned.

Once in her own room she went to the open window and knelt down beside it. The springtime air was fresh and sweet even here in the city. The chestnut trees were all in clustered bloom. The full moon showered a white glory over the buildings and along the streets. So must many a night have looked to the ancient lovers as they listened from their window to the Cathedral bell and the prayer of Compline, the beauty of it all serving as a magic catalyst for the later ecstasies of their love.

Perhaps Héloïse also had had a silken robe that fell about her in blue pools while upon her unbound hair would be her lover's lips . . .

Liza knelt a long time at the window before she dropped her head upon her arms and wept.

CHAPTER III

By the time they were back in New York there was a change in both Dan and Liza. He was less relaxed than in Paris, more fiercely concentrated upon his business. Liza, in her turn, had reached a sort of controlled plateau upon which she fancied herself spending the rest of her life. The emotions of her so-called honeymoon were in a measure spent. She recalled the vicarious rapture and pain she had felt in the story of Héloïse, coupled with her own bitter longings; but she reviewed it now with a slight condescension as though the reactions had been the property of another and weaker woman. From now on she determined to exact from her nature a wordless reticence, even in her own thoughts.

"I believe," Dan said one morning, "that I'll be staying at the apartment for a few nights. I'm going to have late meetings and a few evening conferences which are easier handled there than here at the hotel. All right?" he added as though an afterthought.

"Of course," Liza agreed, promptly. "I'm going to start house-hunting right away, so I'll be busy too. I liked the real estate salesman you sent up the other day."

"I know of him. He's good. And you'd better begin making the rounds of the agencies for a couple. They're not too easy to find. The good ones. Well, good luck to your efforts."

"And to yours. Is it the coal merger or the steel project?"

"Oh, both are on the fire. I don't know what's eating Dunmore. He seems grumpy for some reason. He's always been a cheerful soul and now he's touchy as the devil. I can't figure it out."

"I believe I can."

"*You?*"

"Well, I may be wrong but I think he could be jealous."

"What on earth do you mean?" His voice was sharp.

"You've been pretty close, haven't you?"

"Yes, I guess we have."

"Two bachelors with the same business interests, spending a good many evenings together probably?"

"Yes, he often had dinner with me in the apartment, then we'd thrash things over afterward."

"Now, perhaps he feels there will be a difference since our marriage. Why don't you ask him to dinner often, while you're there? Make everything seem the same."

Dan was staring at her intently. "There might be something in that," he said slowly. "I'll try your advice. By the way, I left my phone number on the desk there. Just in case of emergency," he added.

"I'll keep it for that," she smiled, "though I don't expect any."

"I'm going to take Mrs. Moreland out to dinner or ask her to have me up there some night. I want to talk things over with her and straighten the situation out on this Paula business."

"Good-bye, Dan," Liza held out her hand cordially.

"Good-bye, Liza. Take care of yourself." And he was gone.

Liza went to the phone at once and called Alex Hart, the real estate salesman. It was arranged that they would start their search the next day. Then she called Matt Harvey and the ensuing conversation was sprightly enough.

"Liza! How's the bride?"

"Wonderful!"

"I still can't believe it. You and Dan Morgan! The most unlikely match I ever heard of!"

"Most matches are unlikely, but they do happen."

"How was Paris?"

"It was all I ever dreamed of!"

"Listen, Liza. Did you run into Paula Ruston over there?"

"We did see her."

"The report around here is that she followed you over. She's capable of it. And you know she told someone—it came to me straight—that she was still going to have Dan

Morgan if it was the last thing she did in this world and she
didn't care how she did it. And Liza?"

"Yes."

"I wouldn't say this if you were sensitive, but she added
that she didn't feel you were too big an obstacle."

Liza laughed. "I do happen to have a valid marriage certif-
icate."

"Don't be childish. She wasn't meaning that. She's a dog.
Female." Matt added.

"When can you lunch with me?" Liza asked. "I want to
show you my Paris finery."

"I can't wait. Would Thursday suit?"

"Fine. I'm going to be house-hunting but I'll take that day
off. I'll see if I can round up a couple of the other girls."

"Liza?"

"Yes."

"I think you should warn Dan. Tell him to keep his eyes
open about Paula."

Liza laughed again. It was entirely spontaneous. "I don't
think he needs advice on that subject. Well, see you at one on
Thursday."

The luncheon was a complete success. Liza drew upon all
the hotel resources to provide an exquisite meal served with
perfection in her suite. Flowers everywhere brought spring
into the room, and the guests, friends from college days, were
gay, excited over her new clothes, the little bottles of rare
perfume at their plates, and brimming with questions about
Paris, the house-hunting, and *Dan*. Always the conversation
kept returning to him. They stayed till the afternoon was late,
in hope, Liza knew, of seeing him; but she parried their in-
quiries as to his return, lightly. He was working hard, she
never knew when he would finish, and let it go at that.

But underneath all the usual camaraderie there was an element which Liza would have been less than human if she had
not recognized with a deep satisfaction. The four of them:
Matt Harvey, a year ahead of the others in college, Celia
Darling, Susan Gibbs and Liza herself, had been held together by a close bond through the years, even while the
other three had married early and with distinction and Liza
had remained the unwed secretary with only her salary to live
upon. Now, suddenly, she was a young matron like the rest

and by far the wealthiest of them all. So she saw in their eyes along with the old affection a new gleam. This was the *respect* which one human being accords another when success is not only great but deserved. All that evening as she ate her solitary dinner, talked on the phone with Aunt Sarah, and tried to read, she was conscious of a warm tingling delight in her new status, in relation to her friends. No more would she be the odd girl to fill in at dinner parties, accepting with gratitude the social crumbs that fell from the tables of the *Establishment,* as it were. She now had not only a husband but a fortune as well as so was a woman to be reckoned with. *At least,* she thought as she was falling asleep, *that's one thing important Dan has done for me.*

For two weeks, steadily, she and Alex Hart drove over the suburban countryside. Hart was a slim, leisurely man of forty with a quick perception, a good sense of humor and a well-cut shabby tweed jacket which made him look at home on a country place. Liza herself carefully toned down her new sport clothes to match him as well as she could. At the end of each day after looking at house after house he would raise a quizzical eye to hers.

"No?" he would ask.

"I'm afraid not. I'm sorry."

"Don't worry. We'll find it yet."

And one afternoon they did. As they drove along a pleasant by-road, Alex Hart told her somewhat excitedly for him, about the house.

"I just heard of it yesterday so I posted out here this morning early to take a look. It was built a good many years ago by a Britisher, a Mr. Oliver. Now he's alone and retired and he wants to go back and live the rest of his days in England. The place is not actually on the market yet, I just got a tip, but he wants to sell soon. He's fond of the house, however, and a bit choosy as to whom he lets have it. So, I rather gathered that you will be on trial as well as the property."

He turned the car into a locust-bordered drive. "It's not too far from the road, which gives it a sort of friendliness, but there's quite a bit of land at the back. Here we are," he said as the drive took a turn between yew hedges. "We'll stop while you have a look."

And there it stood, with a welcoming dignity, in palest

flesh-colored plaster with curtains of clematis on one side of the doorway and a tall, spreading rose vine on the other; with the roof sweeping down to overhanging eaves, and three generous chimneys topping it.

"Look at that unusual fenestration!" Hart said excitedly, then laughed. "Architect lingo for windows," he added. "See those two round bull's-eyes above the clematis and the Venetian one below, while on this side of the house there are regular sashes. Gives interest."

He looked inquiringly at Liza who so far had not spoken. Then in a tone of awe she said, "This is it! This is my house, if only my husband likes it!"

"Wait till you see the inside and the gardens at the back! Wait till you see . . ."

"I would buy it this minute with all the rest sight unseen, if I could! It just speaks to me. It's mine."

Hart was delighted. "I've seen this happen dozens of times. It's like falling in love. One look and there it is and you can't explain it. Well, let's get out and see Mr. Oliver."

He left the car in the wide drive which curved at the back into what must have been originally a rambling stable yard, and together they walked along the flagged paving that ran in front of the house and close to it. The step at the doorway was so low that there was the feeling of moving right from the smooth lawn onto the entrance sill. A rather overbearing-looking old man in butler's black opened the door and ushered them through the wide central hall past the stairway and into the library which was evidently living room as well. Here Liza sat down suddenly, as though overtaken by weakness, and looked about her. There was the great, well-used fireplace, the walls of books, the deep, quiet chintz-covered chairs . . .

"I'm afraid to breathe," she said. "Such things as this don't really happen."

"Never distrust fate," Hart said cheerfully. "Sometimes she smiles on you."

Mr. Oliver appeared soon. He was a broad, well-preserved man in his seventies, probably, and extremely reserved. He suggested they go over the house.

"Not much can be said until you have seen it all," he remarked, looking keenly at Eliza.

So she said nothing as she moved through the drawing room, the dining room, what he called "the garden hall," an almost room-sized square at the back with another stairway which Mr. Oliver explained was the *best* one in the house.

From here through the French doors she saw the garden with a beech grove to the side of it where it seemed thousands of daffodils had just ceased blooming. She saw the long, narrow paved terrace that ran past the drawing room, the well-planned upstairs and the servants' quarters.

"For years now I've had just a couple, butler-cook combination, an excellent pair."

Eliza spoke then. "Would they . . . do you think they will be looking for another employer?"

"No," he said, "they are old and want to retire now on their modest savings. As do I," he added with his first smile.

When they had finished the tour he looked curiously at Liza. "You have made no comment, Mrs. Morgan. Perhaps I thank you for that. I had an extremely garrulous woman here yesterday and I felt the house looked a little tired when she left. May I ask whether you feel any interest in the place?"

And then Liza looked up at him, her face glowing. "Mr. Oliver, it's not merely interest. I haven't words to tell you how much I like your house, the garden, everything about it. If only my husband will feel the same!"

"When could I meet him?"

"I'll talk to him tonight. I would hope he could come out tomorrow or the day after. Could you keep it off the market till then?"

"Of course. I'll look for you both as soon as I hear from you. And one thing I should like to tell you. I can take only a few of my favorite pieces of furniture back to England with me. The rest I must sell. Since you are a bride, I understand, I thought you might be interested in knowing this. That is," he added, "if we come to terms."

There was sherry then and a pleasant relaxation on the part of their host. He kept looking at Eliza with apparent approval, adding bits of information about the house. He and his wife had built it nearly fifty years ago, designing it after a small Queen Anne country house they had known in England. His wife had planted the garden. It had been her great joy.

When they said good-bye finally, Liza looked into Mr. Oliver's eyes.

"I want you to know," she said, "that if we are fortunate enough to buy your house, it and the garden will not only be appreciated but," she hesitated, and then added, "but really loved."

"Bless you, my dear," the old man said. "I hope you get it."

As they drove along, Hart was jubilant. "The old boy certainly thawed out, didn't he? Keeping quiet at first was the best thing you could have done. The English, you know, don't care for too much chatter. Well, I thought you'd like the place. One of the odd things about Oliver is that he won't talk price with anyone but the prospective buyer so I can't give you an idea on that. Can you get in touch with Mr. Morgan tonight?"

"I'm sure I can. You've been wonderful, Mr. Hart. I get a queer shudder when I think we might have missed this if it hadn't been for you. If we can go out tomorrow will you come with us?"

"I think not. I believe Mr. Oliver would like to talk business with your husband alone. That is, if it comes to the point of a sale, and I hope it does."

"Not as much as I do," Liza answered.

When she was back in their sitting room her heart was beating fast. Would Dan be annoyed at her call? He had expressly said the number was to be used in an emergency. He had been at his apartment now for two weeks and she had heard nothing from him. She had a feeling that he was testing her by this absence, testing the validity of his freedom. And until now she had made no sign, had remained faithful to his conditions.

She went slowly to the desk and picked up the phone. This was important. This had to be done, she thought as she dialed. A man's voice with an Oriental accent answered. "Yes?" he said politely.

"This is Mrs. Morgan. I would like to speak to Mr. Morgan if he is there."

"A moment, please."

Dan came on almost at once. "Is anything wrong? Are you all right?" he asked.

"No to the first and yes to the second," she said with a little laugh. "But something has come up that I felt you would want to know. Just this afternoon I've found a house. It isn't on the market yet but soon will be. The owner will hold it for a day or two if you could manage to go to see it. Could you?"

"I've got Dunmore and another man coming in tonight but I could pick you up in the morning in good time. I had planned to go back tomorrow anyway. Would ten be too early?"

"That will be fine! I was hoping you could make it tomorrow. Well, I'll see you then at ten. Good-bye!"

"Wait a minute. You really like this house?"

"I simply can't tell you how much. Of course you may not."

"Well, I have great respect for your judgment, so we'll see what happens. O.K. then, tomorrow at ten."

But in a half hour he called. "Liza? I've managed to ditch Dunmore and the other man and I'll be up shortly. I'm curious to hear more about your find. Have you had dinner?"

"Not yet."

"Good. Would you like to go out somewhere? You've been alone for quite a stretch."

"I think it would be more fun to stay here where we can talk in peace."

"That's fine with me. I'll be there soon."

It was like it had been in the old days in the office: the emotional control, the steady determination to monitor her thoughts—it had been like this during the last two weeks. Now the knowledge that she would see him in a brief time sent the blood warmly through all her veins, staining her cheeks. She dressed quickly in a white hostess gown he had not seen her wear, particularly becoming with her present high color, softened her hair about her face as much as she could, and was ready when she heard the entrance door open. She went to meet him with both hands outstretched and he grasped them warmly in his.

"Well, Liza! It's good to see you!'"

"And wonderful to see you. I'm so glad you could come tonight, for of course I'm bursting with news."

"You don't look as though house-hunting had worn you out."

"Oh, quite the contrary. It's been fun, especially today. I've ordered dinner for seven. I thought you would like to relax a little, before."

"I'll drop my bag and be right out," he said.

When he was back in the living room he kept looking at her with (as she recognized) the same approving glances as when she had done an unusually good piece of work in the office. But nothing more! What would happen, she thought wildly, if I flung myself into his arms! But of course she did nothing of the kind. She was her steady, smiling self.

"Now, tell me all about this house. What does it look like?"

"Well, it's Queen Anne in architecture, Mr. Hart says. It has dignity but a sort of demure simplicity. You'll understand when you see it. It's washed plaster in a pale, pale pink."

"Oh, good Lord, I don't think I could take that!'"

"I shouldn't have said pink. It's really a sort of flesh colored cream, hard to describe. There's a clematis and a rose vine, and oh, Dan, you've got to see it to understand how lovely it is."

"How far from the station?"

"Just fifteen minutes and then a half hour on the express trains into the city. Would this be too hard for you?"

"I suppose I couldn't do much better. I don't like commuting but we have to have a home. Does the inside come up to your specifications?"

"Amazingly, except that there's no bay window in the dining room."

"It could be put in, I imagine."

All through dinner they talked of nothing but the house, as Dan asked questions and Liza answered them animatedly. Once she turned serious. "You must remember, Dan, that while *I* like this place, you mustn't be over-influenced by that. You must be as pleased as I am. If you don't feel enthusiastic about it you'll be sure to say so, won't you? Honestly?"

"Just how much do you like it? Honestly!"

She hesitated. "I love it!" she said.

"Very good. We'll go on from there. What's the asking price for it?"

"I've no idea and neither does Hart. Mr. Oliver will only discuss this with the man who wants to buy."

"Not a bad plan. Well, I must say I'm curious. We'll get off in good time in the morning. So, you've managed all right by yourself? I didn't intend to be away quite so long but I ran into trouble."

"Serious?"

"Could be inconvenient, but I hope I can get the best of it. It's about the merger. I was out a couple of days in Pittsburgh seeing Hadley. My own and his are the strongest mines in the area. I could buy Hadley out and I'd rather do that but it's an old company, two or three generations mixed up in it, and he won't sell. He will merge, though, for he's short of capital, if we use both names, the Morgan-Hadley Company. In this deal, if it comes off, I'll hold fifty-one percent of the stock this time and I'll be president. He's agreed to that. He's not young and seems glad to be relieved of some responsibility. But, the thing is, the stockholders have to vote on the merger. Hadley feels sure his will all agree, but who do you suppose bucked me when I spoke of it?"

"I would have no idea."

"No, you wouldn't. It's Mrs. Moreland."

"Why, how could she?"

"Well, it's a long story. I told you I'd gambled plenty in my business. It's been my life and I've liked the excitement of the game. And luck has been with me or I wouldn't be where I am, that's sure. But once about fifteen years ago I was pretty close to a smash-up. It was at that time Mr. Moreland bought a big block of stock and she has now inherited it. Then, as you know, after I opened an office here she was very kind to me socially. Taught me a lot of things."

"And through her you met Paula!"

"That's right."

"Did you have any success with that problem?"

"Worse than none. She was highly indignant when I suggested the woman had followed us over. She says Paula goes over to Paris as casually as most people cross the street. Meeting us was sheer coincidence. Of course," he added thoughtfully, "I suppose it *could* have been."

"Do you really believe that?"

"No."

"Neither do I."

"But Mrs. Moreland went further. In fact she got all wrought up. She says she's known Paula from a child and she's like a daughter to her. She came right out this time and said our own marriage was a great shock as she had still hoped . . . Well, you know what I mean. She never liked Ruston, it seems, so she threw her influence in favor of the divorce. She says . . ."

"Go on."

"This sounds pretty sticky but she says one reason Paula got the divorce was because she had become . . . well . . . interested in me. What a damned ridiculous mess!"

"Will you answer me a question?"

"If I can."

"Did Mrs. Moreland intimate that another divorce might . . . might bring about what she considers the desired end?"

"I won't answer that," he said sharply, "but I will say that *I* lost my temper in a way I'm ashamed of. With an old woman, I mean. And then I got the hell out as fast as I could. I feel as though I'd made matters worse."

"About the merger?"

"Every way."

"What are you going to do?"

"I'm going to sit tight and wait."

"About Paula too?"

"Yes. She hasn't bothered us since we've been back. Maybe she's getting some things through her head. Anyway I can't approach Mrs. Moreland again on the subject. I actually thought she'd have a stroke, she was so upset over my accusations. And I didn't tell her the half," he added grimly. "She's a pretty strong old lady, and I found out she's got a bad temper herself."

"Why didn't she like the merger idea?"

"Oh, she was just sweetly stubborn about that. Mr. Moreland had bought *Morgan* stock and that was what she intended to keep. Very unwise of me to get mixed up with another company. I think I can bring her around on that if I don't press her now."

"Is the merger very important to you, Dan?"

"I'm afraid it's going to be if I get into steel. I'll need more coke, you see. But I'm all right for the moment and I'll have

that ahead of me to work for. It's funny, but I always feel
better when there's a struggle going on. I guess I was born to
be a fighter."

"You don't like to be too sure of anything, do you?"

"No, I don't. It takes some of the zest out of it."

"I'll remember that."

He turned quickly to face her. "Good God! You surely
knew I was talking about *business!*"

"Well," she said demurely, "I just thought I'd inquire."

He laughed at that. "You're always giving me jolts. So at
least I'm never sure what you're going to *say* next."

"How about Dunmore?" she asked. "Did everything clear
up with him?"

"Oh, I think so. I took your advice and had him to dinner
several times. He doesn't favor the merger either but he'll
come round. Did you call Mr. Oliver to tell him we're coming out in the morning?"

"Yes. He seemed pleased."

"We'll leave about ten, then."

"Good. We can breakfast at nine."

Before Liza lay quiet at last that night, she drew a heavy
sigh, then with a smile turned on her pillow. "Half a loaf is
better than no bread, I suppose," she thought.

But long, long after Liza was asleep Dan lay awake. It was
not the prospective merger that was on his mind at the moment, it was a letter in a cramped foreign-looking hand
which had come that day unopened to his desk. In the corner
was written, *Personil,* for he had long ago made clear to the
sender that without this designation there would be no reply.
The letter was from his one-time wife. For months on end
the past, *his* past, lay far beneath his conscious thoughts. Then
suddenly, as now, it rushed over him like dark, engulfing waters.

It had been a hot night in July, with a full moon finishing
the ripening of the big field of wheat just beyond the Harding
mine property, when it had all begun. Dan sat upon the steps
of their house in the Patch, his mother in bed, looking at the
rows of cheap red dwellings like their own, watching darkness settle and feeling the weight on his heart. For only two
weeks before his father had been killed by a fall of slate in

the mine. MacDonald, the foreman, was bitter, for the elder
Morgan had been his friend and he knew that the accident
which took the lives of three men would never have happened if proper precautions had been taken by the owner.
Dan knew this also, and a terrible anger was added to his
grief, while over all a great loneliness oppressed him. Even
with their Scottish reserve he and his father had been close.
From him and MacDonald the boy had learned more about
mining than many a seasoned "digger" ever knew in his life-
time.

For months before the accident Dan's mother had not been
well. Father and son, with hesitant male comments, had felt
they understood. She would be all right when a certain period
of life had passed. But there had been no chance for this passage of time. The tragedy had struck too soon. With its sudden devastation Mrs. Morgan had withdrawn into a world of
her own, with her eyes looking vaguely even at her son.

Dan sat on now, feeling the hot air giving away to a small
breeze. Upon it was borne the sound of accordian playing.
That would be Tony with his bold, roving black eyes and little mustache. Ah, yes, Dan thought. Little Donna Lucetti had
been married that day to old Rocco. At least he must be near
her father's age, a widower, a bad customer, with children
grown and married. And always fighting, always drunk at the
weekends. The men had been talking about the match at
work that day. It was a queer business, they said, for Angelo,
Donna's father, evidently hated Rocco, and yet had felt compelled to give his daughter to him. There was bad blood between the two men, and apparently Rocco held some kind of
power over Angelo. It might have dated back to an old feud
in Italy, for they had all been in this country less than a
dozen years. In any event, the men said, Angelo was known
to have held out as long as he could, then had given in. The
wedding had been that day, and now the merry-making was
in progress. Dan himself had seen the beer wagon depositing
a heavy load at the Lucettis' that afternoon.

There came a new sound of music on the air, a strong, fine
touch, now, on the accordian and a tune that seemed to hold
hot moonlight nights within it. That must be Asa, the Mag-
yar, Dan surmised. Not even Tony could play like him.
They said he was part gypsy. The melody rose and swelled

and fell again with a kind of love and longing. Dan rose, hitched up his pants, tucked his shirt inside and went down the steps. He might walk along and take a look at what was going on. Better than sitting here by himself. Anyone was free to go to these affairs—there was always a box into which the men put a dollar for dancing with the bride, so the more guests the better.

He walked slowly past the back of the houses, all built on a rise of ground so there was a basement under each, opening out to the level. Poor little Donna. She was in a trap now for sure. He'd known her ever since the Lucettis had moved to Hardingville a few years ago. Pretty little thing. With boyish superiority he had tried not to see that she always smiled at him and managed to meet him often at the street pump where the people of the Patch had to go for their water.

When he reached the door into the Lucetti basement he stood a moment watching the scene. Not a pretty one, he was thinking. The place was packed with sweating couples trying to dance as they all milled about, the noise sometimes drowning the music. He managed to wedge himself inside and from the change in his pocket fished out a dollar and put it in the box. He could see Donna in her white dress, her veil now hanging limp from the heat and the many beers spilt upon it. He edged his way toward her, and her partner with a leer surrendered her.

"Well, Donna," he began, but he stopped short. Her arm tightened about his neck. "Save me, Dan," she whispered. "Oh, for God's sake take me out of this! I can't go on. Look at him."

Dan looked and felt sick at his stomach. Rocco stood on a bench, drunk, dripping beer over his wrinkled light blue suit which for some reason the "hunkies" favored, shouting out lewd remarks at which all the men nearby except Angelo were laughing uproariously.

"Save me, Dan. Take me away." Her voice was sheer despair.

Dan didn't think, nor reason. His action was automatic. He held her close and managed to make their way through the hot reeking bodies until they reached the door. Here he waited, pretending to weave back and forth to the music until the moment when the nearest backs were turned. "Run for it!"

he whispered in her ear as they got outside. "Run for the wheatfield!"

They ran, separately, as they could go faster. At the fence her veil caught as she climbed it. She snatched it off and wadded it into a ball, as Dan now took her hand.

"We'll go to the end of the field. They'll never find you there."

As they went through the tall spears, Dan, looking behind, saw the wheat fall together again over the path their feet had traveled, as waves meet and smoothly obliterate the fall of an object into the water. At last he pulled Donna down to the ground beside him where they lay panting for breath. For a time there came to their ears the same sounds of the accordian, snatches of song, and occasional shouts. Then, all at once there was a change. The music stopped and only the shouting intensified could be heard along with wild yells.

"They've missed me now," Donna whispered. "Rocco will fight my father!"

They lay, scarcely breathing, listening to the frightening voices which went on and on until with a startling suddenness all was quiet. Not a sound fell then upon the night air.

"Well, if they had a fight I guess it's over," Dan said. "But all we can do right now is to stay hid. They may be out looking for you."

So through all the night the two young things lay close in the golden wheat with the warm moonlight over them. Donna fell asleep at last, but Dan did not close his eyes. He felt sheer terror as he thought of what the results of this strange night might be. Would he himself have to fight Rocco when the discovery would be made? He had stolen another man's wife in fact, now. What price must he pay? And what was he to do with her? But along with the fears was a feeling of possession new to him and both a shame and a glory in his own strength. He was a man, now.

He woke Donna just before daylight.

"We've got to go," he said, as she clung to him. "I'll take you back to your house."

"No," she shuddered. "I can't go back. My father will beat me, and Rocco! He might kill me, even. Dan, you've got to take me with you. I'll never go back—now."

Dan didn't answer. He pulled her up and together they

started through the field in the faint flush of dawn. "I'll take you to our house until we see what's to be done," he said, through dry lips. "My mother isn't well. She won't understand but she'll be kind to you."

They got there without being seen. All was still within. Dan paused, looking at the heavy-eyed girl beside him. "Go on up to the room over the kitchen and get some sleep," he said. "I'll go up and tell my mother you're here. She won't be awake yet." Donna stumbled obediently up the stairs. Dan made some breakfast for himself and packed his bucket. Then before time for the six o'clock whistle to blow he went up to his mother's bed and shook her gently. She opened vacant eyes and smiled.

"Mother, you know the Italian girl down the row, Donna Lucetti?"

His mother nodded. "Bonny," she said.

"Well," Dan went on, "she was married yesterday to that old Rocco and she's run off. She's afraid to go back. She's here in the back room. "You understand?"

His mother nodded. "I'll take care of her when I get up. Your father will help." And she closed her eyes again.

Dan went to work with an anxiety such as he had never known or imagined. He would likely hear from the other men what had happened last night after he and Donna had stolen away. He heard, his face turning ashen. There had been a double murder. When Rocco found his bride was missing he accused Angelo of breaking his promise and drew his knife. Angelo, as quickly had drawn his. The old slumbering feud flared, and the fight was on, to the death. Angelo, the men said, fell first, with no life left in him, then Rocco after maybe twenty minutes, breathed his last also. The men, as they told it, were subdued. Used as they were to the weekly brawls which left many scars in their wake, they had never known anything like this. Only O'Brien, the irrepressible Irishman, made a joke of it.

"Sure it's just like the Kilkenny cats," he said.

> "There once was two cats of Kilkenny
> Each thought there was one cat too many;
> So they struggled an' spit
> An' they fought an' they bit,
> 'Til instead of two cats there weren't any!"

"Shut up!" the other men cried him down. Even the Super, himself, was going about with a drawn face, getting signatures of witnesses, "for his records," he said.

Dan stopped at the house of mourning on his way back, and talked with Mrs. Lucetti. Donna, he told her, had been afraid, and asked him to help her get away. They had hidden in the wheatfield till this morning and she was now at his house. Could she come back home now? Mrs. Lucetti stopped her hysterical sobbing and looked at him with ancient wisdom in her reddened eyes.

"Tell her come home. Then mebbe soon I talk to priest an' you marry her. You hide in the wheat all night?"

"Yes. No one saw us."

"Donata good girl, got sixteen years, very pretty. Rocco no man for her. You young, nice. You get married." And she resumed her sobbing.

Dan had no one to advise him. As the weeks passed his father's rigid precepts on morality were his only guide. He and Donna were married one day in the tiny frame church on the edge of the town and though he was stunned by the turn of events, in a sort of unquestioning way he loved the girl with a first boyish passion. She had black, glossy hair and hot red lips. She laughed a great deal except when in a temper and gave herself with a voluptuous abandon which, while it sometimes disturbed his innate sense of restraint, he usually accepted with an eagerness matching her own. For it was the overflowing fountain of nature's young ardor, designed not for analysis but for the continuance of the race, which bathed them, laved them, as they lay together in the back bedroom of the Patch house, their bodies touching, their minds as far apart as the poles.

It was after the baby came that MacDonald, the foreman, called Dan into his work shack and told him of a plan. A farmer, Otis, living back over the hill, had a coal bank where other farmers came with their wagons to get coal. Otis was old and slack, the opening of the bank had fallen in, but because of this there was a real opportunity for a strong, ambitious young man.

"You want to stick to the coal, lad?"

"I do. And some day I'm going to get to the top."

"I believe it. You know a good bit already. Well, here's a place you can make a start. Have you saved any money?"

"A little and my father left some."

"Take it all an' get this bank. Lease it for now but find a lawyer soon to clear it up so you can buy it. Maybe the farm itself. I'll bet there's an overlooked vein there. You'll have to work like the devil an' give up your present job. It's a gamble, lad."

"I'll take it," Dan said. "I've got to make a start sometime."

It was the beginning of the Morgan fortune, but it was also the beginning of the disaster which changed his life.

When he told Donna of his new plan she was indifferent. Indeed she had seemed for some weeks apathetic. She laughed less, was querulous with his mother and left the care of the baby entirely to her. Dan looked at the child and touched its tiny fingers reverently. It was all Italian, with not a Scottish feature, but a tenderness for it, coupled with the wonder that it was his, filled his heart.

He worked now from early morning till late at night. With his own hands he cut down the locust trees, and set the posts after he had cleared out the mine entrance. Then the unremitting digging began while the pile of coal outside grew and kept ahead of the farmers' wagons. MacDonald came out evenings and weekends and advised him. He had talked with an engineer who had surveyed much of the Harding veins. He thought the Otis farm was underlaid. The Harding Company had so much to work on right now they hadn't bought up all the surrounding area.

"But some day they'll come to it," MacDonald prophesied. "Then, lad, if you own the Otis place you'll be gettin' a start that will surprise you."

November was rainy and chill, and Mrs. Morgan seemed weak with a hard little cough.

"Oh, it's only a cold," Donna said impatiently to Dan's anxious questions. "She's always imaginin' she's sick when there's nothing wrong with her."

"I don't think she's able to take care of the baby."

"She likes to," Donna said shortly. "Go on about your business. That's all you care for nowadays anyway."

One night Dan was thoroughly frightened. He was up and down during the hours while Donna slept. His mother seemed very hot and her sharp little cough didn't let up until nearly dawn. Just a heavy cold, Dan kept telling himself. But there was something wrong with the baby. It didn't breathe right. Before he left for work he shook Donna awake.

"My mother's really sick, for look, she's not up yet."

"She'll be round fast enough when she smells the coffee."

"And the baby. It's not right, Donna. Mebbe you better take it down where it's warmer. I'll come home early and if they're not better I'll get the doctor.

Donna sat up then, her eyes frightened. "The doctor! We don't want no doctor comin' here. They've just got colds. I've got one too, but *you* wouldn't notice."

"Look out for them careful. I'll come back as soon as I can."

He was there by two o'clock. The house was cold, for the fire had gone down. He made it up quickly. There was no sign of Donna nor of his mother. He tore up the stairs. Mrs. Morgan was lying quiet but the baby's breathing was strange and its little face a bluish color. Dan ran down the row and burst in upon Mrs. Lucetti.

"Where's Donna?"

"She gone."

"Gone *where?*"

"She go off with Tony. I think shame to tell you. But she say you all the time work, no talk, no make love. She young. She want fun. She gone with Tony."

Dan's face was white. He caught her arm. "Go up to the house as fast as you can and see what you can do. There's something wrong there. I'm going to the office to telephone for the doctor."

Mrs. Lucetti put her shawl over her head and started. Dan did not have to go the length of the office as the doctor's Ford was parked in the Patch. They hurried back to the house together. Mrs. Lucetti met them, holding the baby, her eyes red and wild. She caught Dan's arm fiercely.

"You no go up. Just the doctor," she said.

The doctor went but soon came down. He looked carefully at the baby and then told Dan the truth. Two days later he stood at the new graves next to his father's, with a burning hate in his heart greater even than the grief.

Before spring he went to see a lawyer in the county seat, arranged for his divorce and bought the Otis farm. Then one evening in June Donna came back. She was tearful and coy by turns. Tony was no good. He had left her. She never really liked anyone but Dan. She had wanted to come back before this. She besought, she repented, she promised, as Dan watched her, stunned. When she tried to throw her arms around his neck he caught her. "Get out! Get out!" he hissed. "Don't ever show your face to me again! *Get out!*" He repeated it over and over. When she did not leave he flung her from the door with all his force. He heard her cry out, but he only shot the bolt and then went back to the kitchen where he sat down with his head in his hands.

Except for trips to the company store for groceries he went nowhere, saw no one except MacDonald who talked only of the success of the bank (which now had two hired diggers), and the findings of the surveyors. The Otis farm had indeed another and larger vein of coal. One evening the doctor came to Dan's house.

"I'm not sure whether you know about Donna or not," he said slowly.

"I don't want to know anything about her."

"I think you'll have to. When you pushed her out of the door she fell down the steps. She lost a pregnancy and nearly lost her life."

"Good riddance," Dan gritted.

"Now, now, my boy, I know what you've been through, but you did handle her pretty rough."

"I could have killed her!"

"The thing is, Dan I'm afraid she's going to sue you. It might go bad for you with a jury. A man can knock his wife down, but she's no longer your wife. I have a suggestion."

Dan waited. "This is it," the doctor went on. "Give her some money, say a hundred dollars. It will look big to her. I'll get her to sign a statement that she'll ask no more damages. If you're wise, Dan, you'll try this. Have you the money?"

Dan did not reply. He went upstairs and came down with the bills.

"I'll make her sign the paper before I give her these," the doctor promised.

"Mind, I'm not sorry for what I did. I wish it had been worse," Dan said.

"Don't let your hate devour you, Dan. You're young yet. Some day you'll find a nice girl . . ."

Dan's gesture as he raised his hand was purely unconscious, but it was the symbol of an oath. "As long as I live I'll have no truck with women. The way you mean: My heart's dead inside me. She killed it like she killed the others."

For a long time he heard nothing more from Donna until his name in connection with the Morgan Coal Company began to appear in the papers. Then she wrote asking for money, not damages, just *money*. She was married again and her husband had been hurt in the steel mill. Dan was wealthy even then, for by his almost superhuman efforts, coupled with the great sale of the Otis vein to the Harding Company, he was well launched in his career. He sent money through his lawyer, for the fiery hate had by now been somewhat quenched. There was instead, however, a cold stillness in his heart and a shame almost harder to bear. It was made up of the details of those hot, voluptuous nights which Donna had forced upon him, and which now he remembered with loathing.

Through the years the letters, sometimes many months apart, kept coming. Today's had been the worst. Every word was sharp in his memory.

> Dan, I need money for I'm sick. I seen in the papers you got married again. I wonder what she would think if she knowed how you threw me down the steps and all that was after. If ever I seen her I would tell her. I need the money bad so please send soon.
>
> Your first wife
> DONNA

Dan tossed his rumpled pillow aside now and got up. Over at the window, looking down upon the city street, he felt as though the red houses of the Hardingville Patch were so far removed they could have no more power over him. But they had. All that had happened there had left unhealable scars.

He had wondered sometimes if Dunmore might have stumbled upon his secret, for he had made an enigmatic remark once. But it was probably only coincidence. As to the possibility of Donna ever meeting Liza—that was too remote to consider, and he himself could never tell her the truth, not all the truth. Well, the money had already gone, more than usual. It would purchase immunity for him for a year or two, at least.

He walked softly over to the door between the bedrooms, opened it and stood staring at Liza's sleeping figure, as the pale light from the window revealed it. He wondered again as he had many times before just why she had married him. Companionship? Security? It was all he had promised as he made the bargain. There was certainly no loss of dignity in her acceptance and she was fulfilling his conditions to the letter. He gave a shuddering sigh as though mourning for the deadness of his heart, then closed the door carefully and went back to bed. By fixing his mind upon the house she had described to him, which he was soon to see, he fell at last into slumber just as the city was waking to life.

CHAPTER IV

Dan was quiet the next morning and Liza watched him anxiously.

"Are you sure, Dan, that you really want a house? I'm afraid I've pressed you about this."

"I couldn't be more sure," he said. "To have a home after all these years will do me good in more ways than you could imagine."

So they drove out of the city and through the bright countryside, talking little, until at last Liza signed to him to turn into a drive and then stop where he could get the first glimpse of the house as she had done. And like herself he said nothing at once and then drew a long breath.

"I see what you mean. Well, we'll go in and find Mr. Oliver."

The two men, both reserved but mutually friendly, started at once upon a tour of the rooms and the grounds outside, while Liza wandered alone through the downstairs, her heart beating nervously in spite of herself. The final decision must be Dan's, but if it was unfavorable how could she conceal her terrible disappointment? He had been pleased with the outside of the house, she felt sure. If only he liked the rest.

It seemed interminably long before the men came to find her as she sat in the Garden Hall, as Mr. Oliver had called it. Dan was smiling.

"We're going into the library to talk business. Can you amuse yourself a while longer?"

She felt the tension relax. From his expression and an unusual, gentle note in his voice she knew the place had spoken to him as it had done to her.

"May I wander about on the second floor?" she asked Mr. Oliver.

"Wherever you please, my dear."

She had been somewhat inhibited before by his presence as guide and she wanted terribly to check the sleeping rooms more carefully. She walked slowly now through the largest, the master one, facing the beech grove. This would be Dan's, for with it went a rather spacious dressing room which with the addition of a desk and one or two other pieces would serve admirably as a home office, if he wished. There were no connecting bedrooms but just across the hall, with a little balcony overlooking the garden, was one she would preempt for her own. Like the front of the house itself, this moved her with a sort of foreknowledge as though she had always belonged to it. She went over to the fireplace, smiling as she traced with her finger quaint patterns on the blue tiles; she approved the escritoire in the corner and the four-poster with its lacy tester. In fact if Mr. Oliver would sell it, she would like to buy all the furniture. It was right for the room and for her. With a floral paper, she mused, a plain rug and light curtains instead of the heavy hangings, it would be all of which she could dream.

The other rooms were pleasing. The one with Victorian furnishings would delight Aunt Sarah when she came to visit. The whole upstairs, in short, was good. Liza went out on the stair landing and waited there on the windowseat under the oriel window until at last she heard Dan calling to her from the lower hall. When she reached the men they were both smiling.

"All business settled," Dan said.

"I'm glad my house is going to belong to you both." Mr. Oliver's eyes looked a bit misty. "I will enjoy thinking of you here."

"And I couldn't be happier," Liza reassured him. "I know now that I've been terribly nervous all morning for fear something would go wrong. Any time you come back from England you must stay here with us and feel it is still home."

They left with a key to the front door. Mr. Oliver was going to be away for the weekend and very perceptively felt they would like to come out by themselves and go over the place in detail. Also, he left them a list of the furniture he was taking with him, so they could decide what pieces they wanted to buy, "if any," he added.

All the way back to the city Dan was unusually talkative. "You couldn't have made a better find," he said. "I feel I belong there already. I'll keep my apartment of course, but this will be home. I gave Oliver a check for the hand money but I'll get in touch with Hart at once and let him take care of the rest of it."

"Was the price high?"

"So-so. But it's a good buy. One thing, Liza, you must do at once. That is stop at the Agencies and find a couple. You must *never* under any conditions be there alone at night."

His voice was very stern. Liza looked up at him with a little laugh. "You sound almost savage. But I don't mind. I *like* having you take care of me, look after me. After all the years I was alone against the world, so to speak, I appreciate this."

"And I'll tell you something *I* appreciate," Dan replied. "It's the way you have fulfilled the conditions of our . . . bargain. Never once have you put any strain on my emotions, which I would have hated. You know, Liza, you're as easy to live with as an old shoe. I mean that as a compliment."

"Thanks," she said in rather a small voice. "I'm glad you're satisfied."

"The question is whether *you* are."

Liza swallowed carefully. "Have I ever showed the least sign of not being satisfied?"

"No, as a matter of fact, you haven't," he said, relief showing in his voice.

"Well, let's consider your question answered then."

"Very good. This house buying has come up at the best possible time. I've had some problems and I can stand a pleasant prospect to think about."

"Any worries besides the merger?"

"A few. Oh, forget it. That's *my* business."

For the next few months Liza was busier than she had ever been in her life. Mr. Oliver, now a friend, sailed, taking his most cherished possessions with him, after disposing of all that Dan and Eliza did not buy. The servants, Maggie and Horace, a kindly small wren of a woman of astonishing capabilities in the kitchen and a lofty and rather overbearing man, competent it seemed in every other area, had agreed to stay on until the Morgans were well settled, possibly till spring, before they retired. Indeed they evinced a strong eagerness to know what changes were to be made in the house. It was patent they wished to stay long enough to see for themselves. The building of the bay window in the dining room was especially approved by Horrace.

"At large dinner parties, madam, such as we used to have when Mrs. Oliver was well, I could have used an extra serving table here. The one you propose to set in the window will do nicely for that. I take it you will probably do quite a bit of entertaining as time goes on, madam?"

"Oh, I imagine so, Horace," Liza had replied, somewhat vaguely.

As she repeated this question to Dan that night while they surveyed the finished drawing room, Dan took it seriously.

"As soon as the house is in order I would like to have some parties. I've promised Mrs. Moreland we'd have her at the first one."

"Oh, you've been in touch with her again?"

"By phone. I haven't seen her. I'm playing a waiting game, but I have to keep the irons hot while I'm waiting. I need that merger. But I'll get it, eventually. I think it might be very smart to have the Hadleys here when they come on and have Mrs. Moreland at the same time. Everything social on the surface but plenty of business politics underneath."

"Any one you want to have, Dan, will be fine with me, of course, but I would have to meet Mrs. Hadley before I invited her here. And the fact that she lives in Pittsburgh . . ."

"I see. Well, they'll likely be on to New York sometime this fall. Then it would be correct enough for you to call on her at her hotel, wouldn't it? The party plan could be broached then. And I'd want Dunmore, of course, too. They know him. As a matter of fact I'd like to ask him for a weekend as soon as possible. When do you think we'll be ready for guests?"

"It won't be long now. You really like what I've done?"

"I couldn't be more pleased."

"I'm glad. It's been possible only by spending a lot of money. I hope I haven't bankrupt you. Or is it bankrupted?"

Dan looked at her keenly. "Suppose you had. Suppose I should lose everything. How would that affect our . . . our relationship?"

Liza had been rearranging the cushions on the long sofa. She raised startled eyes now to his. "Why, I should hope not at all."

"Those are pleasant words to hear," he said slowly, "but I don't intend to go broke. I think this room is your biggest accomplishment," he added. "It was pretty stiff before, and dull, but now . . ."

"I think it's beautiful myself and I'm terribly glad you approve, for I've really worked over this. And had some professional help too."

She looked about her proudly. There was still dignity here but there was warmth and color as well. They had bought the great Persian rug, but instead of its muted blues which Mrs. Oliver had used entirely in her decor, Liza had picked up its pale rose and gold, using the blue only as accent. The room spoke of wealth and taste but also of the indefinable quality of charm.

"And every seat in it is comfortable," Liza added.

"Thank the Lord for that!" Dan ejaculated. "I sat down hard once on one of those little gold-legged chairs of the Olivers' and I thought I'd smashed both its back and mine. Of course for absolute comfort I'll still take the library."

They crossed the hall together and scanned the room before them. It was larger than either of them had thought at first, perhaps because then it had been a bit overcrowded with furniture. They had kept only the deep chairs with their softly faded chintzes. The massive desk had gone, for Dan would have his own in his "office" and Liza had hers in the Garden Hall. The best pieces from her apartment were now here: among them the antique table and sofa from Aunt Sarah's; her books on the shelves next to the ones Mr. Oliver had left behind; a fine seascape she had picked up once at an auction and a large copy of the Winged Victory for which she had once done without a new winter coat! She had never told Dan that.

"This is what I would call a provocative room," she said thoughtfully.

"Meaning what?" he answered. "A good place for a fight?"

"A good place for conversation. I defy any group to sit here without discussing a few ideas, especially in winter with a fire going. And it's also a lovely room, I feel, to sit quiet in, and think your own thoughts."

Dan was roaming about, studying the book titles.

"You'll have to try your hand at educating me," he said. "Most of my reading has been on coal, steel, and business in general. Maybe I can save a few nights now and then to lap up a little culture, if you'll take me on as a pupil."

"I'll start you in on poetry. I think that's what you need most," Eliza said, laughing. "Well, let's take a look at the dining room before we call it a day."

They had bought the furniture already there, Chippendale, which they both liked, and for the large bay window now completed, Liza had found a small square table which matched sufficiently. "Just for the two of us," she said now. "Very exclusive, this table, probably just for breakfasts. Other times we'll use the big one. Oh, and you must see this!" She opened the top drawer of the buffet. There, shining row upon row was their wedding silver from Aunt Sarah. "Horace dotes on this. He condescends to slang sometimes and he says this has *class*. Good sterling, fine design and a dozen and a half of everything. 'It'll be a pleasure to clean this, madam,' he said. You know, Dan, I'd love to have Aunt Sarah down, soon. She's dying to see the house and I'm getting homesick to see her."

"By all means! Any time you like. I'm getting silly about this place. I'm itching to show it off to everybody, and Aunt Sarah should be first."

"Do you think it would work to have her and Dunmore here for the same weekend? She won't stay much longer than that, I know. She and I could visit while you and Dunmore talk man talk."

"Fine with me. Find out when she can come, then we can ask Dunmore."

They had been living at the house for the past five weeks even while the decorators were putting last touches here and there. Mr. Oliver had taken the furniture from the master bedroom and Dan had bought new for himself in the selection of which Liza would take no part. "This must be all masculine," she insisted. "Then you can feel like a monk or a bachelor with no trace of petticoat influence." And the heavy dark pieces Dan had chosen achieved this effect.

They climbed the wide stairs now together and Dan paused outside his door in the upper hall. "You've really done a marvelous job on the house, Liza. I'm more than satisfied. Well, good-night!"

"I'm awfully glad you like it. Good-night, Dan."

She went on into her room, the one she had planned at once to make her own. It was lovelier now than when she had first seen it. And as Dan's was almost austerely male, so hers was delicately and deliciously feminine. He had crossed the hall to it a few times but he had been then, as always, she thought bitterly, businesslike. She stood for a moment now on her balcony breathing the cool air and watching the silver shadows beneath the trees where the light of a half moon sifted through the leaves. The white flowers in the garden beds—the phlox, the stocks, the petunias—raised pale hands to the night. Mrs. Oliver, her husband said, had been particularly fond of white flowers, and so, by an odd coincidence, was she herself. Yes, this was indeed her home by a strange, intuitive ownership, in which her spirit itself took title. All the hard work of the last months, into which she had put every ounce of her creative ability, had added deeply to her sense of possession but also, alas, to a poignant sense of loss. For in spite of her resolves to remain upon a calm emotional plateau, in spite of the severe monitoring of her inmost thoughts, a hope, fragile but persistent, had arisen. It was that here, together, in the beautiful house that was now *their home,* there would be a change in their relations. That Dan's casual friendliness would become something more . . . But it had not been so.

Sometimes in the stillness of the night Liza would waken suddenly roused by a burden on her heart. For a moment she would lie startled, unable to explain the particular weight upon her consciousness. Then she would remember. "You're as easy as an old shoe, Liza," he had said, *meaning a compliment.* And the slow hours would pass before she slept again.

She looked another minute now at the white garden, then came into the soft light of the room, undressed and settled between the sheets which Maggie meticulously turned down for her each night.

Both weekend guests accepted at once for the date set, Aunt Sarah remarking spicily that if she hadn't been invited soon she would have come anyway. While Dunmore did not go that length it was apparent, Dan remarked, that he was quite pleased at the invitation.

"I've just been wondering," Liza said one evening, "if it wouldn't be nice to start our entertaining with sort of an open-house affair. This way we could each have all our friends at once and then settle down to small dinner parties later on. What would you think of that?"

"Why, I'd think very well of it. Why didn't I get the idea myself? Of course that would be the way to start out. Would you phone or send cards, or what?"

"Cards, I think," Liza reflected. "We have our *Mr. and Mrs.* ones. We could make a list right away and I'll get them off soon. Wouldn't it be fun to have the party the weekend Aunt Sarah and Dunmore are here? You'd want him anyway and I know Aunt Sarah would love it. You remember how she enjoyed our reception *and the champagne.* Well, we could have a big bowl of champagne punch in the dining room for anyone who would prefer it to other drinks. I want to get everyone in there somehow, for the room's so beautiful. I know Maggie and Horace will be pleased about the whole thing. They've hinted that they hoped we'd do some entertaining soon. Oh, I *am* pleased about this."

"So I see."

"The girls have all been dying to come but I've held them off until the house was completely finished. Do you want to know the very worst of me, Dan?"

"I think I could take it."

"I'm just full of vanity and pride. My friends all have lovely homes and I've been invited to them so often. Now *I* have one and *I'll* be the hostess this time!"

"Well, get yourself a new dress to knock their eyes out," he said. And then, "I wonder if everybody can find the way here. They'll all be driving, of course."

"I never thought of that."

"Oh, I know what I'll do. Get a little road map printed. I know a man who would do the printing job in a day's time. I'll have young Colby draw it up. He's good with a pencil."

"Oh," Liza said hastily, coloring, "I don't believe I'd ask him . . . I mean . . . it's just . . ."

"Just what?"

"I dated him quite a good deal and this might not seem exactly graceful . . ."

"You mean over the years you've had *dates?*"

"Why, yes. What did you suppose? I've had my share."

"But you never married," he said wonderingly.

Liza's chin went up as she looked straight into his eyes. "Well, just this *once!*"

It was Dan's turn to color up to the roots of his hair. "I'm sorry," he said. "I deserved that. I won't ask Colby to make the map. As a matter of fact I can do it myself, I guess. What about inviting any of the office people? Would they mix?"

"Oh, yes. I think that would be nice."

"Well, send cards to the ones you want. You know them all as well as I do. There's one thing that has just struck me though. It's the devil, but we'll be in for it. We'll have to invite the Ruston woman."

"Oh, no! Do you really think that will be necessary?"

"Afraid so. After my last talk with Mrs. Moreland I'm sure it would never do to leave Paula out. But in such a crowd . . . how many do you suppose will be here?"

"I can imagine forty or fifty at least."

"Yes. Well, she can't do much harm amongst that number and you can bet I'll keep out of her way."

"If you can," Liza said soberly, and then, "oh, let's forget her and do our lists. It's all right with you to have the party the Saturday Aunt Sarah's here?"

"Heavens, yes. In her black silk she'll give it more tone than we can. Well, let's get to work."

They sat close together at the library table, writing; adding, comparing, striking out, counting up names. At last the joint list was finished, and Liza rose.

"It's been fun, hasn't it?"

"A lot."

"I'm terribly excited over our first party!"

"As a matter of fact, so am I. Well, don't let it keep you awake."

"It may, at that. Good-night, Dan."

Liza had been correct in her estimate of how Maggie and Horace would take the news. They rose to it as trout to the fly.

"Now, this sounds real nice, Mrs. Morgan," Maggie said, smiling. "It's been a little dull round here the last years. No disrespect but Horace an' me like a bit of stir with parties an' that. An *open house* now, will just start things off proper."

Horace was even more animated. It seemed he had a niece married to a caterer. Jennie, she had a fine touch with the hors duvers and her husband he was a good hand *with the corks,* if Mrs. Morgan understood. If she'd say the word he'd get them over for the party and he could guarantee things would go smooth.

"With house guests too, I wondered whether this would be too much for you," Liza put in.

"I'll tell you what," said Maggie. "My friend as is cook over at The Poplars next to here has a girl that goes out betimes to help. I could mebbe get her for the weekend and she could do the beds an' that, and help me with the meals while Horace would be busy with the party. If you'd say the word, Mrs. Morgan."

"By all means," Liza said. "I'll enjoy planning for it more if I'm sure you have plenty of help."

"Just a minute, Mrs. Morgan," Horace said importantly. "I've got something to show you. I tell you I mebbe wasn't just *ethical,* as the sayin' goes, but what would a lone gentleman like Mr. Oliver want with this in a London apartment? I know he forgot about it, bein' put away for years an' all, so I never said a word thinkin' you an' Mr. Morgan was young an havin' likely more use for it. Just a minute."

He went into the storage pantry and returned with a large burden swathed in canton flannel. He set it on the kitchen table, removed the wrappings and stood back, surveying it with pride. It was an enormous silver punch bowl with a heavily embossed border.

"Got it for their twenty-fifth anniversary an' we used it for the party then. Seventy-five or more we had. Isn't she a beauty?"

Liza had clasped her hands in utter delight. "It's breathtaking! Could you set it on the dining room table just to show the effect there?"

Horace bore it in and placed it at one end. "When I get 'er shined up she's goin' to look handsome."

"Are there glasses?"

"Plenty, Mrs. Oliver bought more than what come with the gift. Crystal they are with a bit of silver rim. Very nice an' elegant."

Liza went over and put her hands around the bowl. "I simply love it, Horace. I was going out to buy one of some kind, but I would never have found anything like this. Of course we'll have to tell Mr. Oliver about it. It's too valuable to take without paying him."

"Well you can do as you like," said Horace graciously, "just so long as we've got the bowl. An' I might just say here what Maggie an' me have often mentioned that the house is more cheerful like than it's ever been. Maggie an' me both feel satisfied with the way you've done it up."

"Thank you very much, Horace," Liza said, keeping a sober face. "Mr. Morgan and I both appreciate your staying on with us. I don't know what we would do without you and Maggie."

She walked slowly back through the rooms, her cheeks flushed, her eyes bright. The great silver punch bowl had added a certain last fillip of pleasure to that of all her other possessions. Matt Harvey had one and Liza realized now it was the only thing which had stirred an actual pang of envy within her. Well, *she* had a silver bowl now, much bigger, she thought with a little grin, than Matt's. And then, as she stood looking into the drawing room, something like a chill wind seemed to blow over her. *I've got too much,* she thought, *at least of material things. It's Cinderella stuff. It's too good to be true! It frightens me.*

She walked through the house and out through the French doors of the Garden Hall into the warm sunshine. She checked carefully to see how the last flowers were holding up and as she did so, her spirits lifted. "What an ungrateful and silly attitude that was," she said to herself. "I guess it's my New England blood. I must have been thinking of that awful old hymn Aunt Sarah quotes:

> *You should expect some danger nigh*
> *When most you feel delight.*

Well," she added, "I won't descend to that ghastly theology."

Once in the house again she decided to call up Matt
Harvey. The cards had been mailed and Matt should just
about now have hers. Matt as usual was all bright oral italics.

"Liza! The invitation has just come and I'm simply *breathless* over the party! Tom and I drove past your place one day
but we didn't dare go in after your telling us to wait. Liza, it
looks heavenly from the outside. Are you having a crowd?"

"About sixty if they all get here. You really can come,
then?"

"Just try to keep me away! If you hadn't asked me soon I
was going to come anyhow, in spite of you!"

"That's just what Aunt Sarah said. By the way, she's going
to be here that weekend."

"Wonderful! I'm dying to see her again. I overheard her
setting Mrs. Moreland in her place that day after your wedding and it's been my best story ever since. I suppose you're
not asking her protégé?"

"Paula Ruston? Well, yes. We have to on Mrs. Moreland's
account."

"You're crazy. You know she's going around making the
damnedest remarks about you. You're an angel to have her in
your house!"

"Oh, amongst sixty she oughtn't to show up too much."

"Her!" Matt said ungrammatically. "She looks like the
Scarlet Woman of Babylon no matter where she is. Well, it's
your business. Oh, Liza, can I lend you anything? What
about my silver punch bowl?"

"I've got one, Matt, a beauty, that belonged to the Olivers,
but thanks anyway. Listen, if I read over the list of my special friends will you check to see if I've forgotten anybody?"

Matt gave strict attention. "What about Rose Bascom and
Bill? You met them here one night and they were taken with
you. Didn't they ask you to dinner or something?"

"Heavens, yes. I couldn't go but how dreadful of me to
forget. I'll send them a card at once. Anyone else?"

"Well, just Anne Scott. You remember her. She was in my
class. Her husband, the bastard, walked out on her with another woman. She's free now, unencumbered and as pretty

and sweet as ever but she does get *down*. Any unattached men coming?"

"There may be a few from the office."

"Well, do see they meet Anne. I can't imagine why somebody hasn't snapped her up before this. But then I always said that about you and look where *you* landed. It's uphill work trying to make matches."

"Oh, they're made in heaven, hadn't you heard?"

"Well, I believe in giving heaven a nudge when I can. Liza, I'm just dying to see how Dan Morgan looks in captivity!"

"He's no captive! He's a very free agent!"

"Maybe, but you'd better keep a tight rein on him if you insist on having the Ruston woman around."

"Oh don't be silly. Well, I'll see you at the party. Oh, Matt, I *hope* you'll like our house!"

The preparations moved forward with ease and dispatch. There were lawn tables and umbrellas stacked away in the basement and Liza decided to have them set up in the garden. September so far had been warm and golden and there was a good chance the party day might have bright weather. The umbrellas would add an extra festive and impressive touch to the scene. Sometimes when she had done all she could think of doing inside the house she strolled down the drive and looked back with deep satisfaction. On one of the great gateposts a wrought-iron legend read, *Barmoor House*. The name had been given by the Olivers, and she and Dan had decided to keep it. At the top of the little maps that had gone with the invitations Dan had put: Directions for reaching *Barmoor House*. "That looks pretty dignified," he had said, complacently.

One night at dinner as she surveyed the bare walls where the Oliver family portraits had hung Liza was struck by an idea.

"Why, Dan, *I've* got a legitimate ancestor!" she exclaimed.

"Well, I would hope so," he said laughing.

"I mean there's an oil painting of my great grandfather in Aunt Sarah's attic. I've just remembered. I haven't seen it in years—she wouldn't hang it because she said she always hated him. But if she'll let us have it, think how impressive it would look above the buffet! I'll call her up tonight."

Aunt Sarah was rather scornful of the request. "I don't

know why you'd want that thing. I doubt if it's a very good oil. Just local work, like as not. And the man wasn't much credit to the family. An old pirate if ever there was one. He always scared the wits out of me when I was a girl. So when I took over the house I put him in the attic. You'd better let him stay there."

"Truly, Aunt Sarah, I want him if you don't mind. You see he'll keep us from looking too new and brash. Dan is going to send a car up for you on Friday . . ."

"He'll do nothing of the kind. I'm going on the bus to New York. You can meet me there."

"You can't argue with him, Aunt Sarah, when he makes up his mind. I find he's very obstinate . . ." she looked over her shoulder to smile at Dan, who was listening, "but in a nice way. So you see you can put great grandfather in the car."

"Well, I spose that's the only way I *could* bring the thing. I must say the frame is a good one. They used real gold leaf in those days. I thought once of having a mirror put in it but now if you want the portrait I'm glad I didn't. I guess the trip will be a mite easier in the car and I have some linens I want to take to you, too. Tell Dan I approve of him."

"I will and I'm sure the feeling is mutual. Oh, I can't wait to see you!"

"Well, you've waited quite a spell this time. I guess you can hold out another couple days," was the crisp rejoinder.

On Thursday afternoon Horace found Liza in the garden and announced a caller. "She didn't give her name an' I showed her into the library." He was visibly impressed.

Liza smoothed her linen dress and wished she had changed after lunch. This might be one of her neighbors, none of whom had yet called. She went through the hall with pleasant anticipation and then stopped dead at the doorway. Before her stood Paula Ruston in smart jacket and tweed skirt.

"Hello, Liza," she said with her usual air of condescension. "Of course I'm coming to the party. Couldn't miss that. But I just stopped in now to see the house before it's mobbed. Will you give me a quick show around? I have only a few minutes."

"Why of . . . of course." Liza felt herself stammering with helplessness. "This is the library."

"Yes, so I gathered," said Paula, sweeping the book shelves with an insolent glance.

"Just through here is the dining room," Liza went on. "My aunt is bringing a family portrait down to us tomorrow. It will hang here, above the buffet."

"Good-sized room," Paula vouchsafed.

"I don't imagine you would be interested in the butler's pantry or the kitchen and storage places. If you will come through here," indicating a door at the side, "I'll show you one of our favorite spots, the Garden Hall, as the former owners called it. We find it charming. I do my letters here and a bit of sewing or knitting perhaps, and we read the papers here Sunday mornings. There is a second stairway, as you can see, and the French doors open on the garden."

Paula looked about but made no comment.

"If you will come back now along the main hall I'll show you the drawing room."

When they reached it, Liza could hear Paula give a little gasp of surprise. "Not bad," she said. "Who was your decorator?"

"Myself for the most part, though I had some consultations about this room."

"You!" Paula said. "Where did *you* learn all this? I thought you came from a little back-water Vermont town."

"A very nice one," Liza said icily. Well, I believe that is all, Mrs. Ruston."

"Oh, no," Paula said. "I want to see the upstairs too. Everything."

"I'm just preparing my rooms for weekend guests, so if you'll excuse me . . ."

"That's all right. I'm sure they aren't *that* much disarranged."

She moved swiftly to the stairs and started up. Liza, white with anger, followed her. In the upper hall she said, "There are five bedrooms and four baths. The two front guestrooms share one bath, the others each have one of their own. From here I believe you can get an idea of this floor."

"Oh, I'd like to look into them all," Paula said.

She gave a hasty inspection to the front rooms. "And which is the *master* bedroom?" she inquired.

Liza indicated it and Paula stepped inside, giving an appraising look around it and the dressing room-office beyond.

"Huh!" she said. "This is big enough for a man to house a harem, but I don't see any sign of a woman here. Aren't you going to show me *your* room, Liza?"

"Certainly," Liza said as calmly as she could. "Just there a little farther down the hall." She remained where she stood as Paula looked into the room with interest.

"Pretty, pretty!" she said, with a small sneer in her voice. "Now, I've got to go. Well, this has been most interesting. *Especially* the bedroom arrangements." She ran down the stairs. "See you on Saturday. How many people do you expect?"

"One never knows with this kind of party," Liza said.

"That's right. You catch on quickly. Well, so long till then." And she was gone.

Liza sat down in the library, trembling all over. The woman's insolence and bad manners were exceeded only by her beauty, which was frightening. For she was seductive to a degree. The oval face, the lustrous hair, the great dark eyes, the red, sensuous lips! And, according to Matt Harvey, all this woman's power was to be still directed toward Dan, with a purpose.

"I *won't* be scared," Liza thought. "Dan is a strong man and I'm sure he hates her. But oh, not as much as I do!"

Her first impulse was to tell him all about the call, the minute he came home. It would be a relief to pour it all out. But on sober second thought she decided against this. Dan seemed happier, more elated, just now than she had ever seen him. This would be his first experience in entertaining in his own home just as it would be hers, and unlike her he had no apparent qualms of uneasiness, only a great feeling of pride and anticipation. She decided not to mar this by a recital of the afternoon's experience.

Aunt Sarah arrived well before dinnertime on Friday with her worn suitcase, a box of linens, great grandfather's portrait wrapped in a quilt, a dozen fresh eggs from Mrs. Phinney's chickens and a country-cured ham. She stood in the hall and looked around her with amazement.

"Highty tighty, mighty!" she said "I didn't expect all this

elegance! Well, show me to my room now and I'll wash up a little and then you can pilot me round."

When the grand tour had been completed Aunt Sarah sat in the library and looked at her niece. "Well, as the country saying goes, Liza, when you married Dan you certainly sat down in a butter keg!"

"But don't you like it all? Isn't it beautiful?"

"I'll like it better when I get used to it. I guess I'm more at home in plain surroundings but it's nice, Liza. Very nice."

Which was as far as Aunt Sarah ever went with compliments.

Dinner was quite gay with the old lady's quips and Dan's rejoinders and Liza smilingly aware of the rapport between them.

"I brought you a dozen fresh eggs, Dan, and a Vermont cured ham, so you ought to be fixed with breakfast for a while. You know what wood is best to smoke a ham? Apple." She laughed. "I guess that's why apple sauce just naturally goes with ham. Well, I must say I think you have quite a place here."

"Thank you. For everything. As to the house, the credit all goes to Liza."

"She's a right smart girl," Aunt Sarah conceded.

"I'll go along with that," Dan replied. And while it was not the most extravagant praise in the world Liza colored with pleasure under it.

After dinner Horace brought a stepladder and he and Dan moved the buffet and hung the painting with mild suggestions from Liza and very definite ones from Aunt Sarah.

"That's too low! Now you've got it too high! Over a little to the left . . . It's still crooked!"

But at last it was pronounced in the right place and they stood off to view it.

"He looks a grim old bird," said Dan.

"Curmudgeon!" Aunt Sarah pronounced. "He was the only one of our whole tribe that ever drove too sharp a bargain. Well, you're welcome to him. The frame's good anyway, as I told you, Liza. I cleaned it up some."

Liza studied the painting from all angles. "I rather like him," she said. "His eyes are good even if the rest of the face does look a bit cantankerous. But what the whole thing does to the room is impressive, isn't it, Dan?"

"Quite amazing, I'd say. I wouldn't have believed it. This furniture did seem to demand an ancestor, somehow. Well, now we've got one. There wasn't a portrait of his wife, too?"

"No. She died young, poor thing. I guess he just plain wore her out. Ten children in twelve years or something like that."

"Let's go into the library," Liza said hastily, "and we'll tell you all about the party. There's to be champagne punch, Aunt Sarah."

"Good! I'll relish that. But I'll go at it easier than I did at your wedding. It just seemed like cider to me, but I found it went to my legs. Well, now, tell me all the plans!"

The next day was clear, warm, and mellow with the first faint aroma of autumn. Liza had left the flower arrangements until this morning so now she busied herself with that, enjoying the effect of the yellow chrysanthemums in the drawing room, the red roses in the library and the all white epergne on the dining table where white candles shone in the tall candelabra and the great punch bowl gleamed at the end! She was standing off to survey the effect when Dan came up behind her.

"Yes. White is just right for here," he said.

She turned quickly. "Oh, Dan, do you feel nervous about the party?"

"Nervous? No. Why should I? Do you mean you do?"

"Yes, I'm afraid so. I'm not exactly a stranger to social affairs but I've never been the *hostess* before at anything as big as this and all at once I'm scared."

"Why, you've been so pleased about it all along!"

"I know and I still am but oh, I *hope* everything goes all right."

"Why wouldn't it? The house looks fine and they seem to know what they're doing in the kitchen. When the people all get milling around the only thing you'll have to do is to keep from getting stepped on. Did you get a new dress?"

"No. I'm wearing one of my Paris ones."

"What color?"

"Light blue."

"You look well in that. Liza . . ."

"Yes?"

"You haven't said anything for a good while about your hair."

"Neither have you."

'I think," he said slowly, "that I probably *should* say something when I see it . . . down. It's very pretty."

"Why, thank you, Dan."

"And don't worry about the party. Just try to enjoy it." He turned abruptly and went out.

Dunmore came before lunch which they ate at one of the garden tables to spare the dining room one already laid for the afternoon. He was in a fine mood, admiring everything and exerting all his latent charm. Perhaps, Liza thought, it was only the business side of him that she had distrusted. She could see he was winding Aunt Sarah round his finger.

"You know," he was telling her, "I saw these two here in the office for years and I never suspected anything was going on between them."

Aunt Sarah eyed him sharply. "I don't imagine anything was 'going on' as you say."

Dunmore laughed. "Oh, I didn't mean anything indiscreet. I just meant I never once thought of their getting married. Great idea, though."

"I take it you haven't followed it yourself?"

"Not so far, but . . ."

"But you may have your eye on a prospect?"

"Well, could be. The trouble is I don't think anyone has her eye on me."

"Some women don't show it till they're asked."

"Comforting thought. Dan, if anything could turn a staid bachelor toward matrimony, this place of yours would. It's beautiful. Not too big to seem like a home, yet that drawing room! Spacious enough for anybody. Is there anything I can do to help this afternoon, Liza?"

"Yes," she said quickly, "there is. Some of Dan's friends you know better than I do. If you see me floundering, come to my rescue, won't you?"

"I'll do that. But I can't imagine you out of your depth."

At half past three Aunt Sarah in her black silk and heir-loom cameo came down the stairs and seated herself com-placently in the library. The men soon followed. Liza had not intended to make an entrance but she had waited to rearrange the flowers a little in the bedrooms so when she finally stood in the doorway the three pairs of eyes were fixed upon her. Dunmore whistled, Dan smiled, and Aunt Sarah said with evident restraint, "Well, you look very presentable, Eliza."

"What a Vermont understatement!" Dunmore said, with a laugh.

Liza knew she was looking her best for her mirror had told her so. The gown had Paris written all over it. A pale blue silk brocade with wide bateau neck, tiny sleeves, tight-fitting bodice, a skirt that rippled to her ankles. It bore the unmistakable elegance of the true couturière.

"I'm glad you like my dress," she said, looking as she spoke at Dan, who nodded. "I wish," she added, "that we could open the door ourselves for the first guests at least. It would seem so friendly and informal."

"Wouldn't do," Dan said. "We have to live up to Horace. He's all set to be as formal as possible. Where should we stand? I never thought of that."

"In the hall I should think, until the rooms begin to fill up, then we can move about."

"That's right," said Dunmore. "It's nice to be near the door at first, then later you'll be all over. I think I'm going to lead off to the garden before long. Gosh, it's pretty out there today."

To Liza's relief it was her own friends who came first, Matt Harvey and Tom bringing Susan and Hank Gibbs. There was a bright intimate little flutter of introductions, and exclamations about the house before other guests arrived, then, as though impelled by ungovernable curiosity, there came an early and steady stream of couples. Before one would have thought possible, the rooms were filling up with the usual sounds of chatter and laughter betokening a good party, spreading through them.

When Mrs. Moreland and Paula arrived Dan was in the dining room so Liza had to do her best alone. She returned Mrs. Moreland's rather muted greeting with as much warmth as she could muster but when she turned to speak to Paula she found her busy already with a group in the drawing room. Rude, but typically Paula. Liza gave an inward shrug and welcomed some new arrivals. The first tension had left her. Everything was going well. The service was perfect, so, she knew, were the hors d'oeuvres and of course the punch. A delightful air of pleasure seemed to float through the house.

It was when she was for a few minutes with Aunt Sarah who was holding court in the library that Matt Harvey came up and drew her aside.

"That she-devil!" she said. "You've got to stop her, Liza. She's simply taking over!"

"What do you mean?"

"Go to the drawing room doorway and find out. Come on."

They did not have to listen long. Paula's voice rose clearly above the others. What she was doing was clever, subtle, in a sense beyond criticism but diabolic nonetheless.

"Oh, *Mary!* How wonderful you could come! I was hoping to see you!"

"Tom, you need a fresh drink. Someone will be round in a minute, I know."

"There's one room here you will love, Pearson, and you, Sally, for you're English. It's called the Garden Hall. I think it's Dan's favorite. Come on, I'll show you through. Anyone else care to join us?"

Liza did not wait for any more. She made her way as quickly as she could to where Dan was standing in the dining room. She named him with what to her horror was a little sobbing breath. "Could you come with me to meet some new guests?" She tried to sound normal for the benefit of those who could overhear.

As they started she whispered to him, "Paula is acting as hostess. Can you do something to show I'm . . . I'm . . ."

He caught her hand almost roughly in his own. "You're damned right I can," he replied under his breath.

He still held her hand as they passed through the library, pausing to chat here and there, and finally reached the drawing room where Paula was just shepherding the group back from her tour. Dan planted his considerable bulk directly in front of her and answered a comment from one of the men.

"Oh, the Garden Hall! Yes, my wife and I are particularly fond of that room. Sorry she wasn't just here to show it to you herself. By the way, would any of you care to see the garden? Its best is over but we think it's still worth looking at."

There were a number of interested rejoinders led by Matt Harvey.

"Show them where you're going to put the fountain next spring, Liza," he said, giving her hand a little squeeze as he dropped it. Then he took a step back, practically pinning Paula to the wall, as the others went toward the doors to the terrace.

"You certainly can put on an act, Dan Morgan," she hissed in his ear. "But I'll tell you one thing. If you weren't afraid of me, you wouldn't bother to keep slapping me down."

It was sunny and warm outside, and all at once it was so in Liza's heart. The color came back to her cheeks and an invincibility rose within her as she found herself mistress of the scene and the occasion. Waves of laughter began to run through the garden as more and more guests came out. Dan appeared with Aunt Sarah on one arm and Mrs. Moreland on the other, music flowed out from the Garden Hall where someone was putting records on the player; Horace and his helpers circulated with more substantial hot tidbits and colder drinks, and everyone stayed on and on even when the sun dipped and they all came back into the house.

Before they left Dunmore proposed a toast to the host and hostess in their new home and someone else begged to drink to more parties like this one, and when the cars began finally to roll down the drive there were still sporadic parting bursts of, "For they are jolly good fellows!"

When the last guests had gone, Aunt Sarah put her feet up on a footstool, Liza kicked off her pumps and Dunmore and Dan loosened their ties as they all sat in the library to talk it over.

"I've been to a good many parties in my time," Dunmore said, "but never to a better one than this. Congratulations, Liza. I didn't notice your needing any help."

"Just once, for a moment," she said, looking at Dan.

"Are you all right?" he asked seriously.

"I'm wonderful! The last part of the afternoon was simply perfect. I guess my nervousness had worn off then," she added. "Did you really enjoy it, Aunt Sarah?"

"I certainly did. Only you folks didn't need to pay so much

attention to me. I got along fine. Matt Harvey's a breezy one, isn't she? But I like her. Then I had a real nice time with that Mrs. Moreland."

"You did?" Dan asked in surprise.

"Yes. I thought that day of your wedding reception that she was a little bit uppity with me but today we had a good talk."

"What about?" Liza asked.

"Apples," said Aunt Sarah crisply. "I found out her father had a big apple farm in Dutchess County when she was a girl and she knows them yet, as well as I do. Ramboes, Sheepnoses, Bell Flowers, Spitzenbergs. . . . She likes your house here," she added.

"She's going to sell her city one," Dunmore put in. "Told me so this afternoon. She's taking a big apartment just next to Paula Ruston's. She says she's getting too old to be without any sort of family near and I guess she feels Paula is in that category. They're having a door cut through between the rooms, she says."

"Well, that's news to me," Dan said slowly, "but it may be a good idea. She's not young but she's still pretty husky, I'd say. Hope they don't get in each other's hair. I imagine she'll tell me about it the next time I see her."

"Now this Paula Ruston," Aunt Sarah said with a glance at Dunmore. "She was the good-looking one with the black hair and the red dress, wasn't she? The one you were with out in the garden?"

"Yes, that's the one," Dunmore said, with a trace of embarrassment. "She's been quite a protégé of Mrs. Moreland's . . . They . . ."

Horace had appeared in the door, his usual solemnity broken by a wide complacent smile.

"Excuse me, Mr. Morgan . . . Mrs. Morgan, but we in the kitchen feel that everything passed off very nicely."

Dan and Liza spoke their thanks together. "I'll be out a little later to tell everyone how delighted we were with the service," Liza went on. "It was perfect."

"Thank you, madam, and I would just say that today was like old times, only we thought even better. As soon as the dining room is cleared we'll have a light supper ready for you."

"Don't make it too light, Horace," Dan said. "I think we're all hungry. We were too busy to eat anything this afternoon."

"Just a manner of speaking, Mr. Morgan. I think you'll find there will be sufficient. Maggie an' the girls has been at it while the rest of us were busy with the party. And I'm very pleased, I may say, that you're satisfied."

By nine o'clock Aunt Sarah announced that she'd had enough excitement for one day and was going to her room. Dan glanced at Liza's face, now without its high color, and suggested that she do likewise.

"Besides," he said, "Dunmore and I would be no good as company for I'm taking him up to my office to talk business."

When Liza had removed her Paris gown and put it tenderly away, smiling to herself the while, she prepared for bed and then went into Aunt Sarah's room for a final chat. The latter was propped comfortably against the pillows waiting for her, apparently eager to impart some information.

"Well now I can tell you what I saw this afternoon," she began. "Maybe you know about it and maybe you don't, but I think I discovered the woman your Mr. Dunmore here has his eye on."

"You what?"

"I found out who Dunmore is in love with. It's that Paula Ruston."

Liza gasped. "Why Aunt Sarah, that's absolutely ridiculous!"

"Maybe, but it's the truth. I watched him looking at her. Most men give it away in their eyes. Dan don't but he's different. Dunmore does. Plain as the nose on your face. Trust an old maid to spy that out."

Liza leaned limply back in her chair. "I can't believe this . . . I . . . I don't know what to think."

"Well, I don't suppose you'll have call to think anything. So far I don't believe the Ruston woman is interested in Dunmore. He intimated that, you know, today at lunch. But she seemed to lead him on a little, at that. I think she's a hussy. And also, Liza, I don't exactly care for the way she looks at Dan."

"Neither do I!"

"Ho, hum! So I hit that right too! Well, you needn't worry. I don't think any Jezebel's going to wind Dan round her finger. But you'd better get to bed, now. You look clear bleached out. One other thing I noticed. That young fellow from the office, Colby, isn't that his name?"

"Yes."

"Well, what about him?"

"How do you mean?"

"You know what I mean. Did he take a fancy to you, too?"

"Maybe a little."

"Little or big, I don't think he's over it yet. Well, you've got yourself a good man, Liza, and I'm right glad of it. Now, get yourself some sleep."

As she was leaving the room, Aunt Sarah spoke again. "That dress you had on this afternoon is very . . . I mean you looked very well in it." It sounded as though her customary restraint was difficult.

Liza smiled and passed on to her own room, but there the smile vanished quickly. She stepped out on her balcony and stood there, thinking. This discovery of Aunt Sarah's, if it was a discovery, somehow left her shaken. Dunmore certainly was aware of Paula's reputation. He mingled enough in her set to know as Matt Harvey expressed it, "that she hadn't a moral to her name." If he could actually love this kind of woman it seemed to invalidate to some extent his own integrity. Or was this ever true of men? Did beauty and seductiveness sweep all other considerations aside? On the other hand, could it be that her own instinctive disapproval of Dunmore had been, without her knowing it, based upon a moral rather than a business intuition? At all events in spite of the pleasant even charming façade he had presented here during his visit, she did not wholly trust him. As to how this situation, if true, could affect Dan's unwilling involvement with Paula, she could not guess but somehow it worried her. Aunt Sarah's uncanny ability to discern men's emotions was proven in the case of her old friend Colby at least. He had come to the party and had seemed in a mild way to enjoy himself, but she, too, had read enough in his eyes to cause her a moment of embarrassment. Well, she had seen to it that he met Anne Scott and had noticed they were together for quite a while. Maybe that might prove the answer to his problem. Oh, the conflicting currents of love! How they ran, penetrative, from heart to heart. Like natural streams, sometimes ending in sad trickles of nothingness or in others, sweeping joyous and dominant, through all floodgates away to the sea!

Liza's mind went over and over all Aunt Sarah had said, and all the events of the afternoon, as she settled at last in bed. It was after she had finally fallen asleep that she was wakened by a light knock on the door. She sat up, switched on the light and saw Dan standing there, smiling.

"I wouldn't have disturbed you but I wanted to tell you something I'm rather excited about. I've just asked Dunmore to become executive vice president!"

Liza stared at him with amazement and fright in her eyes.

"Oh Dan," she said, "do you really think that is wise?"

The smile left his face as his features stiffened. "I certainly do or I wouldn't have asked him. I thought you'd be interested. Well, good-night."

And he stepped back, closing the door behind him.

CHAPTER V

The next day, being Sunday, everyone came down late. Aunt Sarah was the first, looking brisk as usual. Dan himself, heavy-eyed and with a little of last night's displeasure still upon him, regarded her with a sort of envy.

"You slept well?" he asked.

"Certainly. I've got a good conscience. And no big projects on my mind. Like you," she added.

"You think I have?"

"More than that, I think you always will have. You're just built that way, isn't he, Liza?"

"I'm afraid so," she said smiling, but with eyes firmly fixed upon the coffee she was pouring. She was conscious of Dunmore's intent gaze upon her. How much he guessed about the quality of her marriage with Dan she was never of course sure, but she always writhed a little inwardly at the thought of what knowledge he might have.

"Now about this steel business," Aunt Sarah went on. "When you were up the last time, Dan, you mentioned you wanted to get into it. What's the idea in that? Isn't the coal business enough for you? I thought you said coal had been your very life since you were a boy."

"So it has, but you see it leads right up to steel and that's where the biggest money is, so naturally I want a finger in that pie too."

"I'll warrant you do, but I still don't see the connection."

"Oh, I can give you that in a nut shell. To make steel you have to have a thing called *coke*. Ever hear of it?"

"Vaguely."

"Well, it takes coal to make this coke. As a matter of fact it takes a ton and a half of coal to make one ton of coke, so it's pretty important. Do you see?"

"Beginning to."

"I'm a coal man. I sell coal. I also make some coke and sell it. But I want to have more coal to make more coke to make more money to buy into a steel firm . . . Now, you know the whole of it, Aunt Sarah."

"Well, you're a mite greedy, I must say, but I wouldn't give much for a man with no ambition. It would have been nice if you'd been a farmer, though," she sighed. "You an' Liza could have lived up there next to me. I own a good farm. Don't get much out of it, but it's been in the family so long I hate to sell it. Of course it'll be Liza's some day, then she can do what she pleases with it. Children ought to have a farm to run over for visits anyway—clover fields, hay fields, barn loft . . ."

"Aunt Sarah," Liza broke in suddenly, "won't you have another muffin? Maggie will be so pleased if she knows you enjoyed them."

"Don't mind if I do. They're good. Now, about this *coke*, Dan, how do you make that?"

Dan laughed. "I'm afraid I can't explain in a sentence. It's made in outside ovens of a certain kind where the coal is burnt. When I was a boy there were great rows of these around the hills, with flames shooting out the tops like hell itself. Pretty sight if you were a distance away but for the poor devils that had to draw out the coke it was hot as . . ."

"You've mentioned the place already," Aunt Sarah said dryly. "Well, what are you going to do next?"

Dan looked across at Dunmore. "Sell more coal, of course. That's what I have an office in New York for. Then maybe combined with another coal company later."

"Oh, yes," said Aunt Sarah, "Liza mentioned that. It's called a *merger*. She explained all about it."

"Well, well," Dunmore said with his faint irony, "so Liza has been learning some business as well as society."

Something in his tone nettled Liza past bearing. She looked at Aunt Sarah.

"And an important thing," she said clearly, "is that if Dan combines with another coal company it must have what is called metallurgical coal, the kind which has the right qualities for making the coke necessary for steel. Under one percent of sulphur, and so on," she added lightly.

There was a second of silence during which Dunmore had the grace to flush and then Dan threw back his head and laughed, all at once in high good humor.

"Good heavens!" he exclaimed. "How many more trade secrets did you pick up while you were in the office?"

"Quite a few," she said demurely. "But I promise never to divulge them to a rival."

"We'll have to watch her, Dunmore, won't we?" Dan said, evidently proud of his wife's acumen. But Aunt Sarah's sharp eyes had missed nothing, so when Dunmore said when they rose from the table that he should be leaving, she spoke at once.

"Sunday traffic certainly gets worse as the day goes on. I hope you won't have any trouble."

"I might impose myself a little longer on you, Liza, but I do have an engagement in the late afternoon. It's been delightful being here and the party was a smashing success! Thank you both so much. I can't reciprocate in kind but I hope you'll have dinner with me at my apartment some night before long, and see a show, perhaps."

His car was brought around as he came downstairs with his bag and goodbyes were cordial.

"See you tomorrow, Dan, thanks so much, Liza. Nice to have met you again, Miss Hanford." And he was off.

Dan settled to the papers in the Garden Hall and Liza and Aunt Sarah went outside in the sunshine.

"Well," the latter said promptly, "neither do I."

"What do you mean?"

"You know very well. I don't like people I can't fathom and I don't get to the bottom of this Dunmore at all. I was very proud of the way you sort of set him down. He can pour on the charm, of course, but somehow . . . What's his background?"

"I think that's part of the trouble. He belongs to the socially elect back in Pittsburgh and I don't think he's ever forgotten that Dan was the son of a coal miner and that I'm a small-town girl. Once in a while his condescension shows through and then I hate myself for *hating* it. He and Dan have been close friends, but sometimes I wish Dan didn't trust him so much. I feel somehow he's a friend you can't depend on. It's a feeling I can't define."

"Have you spoken to Dan?"

"I've tried to but he resents it."

"I expect he would. When he makes up his mind it's made up. Keep your eyes open. About all you can do. Well, I'm glad you did insist on having old grandfather hung."

"Yes," Liza laughed. "I saw Dunmore studying him with a surprised look on his face. Oh, we may be all wrong about him."

"I'm not wrong in thinking he's in love with that Paula person. Will you tell that to Dan?"

"Oh, no," adding to herself, "not unless I have to."

In the afternoon while Aunt Sarah was napping, Liza and Dan sat in the garden where the umbrellas still made a pleasant shade and talked over again their first social venture with satisfaction.

"But now," Liza said seriously, "I've got to think of what I'm going to do with myself as the winter comes on. I've worked so long I feel uncomfortable to be idle. The house is finished now, and Horace and Maggie keep it perfectly. Of course we'll want to do some entertaining, but that won't fill my days. If we were poor and I were cooking your meals it would be different . . ."

Dan rose and walked back and forth for a minute and then stood looking down at her.

"I like you, Liza," he said abruptly.

She knew she was blushing but she kept her voice quiet.

"And I like you, Dan. Especially when you stand with your hands in your pockets. It suits you somehow. And so few men seem to do it."

He laughed then. "Just seems to come natural. But the thing is, I can understand how you feel. Now, I could no more settle to being a country squire with nothing to do but play golf and look after my 'estate' than . . . I think I'd drown myself first. So while it's not the same with you, of course, at least I get your point. Had you thought of some charitable work maybe?"

"Yes, I had. There's a woman on down the road, I hear by way of Maggie, who works as an aid in the hospital. I wish she would call on me so I could ask her about it."

"There's another thing," Dan said slowly. "Miss Ross is very good but she doesn't take your place by a long shot.

Would you care to . . . would you like it if I brought home some special letters for you to do? Some tricky ones?"

"Oh, I would love it!"

"Well, as a matter of fact, so would I. You were always good at making an unpleasant truth sound like a compliment. All right. I'll bring you a few home tomorrow in my brief-case. Miss Ross won't need to know. Though she wouldn't mind, I imagine."

Liza's face was all alight. "The beauty of this would be that I could do the letters in the mornings and still not seem like a hermit to the girls. There will be, I'm afraid, a good many return invitations from our own party of one sort or another. What about that? Shall I always consult you first before I accept?"

"That might make it a bit awkward for you. Why not just try to hold the *couple* parties down to the weekends if you possibly can. There is one dinner especially I want us to give. I did speak of it once. As soon as the Hadleys are in the city I'd like to have them and Mrs. Moreland. Do it up very brown. I need Hadley and his coal, but I like them both, aside from that. Then I always feel I owe Mrs. Moreland a lot."

"I wish, Dan, if you care to, that you'd tell me a little more about that. I *want* to like her and I do in a sense, but I'm sure she was disappointed about our marriage and rather resents me. She simply adores Paula," she added.

"God knows why," Dan said. "Oh, yes, I do understand, in a way. The old lady's absolutely alone in the world so she likes to pretend that Paula is a daughter to her. Wishful thinking, I'd call it, for I'm sure Paula takes all she can get from her and gives as little as possible. Well, about the business."

"Yes, please, if you don't mind."

"I've told you some of this before. I've always been a gambler as far as taking chances is concerned. About fifteen years ago I took a few too many and I was in real trouble. That was before I had the office here but I'd heard of this firm of investment bankers who made a specialty of financing what they considered promising projects. Lasky & Moreland was the name."

"Ah!" breathed Liza.

"Yes, that's how it all started. I came on finally, saw Moreland and liked him from the start. Keen as they come but not the cut and dried banker type. At first he said they weren't doing as much financing right then as they had done, but I kept after him. He finally agreed to send an engineer out to look over my holdings and got a good report back. By this time I'd really gotten him pretty steamed up over it, so he got Lasky to agree to issue new stock on the Morgan Company and try to sell it. Said it would be at least thirty days before they would know and I mustn't count too much on it."

Dan drew a breath as though a weight lay upon his chest.

"And you had to live through those days," Liza said gently.

"They were the worst I've ever had. I couldn't eat, I couldn't sleep." He gave a short laugh. "I even walked the streets at night. I stood to lose my very shirt if I couldn't meet the loans due, and if Moreland couldn't sell the stock —well, that's how it was."

Then all at once he turned and smiled at her. "It was a late afternoon when I got the telegram. My fingers shook so I could hardly open it. It said: SUBSCRIPTIONS NOW COMPLETE. PLEASE SEND DEFINITE INSTRUCTIONS FOR PAYMENT OF PROCEEDS. Do you know what I did then?"

"What, Dan?"

"I went right back to my room and without even undressing threw myself down on the bed and never knew a thing till I woke up the next morning with the telegram still clutched in my hand. Can you imagine that?"

"Yes, I can. I did that once myself when a long tension was suddenly relieved."

"You did? What in heaven's name had been bothering you?"

"Oh," she smiled, "this and that."

"Moreland was the one who really put the thing through. He had faith in me, somehow," Dan went on. "'Lasky wasn't too keen on the financing. But Moreland went further than the banking end. He bought a good big block of stock himself. That's what she holds now of course. They were both good to me when I opened the office here, had me to dinner to meet people and as I can see it now, polished me up a bit.

I needed it. I was very fond of Moreland and missed him when he died. In a way I owe everything to him. So now, that's the story."

"I'm glad I know it, for the picture's so much clearer than it was. I'll be nicer than ever to Mrs. Moreland. Oh, I'll try in every way I can think of to repay her. Why didn't you tell me all this before?"

"Well," he said sheepishly, "for one thing I guess I was a little ashamed to give you all the details. I had been a fool to get into such a bind in the first place. I've been more careful ever since. But of course, when the stock was sold and I'd paid off my loans I had another mine working and two more strings of ovens, so maybe it pays to take a chance, after all. I'll bet *you* never did," he chuckled.

"You'd be surprised!" she said lightly.

And just then Aunt Sarah joined them and the talk turned to other things.

The next week brought several surprises. In the first place there were more telephone calls about the party than Liza had been prepared for. All her own old friends were eager to discuss it and a number of Dan's also from whom she would not have expected a pleasant extra thank you. Everyone mentioned the house itself and these compliments especially she stored to repeat to Dan. She was delighted and proud that her own taste had proved original and pleasing to a sophisticated group.

Of course Matt Harvey was more than ever ebullient.

"What a party!" she exclaimed. "Everybody will be afraid to give one after that. And Liza, what do you suppose all the girls are talking about? How handsome Dan is! They're all crazy about him. And how, I asked myself, did I work across the desk from him for three years and never think he was even good looking? He was always so grim. He never smiled. What have you done to him, Liza?"

"I haven't done anything. It's the house, Matt. You see he's never had a home of his own in his life. And now he's so happy over it, he even *looks* different."

"Well, all I could think of Saturday was, 'all this big handsome hunk of man *and his money too*.' You're lucky, Liza And by the way, you looked like a dream in that blue dress. You could smell Paris on it across the room. Can you and

Dan come to dinner a week from Saturday? And Paula will
not be here. Did you see Dan squash her up against the wall
at the party? The neatest trick of the year if she just stays
squashed. And oh, Liza, I think you've maybe started something between Anne Scott and Colby. Wouldn't that be nice?
I'll have them at the dinner. Can you come?"

When Liza had accepted and finally succeeded in stemming
Matt's conversational tide she turned to her mail and found
there a rather startling missive. It was from René Ronsard,
her erstwhile *guide* in Paris.

> MY DEAR MADAME:
> [the finely etched writing ran] It is my great de-
> sire to spend this coming winter in America. My
> father has already written to your husband about
> a possible position for me. Even if this should
> not develop I intend to carry out my plan any-
> way. My English needs improvement and I have
> other strong reasons which prompt my coming. I
> hope very much that we may be able to share to-
> gether some of the beauties of New York even as
> we did those of Paris.
> With anticipation and warmest . . .

Liza read the letter over and sat thinking, her brows
drawn. There was nothing on the surface of this to be disturbing, and she certainly didn't want to imagine any ridiculous young ardor where it did not exist but the fact was that
while she had paid it scant attention before, she realized now
René had managed to keep in fairly constant touch with
her ever since last spring: a few snapshots; one exquisite little
etching of her favorite Paris scene, "Les Bouquinistes" with
Notre Dame in the background; a gauze scarf for her birth-
day, the date of which he had asked for and remembered; a
poem for her criticism . . . So it had gone. Every few weeks
something had come from René, and now picking up the letter she read again, *I have other strong reasons which prompt
my coming.* Now, just what could *that* mean?

Oh, nonsense, she thought and went on with the reading of
the mail. But that night Dan brought up the matter himself.

"You remember young Ronsard over in Paris, Liza? The
one who acted as your guide that last week?"

"Yes, of course."

"Well, I had a letter from his father today. He says this René is restless, tired of University life and wants to spend a year in America. Says the boy's head is too full of poetry and he thinks a change of scene and some good business training might knock it out of him. In other words, can I give him a job?"

"And can you?" Liza asked.

"Yes, I guess I can. He's a bright kid. Even if it was inconvenient for me I'd still do it, for Ronsard himself is such a good man for us in Paris. I cabled that I'd arrange things. I think I'll put the boy in the office with Colby. He says he can put him up, too, for a little while until he finds a place to live. He's got an extra bed in his room and he's all excited over the idea of practicing his French. So, things seem to be working out. When René gets here we ought to have him out for a weekend right away, don't you think?"

"By all means."

"Only there's Colby. I mean . . . well, you sort of hinted once he had been a bit sweet on you, so would it be awkward either to have him or not to have him?" He looked at her, embarrassed.

"Oh, I can manage that," Liza said easily. "The first time we have René out I'll ask Colby and have a few more people to dinner that night. Matt and I are trying our hands at a little match-making between him and a very attractive girl whose husband walked out on her. This Anne Scott has a divorce now. She and Colby met at the party here and seemed to hit it off right away. You see I could invite her and maybe the Harveys and Susan Gibbs and Hank. Then afterwards René could stay for the weekend and I'll ask Colby if he could take Anne home. See?"

"All too well! That little stunt was practiced on me plenty of times. But this sounds like a good plan. Well, I brought you some work to do. Would you mind if I dictate a few special letters tonight and then you can write them at your leisure in the morning?"

"I'm simply itching to get at them."

They sat in the library after dinner, Dan with a sheaf of papers before him at the table, Liza on a chair opposite with her notebook and pencil. Her eyes were twinkling, though she kept a straight face.

"Good morning, Mr. Morgan," she said.

He looked up startled and then carried on the joke.

"Good morning. We have a heavy day so let's get right to work."

"Not till I tell you this," Liza said, laughing. "Matt Harvey thinks you've grown handsome. She said when she was working for you, you always looked so grim she couldn't see your features properly. She was afraid of you, as a matter of fact."

"Handsome!" he repeated. "I don't know that I like that. I've always thought handsome men were weak looking. What . . . what do you think, Liza?"

"Well, you have several mirrors in your room so you can judge for yourself. But as for my own opinion I would say you have a very strong face which the Lord and your parents between them arranged in good lines. You ought to be thankful, I think."

"Well, you needn't be afraid I'll get conceited over my looks. I might," he added consideringly, "over yours. You certainly look different from the office days."

"It's the clothes," Liza said lightly. "You never saw me then except in a tailored black suit. Now I go in for frou-frou to my heart's content."

"What's that?"

"Oh, fanciness! Elegance. Now, do let's get on with the letters. I want to see whether I've lost my knack."

But she had not. As before they worked as one with his quick, clipped sentences and her swift, exact reproduction until page after page of her book was filled with the familiar pothooks. At the end, he leaned back in his chair and said, "Well! That was wonderful! Not a question or a repeat. Are you tired out?"

"Not a bit! I enjoyed it. Let's do it often. It makes me feel useful."

"Oh, by the way," Dan said, "I met our next neighbor down the road today. West."

"Good. What's he like?"

"Seems a nice sort of chap. I was having lunch at the Club with a man who introduced us. West said he and his wife would be stopping in soon. Said they would have been here before this but she has a young baby. I told him to give us a ring and come in for a drink."

"I hope they will. I've been wanting to meet a neighbor."

They gathered up the papers, put out the lights and went up the stairs. In the upper hall Dan stopped. "Why, I don't believe I thanked you," he said.

"You never used to in the office and you have less reason to now," Liza answered.

"How do you mean that?"

She made a little expansive gesture. "All this beautiful home, all the . . . the *frou-frou*," she added, forcing a little laugh.

"You really do like it all?"

"What woman wouldn't! Thank *you*, Dan. Good-night." And she went on to her own room.

But once there, she sank down suddenly very tired indeed, with a weariness of the heart. "She has a young baby," Dan had said of their neighbor. The words stabbed her with a strange uneasiness which had been building up in her mind. A perfectly illogical one she told herself over and over, a ridiculous one, except that deep within her there was a heavy, still fear which she couldn't throw off. She longed with an aching, desperate desire for a child, for a little head against her breast, reason and justification for her days and for Dan's affluence. And, too, the possibility of his own joy in a family. This would come, she told herself, of course. They had been married but a short time, they were both normal and healthy. And surely the great process of procreation while usually the result of a dual love, still proceeded often without it.

But somehow, the shadow still fell. Only once had she mentioned to Dan the possibility of children and then he had changed the subject almost with violence. And at those times when there should have come from him the greatest ardor there was instead a restraint, a lack of warmth, which seemed to freeze the life-giving instincts of her own body. So she wondered, she hoped, but she feared.

The evenings of dictation were more and more pleasant. Sometimes she knew he was testing her, teasing her, with the speed of his sentences but she always kept up, and at the end they laughed together! Once she stopped him with a question.

"After the stock was sold that time, Dan, what percentage do you still own?"

"Thirty."

"Only thirty? Then you really don't control the company?"

"Oh yes, I do. I'm managing director and unless I ever had to fight any group for control this is perfectly practical. Often happens. Most of the big family companies don't own fifty-one percent of the stock. So don't you worry. I know what I'm doing."

"But . . . if Mrs. Moreland holds out against you? You said she wasn't enthusiastic about the merger."

"Oh, I can manage her. She has always sort of liked the idea of being the big business woman ever since her husband died. Besides it would take several people ganging up on me. That's practically impossible."

"Does anyone else I know own stock, like—well, Dunmore, for instance?"

"Why yes, he bought some at the time. He has money back of him. Family, you know. Well, let's finish up."

A few days later Mrs. West telephoned, and it was settled that she and her husband would come in the next afternoon. Liza was delighted. Her background implied *neighbors,* and even in New York she had been on pleasant terms with others in the apartment. Dan came home a little early and they decided since the day was cool they would sit in the library. Liza had a great bunch of yellow chrysanthemums on the table and she herself was wearing a smart suit of the same color.

"We're really going to have to entertain pretty often if we want to keep Horace and Maggie," she said. "They were quite pleased over the Wests' coming and have all sorts of hors d'oeuvres ready. I thought it would be nice to be quite informal and I would pass the tidbits after I've poured the tea. Of course you and Mr. West can have drinks."

"Here they are," Dan said. "I told Horace one of us would be at the door. I'll go, since I've met West."

The guests were a surprise to Liza. West was good-looking, well-groomed and managed to seem at ease; but she, while very pretty, was definitely nervous and pathetically over-dressed. When the normal amenities had been gone through, Liza got Mrs. West to the sofa beside her.

"We'll let the men entertain themselves," she said. "They like that best, anyway, and we'll talk women-talk, shall we? How long have you lived here?"

"Just a little over two years, and I hate it. We haven't been able to go out much—at least I haven't—and I've been lonely. Of course Henry is busy and sees people every day, but so many days I don't see a soul but the cook. You see, we moved here from a smallish town out in Indiana and I don't seem to fit in."

"You'll soon learn," Eliza said. "I've been longing for a neighbor so maybe we can help each other."

"Oh, *would* you?" little Mrs. West said. She looked over her shoulder at the men, deep in talk, and then turned again to Liza. "I always seem to do the wrong thing. I knew as soon as I got here that this dress wasn't right. And I know Henry will be put out about it. After he's seen what you have on, I mean. And I do so want to please him . . . to be what he . . ."

Liza clasped her hand. "Please don't worry. Forgive me for saying it so bluntly but you're awfully pretty, and you have given him a child. Just think of that! And as to the matter of the right clothes and city ways, *I* had to learn a good deal of that over the years—I came from a little town myself. Let me help you! I'd love to."

"You really would?" Her voice was breathless.

"Oh, truly! May I ask your first name?"

"Helen."

"Mine is Liza. Very old-fashioned. Then it's settled? I'll come up soon and see the baby and we'll talk things over."

Mrs. West's eyes were misty. "I feel as if a weight had been lifted off me. I can't thank you enough. I have to get some new clothes soon—after the baby, you know—and I was dreading it. I suppose you couldn't . . . ?"

"Couldn't I, though! I'd love it. What woman doesn't like to be in on a shopping spree. Why don't we set a time . . ."

After that the talk was easy until Mrs. West whispered, "Shouldn't we be leaving?"

Liza smiled. "I wish it could be longer, but if you want to be correct . . ."

"Oh, I *do*."

As she rose a little note of assurance had already crept into Helen's voice.

"I meant to show you over the house," Liza said regretfully, "but your wife and I, Mr. West, have had such a good visit I forgot all about it. It's been awfully nice of you to come and next time I'll take you on the tour."

There were pleasant goodbyes and the mutual promise of further visits and the guests took their leave.

"Nice chap, West," Dan said when he and Liza were alone. "I think he's made a lot of money pretty fast and it's gone to his head a bit, but he'll settle down. What about her? She looked a little too fluffy ruffly to me."

"I think we're going to be friends," Liza said. "The poor little soul is scared to death. The money *has* come too fast, I think, for her, so she feels out of her depth and I have an idea he's rather critical. I'm going to help her a bit. I'll really enjoy that for I like her."

"Well, you wanted to do some charitable work. You'd better begin on her clothes. Wasn't that thing pretty dressy for this afternoon? By the way, I like that suit you're wearing."

"Thank you. You know I'm in a strange position, as women go."

"How so?"

"Well, all my friends tell me their husbands hit the ceiling when the bills for their clothes come in. You never say anything."

He smiled. "I guess I like paying your bills."

"But if I ever go too far . . . you know it's very heady business for me to buy a dress I like without asking the price . . . if I really overstep you'll tell me, won't you?"

He only kept on smiling.

"But I mean it, Dan. Please promise."

"All right."

It was Liza's turn to smile. "Good!" she said. "It will be quite unintentional on my part so just tell me. Don't scold me."

His face went instantly grave as he regarded her. He knew she must be remembering times when she had overheard the vials of his wrath being poured out on various subordinates.

"I would never scold you, as you say, under any circumstances whatsoever. You ought to know that, I think."

So, in the stillness of her room that night Liza once again kept repeating to herself, *Half a loaf! Half a loaf. That I do have. Maybe I should be content.*

Young Ronsard was as prompt as his letter suggested. He arrived in New York Monday, a fortnight later, installed himself in a small hotel for the time being, reported to Dan and then called Liza, who at once invited him out for the coming weekend, which was fortunately free for them. She checked with Dan at the office and he agreed at once that this was the thing to do and said that he would bring René out along with him Friday afternoon.

"I'll get to work at once on the dinner Saturday evening. I wouldn't bother you now, but what about *Paula?*" Liza asked.

Dan groaned. "Feel Mrs. Moreland out first and if you can't help it, then . . . it will be a big party?"

"As big as I can make it, on such short notice."

"All right then. Go ahead. I'll get the rest of the news to-night."

Luck was certainly with her, Liza thought as the day advanced. Matt and Tom were free, so were the Gibbses; so was Mrs. Moreland.

"Oh, delightful," that lady responded. "I'll brush up on my French. Paula is really the linguist, though. I suppose you are including her?"

"Oh, yes, if she isn't engaged," Liza managed with a private grimace.

"I've moved now, and it's such a comfort to be near her. Don't ever grow old, *alone,* Liza. It's not a nice feeling. She and I will go together then in my car. Shall we dress a bit?"

"I'm saying black tie, and I expect to wear a long dress myself."

"Good! I'm so glad. My legs aren't what they used to be. Thank you and I'll look forward to meeting the young Frenchman."

Paula had an engagement but would break it, of course, and be there. Anne Scott, who was likely to be free, seemed greatly pleased, so *that* was settled. Liza broke her usual rules and called Dunmore and Colby at the office at a time she knew they might be least busy. The former rather rudely asked who all were coming and when he heard, accepted at once. Colby did also.

"I'm having Anne Scott. You remember meeting her at the open house party?" Liza asked guilelessly. "Matt and Tom

Harvey will bring her but it *is* a little out of their way. Would you mind running her home?"

"Not at all," his voice consented quite cheerfully, Liza thought.

She decided on the impulse to include the Wests. There would be enough people to preclude any strain and it might be just what Helen needed to bolster her morale. She would help her pick out a dress before the time, so there would be no trouble about that. The girl had evidently found a good hairdresser herself so her smooth dark hair, very much like Paula's in fact, was nicely taken care of.

On Wednesday Dan called up before noon to say that the Hadleys had arrived in the city the night before and had just gotten in touch with him. What could be done about having them out? Could they possibly fit into the dinner party? It all seemed awkward compared with his former plans and he was worried. But Liza was reassuring. At the moment she had fourteen and the dining room could easily take two more. Horace could get in some extra help and would love the whole thing. Might it not be better to have Mrs. Moreland get acquainted with the Hadleys this way rather than at a more pointed meeting which Dan had first thought of?

"You may be right," he admitted. "I guess it's all we can do, anyway."

"I'll call Mrs. Hadley at once and ask if I may go in to see her. Then I'll invite them for Saturday. They will probably be free unless they have tickets for a show."

"Oh, I can arrange for tickets any night. I know a man . . ."

"You always 'know a man,' " Liza laughed. "Well, we'll hope for the best. I'm getting to be like Horace. Planning a party intoxicates me and this will be a big one, as dinners go. Wish me luck with Mrs. Hadley."

"I do. You may find her pretty stiff."

She was, although she had invited Liza to come to the hotel that same afternoon if it suited her. The older woman was large, full bosomed and regal. She couldn't have been much more than sixty, yet in some intangible way she seemed older. Her speech was precise and her expression unchanging.

"It's so good of you to let me come in today for I'm sure your time is quite taken up," Liza began. "I've looked forward to meeting you, as Dan has spoken often of you and Mr. Hadley. We're hoping very much that you will come out and see us in the country."

"You have not been long married?"

"Just since spring, so this is our first home. We're a little proud of it."

"I remember our first one, very well," Mrs. Hadley said in an odd voice.

When the information was dropped that the Hadleys had a summer place in Vermont, Liza at once was on firm ground. She told of her own little town, of the old family place, of Aunt Sarah, Mrs. Phinney and the cat. As she talked Mrs. Hadley's face relaxed and once a faint smile appeared. When Liza broached the subject of the dinner party the older woman actually looked pleased.

"That sounds very pleasant. May I speak to my husband first and make sure he has no business arrangements for then? I'll call you at once, and thank you very much."

"I do so hope you can come. We really planned the party in honor of an interesting young Frenchman, René Ronsard, who has just come over to work in Dan's office. His father manages the Paris one and we met René there last spring. It will be a rather mixed group, but you and Mr. Hadley will add a great deal to our pleasure if you can come. I'll give you our phone number."

At dinnertime Mrs. Hadley called to say they would be happy to accept for Saturday night and it was most kind of Mr. Morgan to suggest sending a car for them.

During the next days Liza had her wish to be busy. This dinner party, even though planned hastily, would represent more than the At Home, her success, failure or mediocrity as a hostess. Dan himself seemed to take the present plans more seriously than he had the others. One strong support was Horace, who with Maggie delighted apparently in all the work that led up to the occasion. They had engaged the extra help needed, accepted Liza's menu with a few wise suggestions, and by four o'clock on Saturday had the dining room table extended to its full length and laid with the best crystal and silver. Liza as before had done the flowers, this time with the help of René, who had arrived Friday afternoon as planned. He was more handsome than she had remembered with a little added maturity he had somehow picked up. But his manner was charmingly easy and casual and Liza blamed herself for having had even a thought that he might be interested in her as a woman.

She wore that night the blue chiffon she had worn in Paris when they had first run into Paula and to her surprise, Dan remembered it.

"That's the dress you had on the night you took that nervous chill or whatever it was in Paris."

"Yes, it is."

"That was a funny thing. I mean the chill. You've never had one since?"

"No."

"I like the dress. Well, I hope Mrs. Moreland and Hadley will hit it off all right."

"I had a time with the seating plans but I've put Mr. Hadley to my right with Mrs. Moreland next to him and then Mrs. Hadley beside you. I thought perhaps I should have René at my other side since in a way the party is for him."

"I think so. Who have you put next to him?"

Liza gave a small giggle. "You'd never guess. Little Mrs. West. I went out with her and helped her select a black dress and she really looks ravishing in it. She went to a convent school, I found, and knows some French so I think it will work out. At any rate it's worth a try to bolster her up. She's such a nice little thing."

"Well, your hunches are likely to be right." He looked around the drawing room. There were bouquets of autumn flowers and a glowing fire on the hearth for the evening was chill. "If any man had told me a year ago," he said, "that I would be entertaining sixteen people for dinner in my own home and *liking it,* I would have said he needed to have his head examined."

"We'll do it often," Liza said. "It will be good for both of us and I have a feeling this evening will work out well even with our mixed elements."

As a matter of fact she had prepared Matt Harvey some days ago for the Wests. "He's made oodles of money very fast and it shows a little, but she's a dear little scared rabbit

and I do hope you and Tom will take her under your wing a
bit."

Liza had had a surprise that morning. While she was ar-
ranging the flowers for the table and Dan was in his study
she heard music. She hurried to the drawing room door and
found René playing her favorite Chopin étude with a skilled
hand. When he looked up and saw her he rose, embarrassed,
as she hurried over to congratulate him.

"René! I had no idea you played!"

"Oh, just a little, perhaps."

"Not a little. You have a beautiful, a marvelous touch. Oh,
would you do something for me tonight? It's a great deal to
ask of you, but would you help me?"

His eyes looked straight into hers. "Surely you know, madame, that I would do anything for you."

"This is it," Liza said. "We'll have coffee in here, of
course, but just after it I've noticed there is sometimes a
small lull, as though everyone was a bit 'talked out.' After
we've lingered over the coffee and liqueurs would you play
for us? Oh, *would* you? It would be such a delightful surprise
for everyone. I won't even tell Dan."

"I do not play as well as that," René said slowly, "but if it
would give you the slightest pleasure . . ."

"Oh, so much and the others too. And you *do* play beautifully. I know enough of music to be sure of that."

"I'll have to choose what I can remember. A little Schubert
perhaps . . . nothing heavy, I think. I'll run over a few
things now, if it won't disturb anyone."

"Thank you *so* much, and don't forget to do the Chopin
again, for me."

"For you," he said, smiling. "And may I tell you again
how much I like your house? It is so different from France. I
think with us the building, the décor has a tendency to domi-
nate. Here, all this beauty is just the background for something still more charming. Or someone," he added.

She thanked him and hurried away. He had of course a
Gallic knack at pretty compliments, that was all. But the
music was an inspiration. How well he played! It would in-
sure the success of the evening.

It didn't need insurance as it developed, for from the beginning things went smoothly. The Wests were the last to

arrive and when Helen, in the form-fitting black dress, appeared in the drawing room doorway, the men were on their feet a little more quickly than usual, for the shy, half-appealing smile coupled with the utter sophistication of her gown was irresistible. Liza acted her own part with an ease she would not have believed possible in her old secretary days. It came, however, partly from the acquaintance with all types of people which a small town affords, partly from the dignity of Aunt Sarah's home where three generations had lived before her, and partly of course from the assurance which Dan's wealth had brought. So she made her guests immediately at home. René himself bridged the only awkward moment. When Paula had arrived Liza said, very quickly, "Mrs. Ruston, I think perhaps you met Mr. Ronsard in Paris, did you not?"

"I certainly did," Paula returned crisply. "I invited him to lunch with me and he refused."

"Ah," said René, as though making a great effort to recall, "really? There must have been an important previous engagement. You must forgive me. How pleasant to see you again." And he turned at once to acknowledge the next introductions, while Paula, her color very high, glared at him.

The dinner was superb and the talk around the table animated. Mr. Hadley, gray-haired, handsome and not devoid of humor, seemed to be enjoying himself between his hostess and also Mrs. Moreland, who was playing up to him with an archness that belied her years. Well, Liza mused, the blandishments of Eve will have more effect than business pressure, and the other way round, his gallantry may win her when Dan's logic couldn't. Her thoughts were broken in upon by a voice beside her.

"After all, I am the man at your left!" it said.

"Oh, René, I'm sorry. Have I been neglecting you? You wouldn't guess it, I hope, but some unexpected currents developed in your dinner party. I'll tell you tomorrow. How have you been doing?"

"Very nicely. Mrs. West has been well taught. There was a French nun in her convent school so her accent is remarkably good. But I prefer to speak English with you. May I make a comment?"

"Of course."

"From that sudden meeting in Paris I thought that a certain lady was persona non grata and yet I find her here tonight."

"That is another thing I'll explain tomorrow. It must look puzzling at the moment, but there's a reason."

"I hope you're going to show me New York. I would like to see it with you."

"But of course. We'll find a time. I'll take you to the regular tourist places first—the top of the Empire State Building, and so on—and then to a few pet spots of my own. I hope Dan can join us."

He made no response to that and a little later Liza gave the signal to rise. Back in the drawing room there was an easy regrouping of guests—Colby sauntered over casually to a seat beside Anne Scott, Dan crossed to Mrs. Moreland, Mr. Hadley shared a sofa with Helen West, with rather obvious pleasure, Liza moved about, seeing that everyone had a new partner, so to speak, for the rest of the evening. Only Paula sat a little apart in a sort of sulky isolation. For once, Liza thought, she's not the best-looking woman in the room. Helen West's beauty was rather like Paula's own, only repeated with a dewy freshness.

When the cups and glasses were finally emptied Liza made her announcement to the group.

"I have a surprise for you which I'm sure you will enjoy. Only this morning I discovered that Monsieur Ronsard plays the piano beautifully. Oh, yes, you do, René, in spite of your disclaimers. He's very modest, but he has agreed to my urgings and is now going to play for us."

"I'm truly embarrassed," René said, "and you must be— how do you say—charitable. I do not play for . . . for people and only now at Madame's request."

"And since I've asked him to play as many selections as he will, perhaps it would be best if we reserve any applause until he has entirely finished."

René went over to the piano and sat down. He began with Schubert's Minuetto and from the first bright flashing chords on to the delicacy of the second part with its faint haunting minor, Liza could feel the quality of her guests' listening. The Gibbses, Mrs. Moreland, Anne Scott who had studied piano as a girl in Italy, these she had been especially sure of, but the others were all to some extent knowledgeable and she could tell that they were now *feeling* the music as René brought it to them. It was not only his technique which seemed to her extremely good, it was the heart to heart transference which was holding them captive. At the end he spoke.

"I will conclude this very impromptu little recital with a Chopin, the étude in E Major which happens to be a favorite of Madame Morgan's and also of mine. You will all recall that Chopin as a young man of twenty-one came to Paris and there fell in love with a woman somewhat older, Baroness Dudevant, who is better known by her writing name of George Sand. It is believed this étude had particular significance for them. One other thing might interest you to know. I had the pleasure last spring of acting for a little time as guide to Madame Morgan when she and her husband were in Paris. One day we stood together at Chopin's grave in Père Lachaise cemetery. Always to me a moving experience. So now, I shall try to play the étude."

The first tender, yearning notes seemed not so much a piece of music as a lover, speaking to his beloved. Even Liza, who knew every phrase, every cadence, caught her breath, for she had never heard it played with such meaning before.

When he finished there was a second or two of absolute silence, and it was then that it happened. Into this hush as a pebble in a still pool there came—not a voice—rather a faint whisper which was almost a hiss: *"You crazy fool!"* Then at the instant the applause broke and lasted until Liza wondered if she had imagined the words which were no more than a breath.

The music, instead of concluding the evening seemed to have started conversation afresh. The plaudits to René were touchingly sincere and everyone's experience of Paris, enjoyed or imagined, was revived as questions and answers flew back and forth.

"Now this cemetery you speak of. Are there other famous people buried there?" Dunmore asked.

René enumerated a number in which they might be interested and ended with Héloïse and Abelard. Matt Harvey exclaimed at once.

"Oh, *them!* And to think I never knew it, when I was in

Paris. I simply wept buckets of tears over their love affair when I studied it in college but I've forgotten a good many details. Won't you tell it now for us all? It's supposed to be the greatest."

René looked embarrassed but Liza nodded encouragingly. So, briefly, but dramatically he told the old story again. As with the music this seemed to stimulate more talk, and opinions on the philosophy of love in general were discussed with that zest which comes from treading delicately upon thin but fascinating conversational ice.

It was after midnight when the guests left with expressions of unfeigned pleasure. When they were all gone René accepted Dan's and Liza's thanks gracefully, offered his own for the evening and went on up to his room. Liza and Dan went back into the drawing room where she plumped up the sofa cushions and he settled the dying logs and put up the fire screen.

"It really was lovely, wasn't it, Dan?" she asked.

"A great success, I'd say. And I think Hadley made a good impression on Mrs. Moreland. There's just one thing, Liza?"

She turned at once. "Yes?"

"Did you hear something just when René stopped playing?"

"Yes, I did. At least I *thought* I did."

"Where do you think it came from?"

"It seemed to me it had to come from either Mrs. Hadley or Paula."

"Mrs. Hadley?"

"Well, he did seem to be paying a little more attention to Helen West than was necessary. And she really looked beautiful, didn't she?"

Dan's expression was vague. "I guess so. I can't get it through your head that I don't pay much attention to women." He caught himself up sharply. "But *you* look nice, tonight. Very nice. As to Mrs. Hadley, though, that's ridiculous. She's a lady with a lot of dignity. She'd never stoop to a thing like that, no matter what she felt. No, it had to be Paula and of course she must have meant me, for it sounded so bitter. *I don't like it!* I've stood a lot from her but this is just too much. Here in our own house in a group of people. Do you suppose everyone heard it?"

"I don't know." Then she went over to Dan and in a rare gesture laid her hands on his arms. "I'm frightened. I have sort of a premonition that she will bring us trouble. It worries me."

"Oh, nonsense! She can't hurt us, aside from being a damned nuisance. I haven't any premonition. I'm just *mad,* mad enough to wring her neck."

"Do you think if you went to Mrs. Moreland and laid it all before her it might do some good?"

"Not a chance. In her eyes Paula can do no wrong. It's pathetic, for I've an idea Paula gets a little fed up with the old lady's devotion. But, there it is. I guess I'll just have to *thole* it, as the Scotch say. Well, anyway, outside of that, it was a fine party, and you have a wonderful knack of keeping things from being too formal. I'll put out the lights. I told Horace to go to bed. He and Maggie had a big day."

"But they liked it?"

"Oh, heavens, yes. He whispered to me after dinner, 'This is like livin' again, sir!' And by the way, wasn't René the star of the evening? Why didn't you tell me about the music?"

"Maybe I should have. I wanted to surprise you."

"You certainly did and I liked it. Now, you'd better get on to bed yourself. You're probably as tired as Horace. But I'm very proud of you," he added.

CHAPTER VI

The next day Liza had a phone call from Matt Harvey.

"Well, you've done it again. That was a simply fabulous party. If you don't look out you'll be hostess of the year, or something. And Liza, your young Frenchman is absolutely divine, at the piano or any place else. But listen, you. Don't you pull any more scared rabbits like the little West out of your hat or none of us will have a husband left. The men couldn't take their eyes off her and I really didn't blame them. Such a figure! Ye gods! This settles it. I've got to cut out the butter."

Liza laughed. "The thing I was interested in was that her own husband couldn't keep his eyes off her. I've been afraid he wasn't appreciating her as much as she deserves."

"Well, I think you can relax now. But Liza, I want to ask you a question. Just when René stopped playing did you hear something? Like a devilish whisper?"

"Y . . . yes, I did."

"Thank heaven. I was afraid I was going balmy, for Tom didn't hear anything. He said I imagined this. Of course it was Paula. It sounded to me like, *you crazy fool,* so she could only have meant Dan. I wish to goodness you'd stop having her at the house."

"I'm going to."

"Better late than never. Well, thanks again for the lovely party. The Gibbses said they hadn't been to as good a one in years and they certainly get around."

The autumn weeks melted swiftly into each other with the latest chrysanthemums defying the frost, the smell of the last burning leaves in the air, and November's first tentative snowflakes now and then. Inside, the house, to Liza, seemed more attractive than ever, and Dan, too, loved an open fire. So there were cords of wood stacked beside the garage and each afternoon and evening a warm, crackling glow in the dining room and library fireplaces.

"The wood really talks, you know, Dan," she said one night. "When you have to be away I hold conversations with it. It's company!"

"I'm sorry I have to be away so much. You're not afraid here, are you?"

"Oh, mercy no. Not with Horace and Maggie in the house."

"I have to be back in Pittsburgh pretty often now. Things are shaping up well for the merger. In fact, as the Scotch would say, I feel *lifted*. Hadley has been more friendly ever since they were here but I've learned that he can't or *won't* move fast. In the meantime, though, our coke ovens are going full blast and I've just got a long-term contract with Premium Steel, which is the company I hope to buy into after the merger."

"So, you're happy."

"Happy?" he said in surprise. "That isn't exactly the word for business. Let's say at the moment I'm reasonably satisfied."

"But just for the moment."

He laughed. "I guess so. This whole manufacture of steel has gotten into my blood. You should see the mills! The furnaces roaring! The great molten mass being poured! Why, it's *power*, that's what it is. It's what makes the world go round. Take all the steel out and what would you have left? And I'm going to get into the thick of it or my name's not Dan Morgan."

He leaned back in his chair. "Well, we've no letters to do tonight. Maybe you'd better improve my mind a little. Help me relax. I've been going a pretty fast pace."

Liza had been quick to act upon his earlier suggestion that he become better acquainted with some of the books on the shelves, so during the autumn weeks when there was a free evening she had with great care selected poetry that she felt he might like, narratives first, when she found how limited his knowledge was, and then fragments from here and there.

"This is you, Dan," she had said once and read:

> *"As garment draws the garment's hem,*
> *Men their fortunes bring with them.*
> *By right or wrong*
> *Land and goods go to the strong."*

"Who said that?"

"Emerson."

"I thought he wrote essays."

"He did some poetry too."

"H'm. Well, he could be right, I suppose."

But his favorite poem was Henley's *Invictus,* insisting he would have written these very words if he could:

> *I am the master of my fate;*
> *I am the captain of my soul.*

He asked for it again tonight and she read it. She mused for a moment and then said, "I believe I'll read something quite different by the same author. Shut your eyes and try to get the picture." She read slowly and with feeling:

> *"A late lark twitters from the quiet skies;*
> *And from the west,*
> *Where the sun, his day's work ended,*
> *Lingers as in content,*
> *There falls on the old, gray city*
> *An influence luminous and serene,*
> *A shining peace. . . .*
>
> *So be my passing!*
> *My task accomplished and the long day done.*
> *My wages taken, and in my heart*
> *Some late lark singing,*
> *Let me be gathered to the quiet west . . ."*

He looked up quickly. "Is that all?"

"I skipped a little."

"Strange the same man wrote that who wrote the captain of my soul bit. You know there's more to this poetry business than meets the eye. At least that has ever met mine. Won't you read that one over, Liza, and don't leave anything out this time. I sort of like it."

He sat very quiet when she had finished and then decided that was enough for the evening. He was tired and would go on up but would take the book along if she didn't mind. At the door he turned suddenly.

"Oh, how are you getting along with showing René the town?"

"I hope all right. We have only occasional late afternoons and spots on weekends but I've tried to let him see as much as possible. After all, if he plans to stay here for a year there's no real hurry."

"I've been thinking about the evenings. He may find them a bit lonely when he's a stranger. I feel responsible for the kid, and I'm very much pleased with the way he's working out at the office. He's not all poetry and music by a long shot. He has a good head on him. I've written his father so. The trouble about his evenings is that I think Colby is off on his own a good deal now."

Liza smiled. "Oh, he is. I get the news from Matt and it's wonderful. I really think between us we've made a match."

"Well, that's all right with me but I don't want René to get bored. What about opera? You said once you liked it."

"I love it!"

"Well, I'm afraid you'll have to count me out on that. The Morelands used to invite me and I suffered through it when I had to but I'm not going to try it again. Young Ronsard probably likes it, though, being musical. I'll see about some tickets. Any special program?"

"No. I just like opera, period."

"Box or orchestra?"

Liza laughed. "I guess anyone would prefer a box if it's in a good location, but I think they're pretty hard to come by."

"I'll look into it," Dan said, picking up the book of poems. "I may read that one over again. It sort of got me, somehow. Well, good-night, Liza."

Two days later Dan announced that he had gotten a good box for every Wednesday night. Would Liza care to go as often as that? She would, she assured him with a misty-eyed rapture, exclaiming that this was one of the nicest things that had ever happened to her.

"You see, I'm used to going seldom and sitting a little higher up."

"The thing is," Dan went on, "you've been spending a good many evenings alone when I've been away through the week. Even when I'm home I don't like to go out except on weekends as you know. Now René is a gift from heaven. You've got an escort made to order. Make a list of the plays you'd like to see and you can work some of them in too. Killing two birds. Letting you have a night out when I can't take you and giving René some fun. And another thing about the opera box, you can ask another couple or two to go with you. Nice way to entertain."

With Liza's keen sense of humor to the rescue, she dressed for her first night of opera with an inner delight, for though she was amused by the words, she knew that the Box was a status symbol, and that for her, accustomed as she had always been to sitting in the far upper reaches of the great Opera House, her position tonight would be the outward and visible sign of her new state of financial grace—to paraphrase the catechism. She had invited Anne Scott and Colby as the first guests since the latter had been unusually kind to René. The young Frenchman himself had been in a transport over the idea of being at Opera every week.

"And to be there with *you*," he had added meaningfully to Liza.

"Yes," she had returned in a matter of fact tone, "it will be so good for me to have your comments on the music."

She wore a black velvet gown that night with her new mink jacket, which she caressed as though it were a child. Dan looked her over approvingly at the front door.

"Don't most women have *long* fur coats?" he asked.

"Yes, but I like this better. Oh, Dan, thank you for everything."

"Why, you're welcome," he returned, pleased. "You're most terribly welcome. Have a good time and I'm glad I don't have to go along."

They laughed together as he saw her to the car where John was waiting.

Once in the box the four young people sat at the front, side by side, with the men at either end. Liza's heart was beating fast as she surveyed the great house. It was all an unbelievable dream, come true.

"Well, this is a little different from the night we sat up in peanut heaven, isn't it, Liza?" Colby's voice was cheerfully casual, she was glad to hear.

"But that was fun too. And the house was sold out that night, don't you remember? So we were lucky to get in at all."

There was no doubt of the interest Colby and Anne were feeling for each other, and it added an intangible note of happy suspense. René was at his charming best so a mood of pleasure fell upon them all as they waited.

"It's *Aida,* as of course you know," Liza said, turning to René. "The music critics call it the good old war horse."

He looked puzzled. "Because there are horses on the stage?"

"Oh, no," she laughed. "Because it's such a good, dependable old opera. I've seen it often but I still love it and I'm sure you will too."

"Madame—or may I say Liza?"

"Of course."

"I would enjoy anything sitting beside you!"

"Now René, no more pretty speeches!"

"That was not just a 'pretty speech,' as you call it."

The overture began, so Liza was saved from further comment. *But I must be careful,* she thought. *He's such a darling, but he mustn't get out of hand.*

At the end of the first act Liza noticed that the box just two beyond theirs, which had been empty before the curtain rose, now had occupants. Mrs. Moreland, Paula and *Dunmore* were in it. They all saw each other at once and nodded. When Paula and Dunmore went out Liza suggested to René that they go over and speak to Mrs. Moreland. He kissed the old lady's hand gracefully and she looked flattered.

"Where's Dan?" she asked at once.

"He doesn't like to go out week-day evenings," Liza said. "He's working too hard just now. As usual."

René and Mrs. Moreland were deep in musical criticism when the other two returned to the box.

"Well," Paula began, "where's Dan?"

Liza repeated her explanation.

"How nice for you," Paula said with the familiar tiny sneer in her voice, "to have such a charming *substitute.*"

René was quick. "I am not a substitute, Madame. Any man I'm sure would be honored to be Madame Morgan's escort."

"There goes the curtain," Liza said, and with hasty good-byes she and René left. Once in the corridor he spoke.

"I do not like this Paula woman. She seems to me a *serpent dans . . .*"

" 'Snake in the grass,' we say," Liza helped him out.

"Exactly. If I were you, I would see her as little as possible."

When she got home that night Liza found Dan in the library waiting up for her.

"Well, how was it?" he asked eagerly.

"It was beautiful! It was heavenly! Oh, that box, Dan, is going to give me more pleasure than you can ever imagine. And not just me. It will be such fun to share it. By the way, Mrs. Moreland's is just two beyond ours to the right. She was there with Paula and Dunmore."

"Dunmore! What was he doing there?"

"Why, quite evidently squiring Paula," she said, laughing.

"Well, I'll be damned. I'd wish him well with it, if he weren't a friend. But Liza, I got some bad news tonight."

"Aunt Sarah?" she breathed.

"Oh, no, no. I didn't mean to frighten you. It's Miss Ross. She went home Monday with an awful cold and her mother called up to say she's got pneumonia and this afternoon they took her to the hospital. The doctor thinks he's got it in time but of course she'll be away from the office for several weeks. It's caught me at a bad time and I hardly know which girl to have in. Who would you suggest? It's my own fault for depending too much on one secretary. I'll have an understudy ready after this, you can be . . ."

"Dan! I'm going into the office with you tomorrow morning and no ifs or buts from you, sir."

Instead of any remonstrance a wide grin spread over Dan's face. "If I ever heard a hint that was one I gave you. But Liza, really I wouldn't ever have *asked* you to do this. I just had a sneakin' little hope you might offer. It would really save my life to have you help just now. You're sure you won't mind going back again?"

"Mind? I'll love it. I'll set my clock and be up to have breakfast with you . . ." She started at once for the hall.

"I'll have John take us in. I *won't* ask you to commute."

"Fine. I'll be ready. I'm not so sure," she called back, "that I won't enjoy this almost as much as the box."

He regarded her as she stood on the lowest stair, her face above the black velvet flushed with excitement, the fur jacket pushed back on her shoulders.

"You're a funny girl," he said in a strangely soft voice, "but a good one."

The next morning in the outer office Dan strode through as usual with a curt nod to right and left as he went. Liza tarried long enough to shake hands with the girls and explain about Lila Ross.

"Why you're just the same, Liza!" several exclaimed at once.

"Well, I should hope so. It's nice to be back. I'll be seeing you every day for a while."

She glanced automatically at the big clock and then opened the door marked *Private* and in a minute was seated in her old place.

"I'm ready, Dan," she said.

"I'm in a spot of trouble which I hope we can clear up right away. I told you about getting a long-term contract to sell our coke to Premium Steel. Well, one of their men called me up yesterday and said the coke is faulty, not right for steel. I'm sure there's been some crazy mistake, but it's serious. I'm going to have Dunmore in now to discuss it, but I want you to hear. I'll call this man up, of course, but I'll want you to write a follow-up letter—the kind you do so well —making him think I'm his brother and all that." He pressed a button and in a minute Dunmore appeared. His eyebrows went up in a quizzical stare as he saw Liza.

Dan told his story quickly and Dunmore concentrated upon it.

"A little too much sulphur."

"What makes you say that?" Dan snapped.

"Well, it's the coal from the Magnus mine we're using and it's always made good coke. But once when I was out at the ovens I thought there was just a little too much yellow in the flame . . ."

"Why the devil didn't you tell me?"

"Oh, I didn't think too much about it. And you were so

hellbent just then to get the contract from Premium you probably wouldn't have listened anyway."

"I resent that," Dan said angrily. "Of course I was after the contract but you know I'd never sell inferior coke if I knew it!"

"O.K. Keep your shirt on. What do we do now?"

"I want the best metallurgist out there to test the Magnus coal and the coke. Who do you think is the best man?"

"Hankinson."

"So do I. I wanted to be agreed on that. Will you take this part over? Call Hankinson as soon as you can get him and explain how urgent the matter is. Ask him to phone one of us the moment he's made the tests and then send two written reports of his findings. Build a fire under him. And thanks, Dunmore."

Dunmore still stood, looking now at Liza. "Well, this is a switch," he said. "Grand lady at the Opera at night, secretary in the morning. How come?"

"Oh, I like variety," Liza began, but Dan cut in swiftly.

"Miss Ross has pneumonia and I've got some stuff here that has to be handled with kid gloves so Liza's helping me out."

Dunmore turned to the door. "Pretty soft for you, Dan," he threw over his shoulder as he left.

Dan made a slight grimace. "We've been friends for years," he said, "but once in a while he gets under my skin, somehow. Well, let's get started."

It was a hard morning but Liza gloried in it. She felt closer to Dan as they worked together, sitting in their old places, than she ever had before. At one o'clock he leaned back in his chair and looked at her with a twinkle in his eye.

"I've never approved of businessmen taking their secretaries to lunch but today I think I'll make an exception. How about it?"

"Your secretary has no inhibitions whatever about lunching with her boss. And I'm starved, aren't you?"

"Absolutely. But we've put through a lot of work, Liza, bless you! Well, come on, let's go."

"About that coke," she said as they went out. "The steel company must buy from a number of firms. Could somebody possibly—this may sound crazy—have made a mistake? Maybe it's some other firm's coke that's wrong."

"That same idea occurred to me, but it seemed too good to be true. I still have faith in my own product, though, so we'll wait and see what happens."

Over lunch Liza brought up the matter of Christmas. "It's less than four weeks away," she said, "and we should be planning a little. Where have you gone other years for the day?"

"Oh, always to Mrs. Moreland's with Paula there and sometimes a few others. I've hated to mention it to you for I didn't see how we could get out of it this year if she asks us."

"But there's a perfect way! I've always gone to Vermont to Aunt Sarah's. Don't you think we should go there? We couldn't disappoint her. Wouldn't you like it?"

"Like it? Great heavens, I'd love it and the idea never hit me before. It's a perfect *out* for me with Mrs. Moreland. There's just one thing . . ."

"What's that?"

"René. We can't wet nurse him indefinitely, but this first Christmas it would seem natural to have him with us."

"Why not take him along to Vermont? He would see an entirely new America there. He would kiss Aunt Sarah's hand and she would say, 'Tut! Tut!' and give it a shake but inside she'd feel she had really *lived* for once."

"Do you suppose he would go?"

"I rather think he would," Liza said quietly. "You ask him. Then he might find it easier to refuse if he wishes to. Oh, Dan, I wish I knew what I could get you as a gift. I'd so like to please you!"

"You pleased me this morning. I call that quite a gift."

"Oh, you know what I mean. Now a really fine cigarette lighter would be just the thing, but you have one."

Dan drew it from his pocket and laid it on the cloth between them.

"It is a beauty, isn't it? Look at the engraving of my name and that tiny carved border. I think it must have been specially designed. Mrs. Moreland gave it to me at Christmas two years ago."

Liza fingered it admiringly and handed it back. "Well, that's out. I'll have to think of something else."

"I believe I have you settled."

"Oh, please don't give me anything valuable. I have so much. Count the Opera my real gift and then get me a pair of long white kid gloves, size 6½. That would be perfect. And just enough."

He drew a little book from his pocket and made a note in it. "I'll remember that," he said gravely though she could tell his eyes were amused. "I'm certainly pleased over the plan for Christmas. When does the day fall this year?"

"Sunday."

"Good. We can drive up Saturday and home Monday."

"I would want to leave quite early on Saturday then, for there's so much to do that afternoon. Trimming the tree and everything."

"Oh, do we have a tree?"

"I should say so! One of the neighbor men usually cuts one for us but I think you and René can manage this time. There are plenty of young pines on the farm. I'll get a few elegant new ornaments to add to the old ones. Oh, it's going to be fun!"

"I won't speak to René until you've called Aunt Sarah. Well, are you able for a little more work now? We ought to be getting back to the ship. That letter you wrote the Premium fellow was a pip. When he reads that he'll probably be willing not only to buy my coke but to *eat* it. You certainly have a way with words. We'll stop early this afternoon. John's to pick us up at four. That will give you time to rest a little before dinner. O.K.? Let's go."

When they finished that afternoon, during which Liza had typed the rest of the letters, rearranged a file the way she knew Dan liked it, and taken notes during a conference, he said, "I'll never know how I had the courage to ask you to marry me when it meant giving you up here."

"Is it worth it?" she asked with a twinkle. He only grinned as though embarrassed.

For the next two weeks Liza went every day to the office, where matters seemed to be slowly righting themselves. The report from the metallurgist pronounced the Magnus coal and its coke unflawed. A manager of the coke yard at Premium admitted his own mistake. Dan was enormously relieved. He had evidently been more worried than he had shown.

"And don't ever think that letter you wrote, Liza, didn't help to oil the wheels to get us going in a friendly way again. The trouble with me is I'm too blunt and Miss Ross never tones me down."

The reports from Miss Ross were increasingly good, so the week before Christmas Liza was free to do her last-minute shopping. Meanwhile the nights at the Opera had been sheer delight. She had invited two other couples each time which made it easier to place another woman next to René, who in his turn did some manipulating at intermission so he would again be beside her. On the surface he was charming, indeed quite captivating it would appear to the female guests, but in Liza's heart an uneasiness was mounting. As they stopped outside his apartment one night, he quietly stripped off her glove and pressed his lips to her hand, not in the light conventional gesture but rather with a distinct caress. Liza freed her hand as soon as she could, hoping John had not seen.

"Good-night, René," she said distinctly, "A wonderful performance, wasn't it?"

She was pleased with her Christmas selections. It was exciting to buy without limitations of the purse. She had found for Dan a beautiful silver tray for his pens, with his name and the date engraved on the bottom. Aunt Sarah and Mrs. Phinney were never hard to please but she had bought for them both very fancy "breakfast shawls" as they insisted upon calling the little sweater capes, and a really elegant pin for Aunt Sarah. Dan had done his own shopping and included René on his list so when she had found the most unusual odds and ends available for her closest friends and taken care of Horace and Maggie, she was ready to enjoy selecting the new trimmings for the tree, and the gourmet items, unknown to the small-town store, which she always took with her.

They set off gaily in a delicate snow early on Saturday morning, the twenty-fourth. Even Dan talked more than usual as the miles passed and before it seemed possible they were pulling into the familiar drive and were being greeted by Aunt Sarah at the front door. The fireplace in the sitting room was ablaze and delicious Christmas smells of warm mince pies and turkey stuffing in process of being made filled the house.

"Oh, it's so good to be here!" Liza kept repeating while Dan echoed it, and René kept making delighted remarks of his own which Aunt Sarah evidently found gratifying, though she had promptly withdrawn her hand when he had bent to kiss it.

"We've got to unload the car the first thing," Dan said. "This snow may get deeper. Come on, René, we'll bring in the dunnage."

"Use the kitchen door, then," Aunt Sarah called. "No need to track up the house more than's necessary."

Under Liza's direction, the gift packages were all put in the corner of the sitting room, the parcels of goodies in the kitchen, and Dan's special box in the pantry. "Champagne, ma'am," he said to Aunt Sarah, with a bow. "Your favorite beverage, I happened to remember."

"You're a bad boy, but I like you, Dan. I'm ashamed to say it but I'm glad you brought that. It will just top off our dinner nicely. And you can hold me up afterwards till I get to the sofa. Now, Liza, you can show them to their rooms. René is over next to me and you and Dan in your usual ones. Then come down and have a cup of tea to warm you up. Laced, if you want. Remember I'm descended on one side from sea captains. And if it won't spoil your supper we've got fresh doughnuts."

It was a jolly tea. Supper or no, they fell ravenously upon the doughnuts, René declaring Paris could produce nothing like them. Liza was wearing a bright red dress and her cheeks, from the cold air and now the fire, matched it. Aunt Sarah tried to speak casually.

"Well, I must say you look fairly well, Liza. Dan's been taking good care of you apparently."

"No," he said laughing, "I've been working her to death and she hasn't had the sense to complain."

"His secretary was sick and I filled in at the office for a couple of weeks," Liza said, "and enjoyed every minute of it. I think work agrees with me. But now, my good gentlemen, I have work for you. We must go after the tree before it gets any later. Is the hatchet sharp, Aunt Sarah?"

"Sharp as a shrew's tongue. Mind, you don't cut yourself with it, any of you. I would have had Tom Lewis down the road cut the tree and have it here all ready if you weren't so set, Liza, on picking it out yourself this year."

"But I am. You remember once Tom brought one in that was so lopsided we grew cross-eyed looking at it? No, I want a perfect little tree. Come on, Dan and René. We should hurry."

Dan groaned as he stretched his long legs toward the fire. "You don't need me," he said. "Here's René, young and strong and full of pep. Let me stay here and toast myself and visit with Aunt Sarah."

"But I thought it would be sort of a ceremonial, since this is your first Christmas here." Liza's voice sounded disappointed.

"Well, I'll tell you what," Dan said. "You and René go out to the pine grove, you pick the tree and René I'm sure can cut it down, can't you?" he asked, appealing to the young man.

"But certainly! It will be to me a pleasure. I need the exercise. I am growing—how do you say—*soft!*"

"Then," Dan added. "I'll come to meet you and drag home the tree. Bringing in the Yule, wasn't it called? How's that?"

Aunt Sarah brought the hatchet, René helped Liza into her red coat with its fur collar, fastened her boots, equipped himself and they were ready.

"Lazy-bones," Liza smiled at Dan. It seemed easier somehow to tease him here than at home. "Don't be too long coming after us."

It was the gentlest time of the day, with just enough light left of the afternoon while a growing gold and pink along the west spoke the coming sunset. Tiny flakes like bits of feather still fell, and the air was soft with the clean vibrant peace of a snowfall. Liza was filled with a great happiness, a tremendous elation. Here she was at Christmas time on the familiar ground of her childhood, with Dan sitting content beside the old fireplace, he and Aunt Sarah enjoying each other! At the moment it seemed she could ask for nothing more. She all but forgot René beside her as she moved surely over the snow-covered path, through the gate into the wood-lot and at last into the grove of pines on the edge of the farm. The trees had been thinned out so it was easy to move about amongst them as Liza did now, studying the smaller ones from every angle. At last she settled upon a shapely balsam fir.

"This one is perfect, isn't it? And it will perfume the whole house."

She stood then, her coat open at the throat, her head raised in a sort of rapture as she drank in the sweet piney fragrance and glimpsed the early sunset through the trees. Her hands were spread in an unconscious gesture of abandon.

"Isn't it all beautiful!"

René dropped the hatchet and came close.

"You are beautiful!" he said thickly. "To me you are irresistible. I love you!" And before she could draw a breath his arms were about her and his lips on hers.

For some seconds she yielded herself completely. Often afterwards she wondered how long this had been, for she did yield, not to René but to the kiss itself, the like of which she had never known. There had been others of course over the years, but light ones. Never one like this, a lover's kiss with a man's whole strength behind it. *This,* then, was what her heart had been craving from Dan. This was what she had missed. Would always miss.

She freed herself with difficulty. "René," she half sobbed, "how could you have done this to me?"

"But I love you. Surely you know that. A woman always knows. Why do you suppose I came to America? I've loved you since the moment we stood together in Père Lachaise. There will be some way for us. Love like mine cannot be denied . . ."

But Liza had turned and hurried from the grove, the tears streaming unheeded down her cheeks. She ran through the wood-lot and over the front lawn until, blinded, she got off the path, tripped over a snow-covered root and fell headlong just as Dan emerged from the front door. He was beside her in a moment, helping her to her feet and brushing the snow from her coat.

"Are you hurt? Liza, are you hurt?"

"No, no. I'm not hurt at all. I'm just shaken a little from the fall. I . . . I was running . . . it was so silly . . . and missed the path."

"But you're crying. You *must* be hurt. Were you coming to meet me?"

She let this explanation go as unexpected beneficence. "I'll be perfectly all right when I've rested a few minutes. Will you help René with the tree?"

"Not until I'm sure about you." He guided her to the hall, shook the snow from her coat and went up with her to her room.

"You're sure it's not another of those *chill* things?" he asked anxiously.

"No, absolutely. I'll lie and rest a little while and then be down before dinner." The trouble was she could not stop the tears. When he handed her his handkerchief she accepted it gratefully. "I don't know whether I even brought one," she said shakily, "they seem to be going out of style."

"I'll get you some brandy," he said and was back in a moment with a flask and glass.

"Man's infallible remedy," she said, trying a smile, which ended to her intense embarrassment in a sob. He felt her hands.

"They're cold as ice. Why don't you take a hot bath? That will soak the stiffness out of your bones and calm your nerves at the same time. I'll look in on you after we get back with the tree and see how you are. Shouldn't I tell Aunt Sarah?"

"Please don't. If she misses me later just say I'm changing my dress. And thanks, Dan."

When he was gone she dropped the snow-covered red gown indifferently to the floor, put on a robe and stretched out on the bed. She lay very still and very tense beneath the coverlet. Part of the strange anguish she felt was that she had loved the kiss. Had wished then that it might have gone on and on. But she knew her heart was faithful. It had been Dan's lips she had felt upon hers; it had been his arms she had felt around her. René? He meant less than nothing to her. Her agonized wish now that it had never happened was not born of the slightest compunction. The sorrow which still made her tears flow was that now what she had only before imagined had been made real. And her loss was therefore irreparable.

She lay until the tears had stopped, thinking it was well

that she was so conditioned to restraint, for this Christmas Eve must not be marred. After a warm bath she began to get control of herself, dressed quickly in a green dress, also seasonal, she thought, and with a little extra make-up went down to join the others. Dan was sitting on the sofa, looking pensively into the fire, Aunt Sarah was bustling about with the tree ornaments and René nowhere to be seen.

"Hello," Liza said. "Guess what, Aunt Sarah. I fell over that old maple root and went down in the snow, and had to change. Isn't this tree a beauty?"

"So that's what's been keeping you so long. I thought you and Dan must have had a fight."

"We don't fight, Aunt Sarah. Dan's a very pleasant person to live with."

"Well, I may say, you are too. She never gets mad, does she, Dan?"

"I've never seen her," he said, adding as Aunt Sarah turned for a moment, "are you all right?"

"Perfectly. The brandy, I think, did the trick."

"Your young Frenchman seemed a bit quiet," Aunt Sarah said, coming back from the tree. "He's maybe homesick, poor lad. I sent him to the kitchen. You can never be lonesome in a kitchen, and now he and Mrs. Phinney are thick as thieves. He's making little do-dads out of those things you brought, to go with our blackberry wine. Of course, Dan," she added, "as you know I always keep a little whiskey on hand in case of snake-bite and if you'd rather have *it* . . ."

"I might at that," he said.

But in the end they all had Aunt Sarah's own brew with René's delicate hors d'oeuvres to accompany it. As soon as he had seen Liza's smiling face he became his usual animated self, assuming, apparently that the incident in the pine grove was either forgotten or approved, so an outward happiness settled upon the group, over the dinner table and later as the little balsam was being laden with its glittering ornaments. They all took part in the trimming and stood back at last to exclaim with pleasure over their work.

"And now," said Aunt Sarah, "I hear, René, that you can play the piano. I've had the old one in the parlor tuned as much as it can *be* tuned . . . It may still be bad enough, but

I would be pleased if you could play a few carols. Liza always used to but she says . . ."

"Please, Liza, will you not . . . ?" René asked.

"Not when you are here. That is certain. Really, René, you can give us all a great deal of pleasure."

So René, after exclaiming over the great square piano which seemed to fill half the room, managed to manipulate the old yellowed keys until the familiar melodies came from them, ending, of course, with the "Cantique de Noel."

"It's been a heavenly evening," Liza said, as he came out again, "and that of course is always the perfect ending."

"And now about tomorrow," said Aunt Sarah, "and thank you, René, very much for the carols—we've always had Christmas the same way and we're always going to, as long as I'm alive. At seven-thirty sharp, Mrs. Phinney rings the bell and we all come down to the fire in our dressing gowns and take plenty of time to open our presents. Then we have a light breakfast and everyone can go after that to dress for the Day. Dinner is at two. How does that sound to you, Dan?"

"Wonderful! Couldn't be better."

"It is a marvelous plan, Madame," René said earnestly. "You cannot know what it means to me to be here."

They watched the little tree twinkling quietly, for a time, and then Aunt Sarah announced she was going to bed and would advise everyone to do likewise since they would be awake early.

"I'll fix the fire and put out the lights," Dan said, "and maybe have one more cigarette before I go up. It's been the nicest Christmas Eve I've ever had, by the way."

As Liza went through the hall she opened the front door and peered into the night.

"It's snowing, but just a little white mist. Not enough to block the roads, I'm sure, but just right for tonight. Merry Christmas, everyone. I said it first!"

In the morning, as Aunt Sarah had planned, they all gathered before the fire with the beribboned packages about them. Liza and René sat on the floor, Dan said his legs were too long and Aunt Sarah and Mrs. Phinney said theirs were too stiff, but they were all close together as they opened, cried out, passed the gifts about for all to view and then exclaimed again in the medley of thanks. Aunt Sarah brought the laughter. She looked at her shining pin and then restored it promptly to its velvet bed. "Now there's no sense in spending all that money on me at my age! You just take that right back, Liza, and get something practical. Of course," she added slowly, opening the box again, "it would brighten up my dark dresses a mite."

Everyone was pleased: Mrs. Phinney with her little bedroom clock, René with his cufflinks, Dan really exuberant for him, over his pen tray. There were charming gifts for all from Paris, and careful handwork from the two old ladies, with smaller remembrances all around. The last package on Liza's knee was a long, narrow one tied with white ribbons. She took it up finally and looked across at Dan. "I think I know what's in this. The very thing I asked for!"

She took off the lid and drew out a long white glove. "Oh, it's beautiful!" she cried. "I've never seen such lovely, soft kid." She laid it gently against her cheek. "And look, everyone, shoulder length! Thank you, Dan. Now, I *will* be ready for the Opera."

He was watching her with a quizzical smile. "Hadn't you better be sure there's a pair there? That seems to be tissue paper in the middle."

"Why, of course there will be a pair." She removed the tissue and then gave a little gasp. She could see that there was a small bulge in the second glove. She shook it gently and a jeweler's box dropped into her hand. She stared at it, speechless, while all eyes were upon her.

"Open it," Dan said. "It won't bite."

She pressed the spring and three beautifully cut sapphires in a row looked back at her.

"Mon Dieu!" René murmured as he saw them. "Quelle baguette!"

"Try it on," Dan was urging, "and see if it fits." There was a look of pride on his face.

Liza slipped the ring on her finger and held it out for all to see. "It fits perfectly, but I'm afraid I simply have no words . . ."

"Well," said Aunt Sarah practically, "you might give him a kiss. Seems to me I've heard of that bein' done sometimes."

"Oh, no," Liza said quickly, "Dan is shy, but I think he

knows how utterly overwhelmed I am over the ring, don't you?"

For answer he held out his hand. "Let's see how it looks on you."

She put her hand in his and he turned the stones slowly this way and that. "Well," he said, as though explanation were needed, "I knew blue was your favorite color and I thought your right hand did look sort of bare."

"It won't be any more," said Aunt Sarah. "This has certainly been a big climax but I must say I think we've all fared pretty well. Come on now, Mrs. Phinney, an' we'll set down some food."

Aunt Sarah's "light breakfast" proved to be sausage with pancakes and Vermont maple syrup, but she assured them it was early yet and if they all took a walk they would be ready for the turkey by two. Liza for her own reasons did not go along but she managed a minute alone with Dan before he and René set out.

"I can't believe it's mine," she said. "It's the most beautiful ring I've ever seen in all my life and I still can't find the right words to tell you . . ."

"You don't have to tell me anything. If I had needed thanks, which I didn't, the look on your face when you first saw it would have been enough. Glad you like it!" And he was gone.

They lingered over the dinner as the mammoth bird became gradually dismembered and gave place at last to the mince pies and champagne. Three o'clock came and four and the world outside was white and the sunset a growing gold; inside, the little balsam shed its fragrance as it twinkled, and the men smoked by the fire while the cheerful, homely sounds of dishes and silver being put away came with the women's voices.

"Now, mind," Aunt Sarah called from the kitchen door, "we never have supper Christmas evening."

"Good Lord, I would hope not," Dan exclaimed. "I don't expect to eat again for a week!"

"I've heard that kind of talk before. By bed-time you'll all be ready for a sandwich, and everybody makes their own out here."

She was right. At ten o'clock after quiet talk and more carols they were all wrangling cheerfully in the kitchen over the makings Aunt Sarah had set out for them, then their snack by the fireside and the end of the day.

"I always feel sad about the tree," Liza mused. "It was growing so contentedly until it was cut down and now its bright little life is so short."

"It will have till Twelfth Night to keep on twinklin'," Aunt Sarah said, "then I always get young Lewis to cut it into very small pieces and put them in the wood-box on the porch and we use them up little by little. Makes a pretty smell and a nice light."

"I'm glad it all goes out in brightness, somehow," Liza said. "I still feel sorry to leave it."

"Do you want to stay on?" Dan asked quickly.

"I always like to be here, but I do need to get home this week. It's been perfect, though, Aunt Sarah. Thank you for a lovely, *lovely* Christmas!" And she kissed the old woman's wrinkled cheek tenderly.

The driving was bad the next day and Dan concentrated carefully upon it. There were several unpleasant skids and light conversation seemed unsuitable. Besides, René's face had a moody expression and Liza, sitting between the two men with René's arm along the back of the seat touching her shoulders, was irritated by his position, although she knew it was probably the most comfortable one for him since she was giving Dan all the space possible.

They reached the city in grateful safety—they had passed several wrecks by the way—dropped René off and finally entered their own drive, where Dan left the car for John to put away and bring in the bags. When Liza came downstairs she went at once to the kitchen to tell Horace and Maggie the news and hear their thanks for the gifts left them. As soon as Dan was down, dinner was served. But it was a silent meal.

"I'm so glad I put up the greens before we left," Liza began, looking about her. "We'll take them down on Twelfth Night, and have a little ceremony burning them. That brings good luck for the new year, did you know?"

"No, I didn't," Dan replied, and then said nothing further. When she rose from the table Liza, filled with concern, went into the library and sat down. As soon as the dining room was cleared and darkened, Dan came in and stood with his back to the fire, facing her.

"Liza," he began, "I don't want to sound inquisitive but I'm no fool. I know something went on when you and René were out there getting the tree. You weren't hurt by the fall but you were terribly upset and it bothers me. I would appreciate it if you told me exactly what happened. René seems a nice chap and Colby likes him, but he did tell me once that René has a pretty good stock of French jokes, and I just wondered . . ."

Liza turned her new ring upon her finger, looking down at it.

"I certainly wasn't being secretive, Dan, but I didn't want to speak of it up there. And you must believe me now, that I really couldn't have prevented it. We were standing in the pine grove and it was all so beautiful, with the light snow falling and the sunset showing between the trees . . . I was looking at that, not even glancing toward René, when suddenly I found his arms round me and he was kissing me."

"*Kissing* you!" Dan repeated in astonishment. "Why the impudent young pup! I ought to go out and thrash him. What on earth possessed him to do such a thing?"

"He said," Liza went on slowly, "that he was in love with me. Had been since that first day we were together in Paris . . ."

"In love with *you!*" Dan interrupted. "Why that's the most preposterous thing I ever heard of. It's incredible!"

Liza rose and looked squarely into his eyes. "Yes," she said, and her voice was pure ice. "It is incredible, isn't it?"

She turned, crossed the hall and went up the stairs. Then the door of her room closed. Audibly.

CHAPTER VII

The next morning Liza delayed coming down until she was sure Dan would be gone. But as she entered the library he was still there, pacing back and forth.

"You haven't left?" she asked in surprise.

"I couldn't go until I'd seen you and explained about . . . about last night. What I said must have sounded sort of insulting to you. You see René seems such a youngster to me, such a kid, just a college boy, and you are older and *married* and that's what I meant about its being incredible for him to be in love with you. Don't you understand? I'm afraid you took it up the wrong way, didn't you?"

"I'm afraid I did. You must forgive me."

"I'm the one to ask that. Is it all right now?" he said anxiously.

"Yes. Entirely right. I was just foolish, that's all."

"And you'll put your ring on again?"

"Oh, you noticed?"

"Of course."

"I'm ashamed of myself. I'll go and get it right away."

"No, wait a minute. There are two other things I have to say." He swallowed painfully. "René is young and good looking and romantic and likes Opera and a lot of things you do. Have you . . . have you any interest in *him?*"

"Good heavens, *no!*" Liza answered explosively. "How could you ever dream of such a thing!"

"Well, I didn't really think it, but I felt it was only fair to you to be sure. I lay awake a good while last night weighing the matter. Needless to say, I'm relieved. But the other thing is what the devil I'm to do with the boy now. Of course I'd *like* to tell him to pack his bags and get back to Paris as fast as he can go. And that's what I *will* do if he's going to be an annoyance to you, but I'm in a spot about his father. He's a good man over there. I need him if I can decently keep him."

"I think there's a way we can manage it," Liza said slowly, considering. "You act with René just as you always have. He will assume you know nothing. Then I, on my part, will see to it that I'll never again be alone with him. Anywhere. We can have him out, but only to a dinner party. Other times I'm sure I can take care of it. If I keep this up, I believe in a few months he will go home of his own accord."

"You think it's as bad as that with him?" Dan asked gravely.

Liza flushed. "I think he'll go back to the University where he ought to be now, and fall in love with a pretty little French girl and forget all about . . . America. Then, you see, if he leaves voluntarily you can honestly tell his father how sorry you are to lose him in the office, and he can report that he didn't like this country as much as he had expected, and there you are!"

"Sounds good, if it only works, but we'll try it. Well, I've got to get going."

Liza touched his arm lightly. "Thank you for waiting, Dan. You could have explained tonight, but it wouldn't have been quite the same as staying now. I'll always remember this."

He gave her hand a little squeeze. "Glad it's all right. I'm such a blundering ass sometimes."

Liza was always to recall the months between that Christmas and the spring when the world fell to pieces beneath their feet, as a happy time. In the first place she had become entirely mistress of her own charming domain. When she entertained now, which was often, the old nervousness was completely gone. She knew that she was making a place for herself in the social group in which her old friends moved and in a more important one which impinged upon Dan's business interests. He was not only content, but proud of her success. They had made new acquaintances in their own community, also. The larger estates on down the road from them had become places to know and enjoy. The men who lived there had important city connections and they and Dan had a certain mutuality. The women, while not all congenial, were in one way or another interesting to Liza. One in particular, a Mrs. Carstairs, was on the board of a Children's Relief Organization and when Liza asked hesitantly if there was any help she could render, the older woman looked at her with real interest, and also hesitation.

"I suppose you didn't learn to type when you were in college?"

"But I *did*. I can take dictation too."

Mrs. Carstairs drew a long breath. "It's in the office we are absolutely at an impasse at times. It's hard to get good typists who will work for nothing and we are always in the red, anyway. If you could come even one morning or one afternoon a week . . . ."

"Of course I can. I've been wanting something of the sort to do. I could give a whole day occasionally when you needed me most. But I'll come every Monday morning at least, if that suits."

After a few weeks Mrs. Carstairs eyed the neat desk in the office one day and looked quizzically at Liza. "You didn't say so but I believe you're a *professional*, aren't you?"

Liza smiled. "I guess I am. I was Dan's secretary before we were married."

Mrs. Carstairs, who Liza knew came from the crème de la crème of New York society, did not look shocked. Instead she smiled back. "I admire you, Mrs. Morgan. Or may I say *Liza?*"

So another new friendship was cemented.

As to René there had been a few difficult times with two insistent visits by way of taxis, and many passionate appeals by letter. To all of these Liza had made one constant reply. She was completely devoted to her husband, would tolerate no extraneous love-making, would like to continue the pleasant friendship but it must be within the prescribed limits. She was quietly adamant, an attitude which evidently impressed René more than a highly emotional one would have done. So Liza's weeks went on, busy, and in the main contented except when the memory of the kiss in the pine grove woke intolerable desires within her, and when the longing for a child beat in her bosom. She had gone to a doctor who reported there was no reason why her wish should not be fulfilled, and she could not tell him that her own heart knew the answer. Meanwhile she went often to Helen West's and begged to spend the time in the nursery.

On Dan's part there were many problems to plague him in addition to the routine pressures. One was another letter from Donna. They had moved, she said, to New York State, the part that was just over the line from Pennsylvania. Her husband had heard of a job there through his brother, but it wasn't a very good one and they couldn't bring their furniture and she needed money to buy some new and would he please send as much as possible at once.

This was the gist of the letter and it arrived on a bad day for Dan. He had had another argument with Dunmore, the frequency of which now bothered him greatly. There were incipient labor troubles to be smoothed out back in Pittsburgh, one of his best foremen, the manager of the Magnus, was fatally sick, and a big export order had been canceled. Donna's letter was the last unbearable straw. It was not the insolent demand for money he resented as much as the opening of an old wound that would not heal. He drew a sheet of paper toward him and wrote to his lawyer through whom all moneys had passed. He explained that he was through, finished, *washed up;* that never again would he give her another cent; that if she had taken any care of what he had sent her over the years she would have enough now to live on; that no letter of hers would ever again be opened, and *never again* would any money be sent to her!

He felt better after he had written it. Better still next day when a wire came from his lawyer: GOOD FOR YOU. I HOPED SOME TIME YOU'D TAKE A STAND. I'VE WRITTEN A SCORCHER AND DON'T THINK YOU'LL HAVE ANY MORE TROUBLE.

So, Dan thought with an enormous sigh of relief, he'd heard the last of Donna after he had gone far beyond the call of duty over the years in helping her while he hated the very thought of her. He wondered, as often before, how much of his tragic early story Dunmore knew. There were some old miners still around the "works" who would remember and Dunmore might easily have heard it all from one of these. While he tried not to dwell upon the possibility, there was still the miserable feeling that Dunmore held an ace in the hole which he could use in some way whenever he cared to do so. Sometimes in the dead of night when the past rose in sorrow and anger within him he pondered upon whether it would be better to confess it all to Liza. But the hard closed door of his heart would not allow it, would not open.

There was one thing, however, which he felt increasingly able to share with Liza: this was information about his business itself. Often now in the evenings before the library fire he talked of it as Liza listened eagerly and asked her intelligent questions. Labor troubles for example. He had had fewer than most operators because the union heads knew—and the men knew—that he had come up from the ranks himself; that he and his father before him had dug coal in the pit.

"It makes a difference," he said one night. "They realize I know what I'm talking about. I don't kick about good wages as long as I'm making a reasonable profit. I've always gotten on well with Lewis. Now *there's* a man! Strong and stubborn but honest. If he gives his word he keeps it. I really admire him, though," he laughed, "there are plenty that don't, I can tell you."

"He's just a name to me," Liza said.

"He's a pretty big name in the coal industry now. He made his big impact last year. Oh, I won't go into all that to bore you, but the gist of it was the right of workers to organize. One day Lewis and I had a real man-to-man talk. He's smart as the devil and farsighted. He thinks as I do that in not too many years there will be mechanization beginning in the mines and that will mean laying men off. Well, he said an amazing thing. That he'd rather see half a million men working for good wages under good conditions than a million working in poverty. Good man. Good fighter. I tell you, Liza, the coal business has been through the wringer several times but right now things are good, I'm thankful to say."

"What about your merger? It seems to me it's been hanging fire for a good while, but I suppose it does take time."

"I've had trouble off and on with Hadley. One week he would be all set, and then the next he'd come to see me and say his company had been in their family for three generations and would I mind if the new one would be called simply, *The Hadley?* And of course I did mind. I pointed out that my name in the business meant something and I would agree to nothing less than Morgan-Hadley for our new title. I think he's coming round and he's got his stockholders lined up."

"And how about Mrs. Moreland?"

"Oh, I feel sure she'll be all right when it comes to the vote. I've had several telephone talks with her and she sounds pretty agreeable. I wish we could have her out for dinner again but that would mean Paula too, and I've got enough problems without getting mixed up with her any more than necessary. Have you ever seen Dunmore with her again?"

"Every week at Opera, and Matt says she saw them once at the theater together."

"I've had some trouble with Dunmore," Dan said slowly. "It's hard to put a finger on, but I'd say he's *edgy*. Seems to take very little to start an argument between us, and it was never that way before. I can't understand it."

"Suppose," Liza said, "that he really enjoys Paula's company and yet all the while suspects that she is . . . is interested in you. Wouldn't that possibly affect his attitude? Toward you, I mean."

She spoke hesitantly but Dan did not seem to resent the suggestion. "Oh, I think that's rather far-fetched. Well, come on, now, tell me your news. I've been doing all the talking."

Liza would tell then of her own days as brightly as possible in the hope that the lines on Dan's forehead would smooth out. As a rule she had the relief of seeing him relax before the evening was over. So the winter nights kept slipping by with easy talk, occasional letters to be done for Dan and sometimes at his own request, some reading. Liza felt sure he looked forward to these hours together even as she did.

At the end of February René came into Dan's office one day and with real embarrassment confessed that he had decided to go back home.

"It is very sudden, I know, and I feel quite foolish but I believe I am homesick. For my family, yes, but even more, perhaps, for Paris. All at once I have this feeling . . . it is hard to explain."

"Not at all," Dan said kindly, as he tried to register surprise. "Everyone is a bit lost in a foreign country. But we'll miss you, René. You've done good work. Will you come out to the house for dinner before you leave? I'm sure Liza would . . ."

He fumbled for words but René saved him. "When I made
up my mind to go I decided to do so at once. I finish what is
on my desk and try to get a sailing for next week. Since I
was at the delightful party at your home so recently I will not
tax your hospitality further, but you and Madame . . . Liza
. . . have been most heavenly kind to me. I will call her before I leave and you will perhaps carry her my thanks also."

They discussed a few matters of business and then with his
usual small, courteous bow René went out. When Dan
reached home that night he hurried to find Liza in her own
room where she had just finished dressing for dinner.

"Guess what? Another of your *hunches* has come true!"

"What do you mean?"

"René expects to leave next week for Paris. He's homesick,
he says, and made a quick decision. Since he was just here
last Saturday at the dinner party he won't be out again. I
asked him. But he'll call you on the phone and he wants me
to give you his thanks. Well, what do you think of all this?"

"I'm not really surprised and I'm terribly relieved, but do
you know . . ."

"Yes, I think I know what you're going to say. I felt the
same way. I was sorry for the kid when he was in the office.
His face looked sort of pinched and it made him seem younger than usual. I wish there was something we could do for
him. I'll ask Colby to give him a little office send-off. They
all like him there."

"And what about some sort of gift from us, that he could
keep? I've noticed him admiring your cigarette lighter."

Dan laughed. "I don't believe we could duplicate that for
him but we can certainly get him a nice one. I'll see to it first
thing in the morning and browbeat someone into engraving it
at once. His name and the date, don't you think?"

"That will be wonderful. Maybe we can see him off when
we know the time. I feel I owe him that much," she added.

They decided during dinner that Dan would find out the
time of departure and if Colby was willing, John would drive
Liza into the city, pick up Dan and Colby and then René
himself with his bags and drive them all out to the pier.

"Does he ever call you by your first name?" Liza asked
suddenly.

"Never."

"Even so I think it would please him to have *From Dan and Liza* put on the lighter. What do you think?"

"I agree. It would probably please his father, too, for he calls me Dan. Well, I hope the plans work out."

They did, to René's apparent surprise and pleasure. Just before time for him to board his ship he shook hands with the two men, voicing his thanks with touching warmth, then very slowly kissed Liza's hand and held it for a moment against her cheek. She gave him the small box and told him to open it when he was really out to sea.

"Just a little remembrance from Dan and me," she said.

When his figure on the deck had grown small and they were back in the car again, Colby said, "I'll miss him. He's got some pretty French ideas about some things, but at heart he's a nice chap. And a brilliant one, I'd say." He looked at Liza with a straight glance. "Wasn't his leaving rather sudden?"

"He's very young," Liza answered in what she feared was a slightly muffled voice, "and young people are likely to make quick decisions."

"I guess so. Well, I wish him everything that's good."

"So do I," Liza answered, and then remained silent the rest of the drive, leaving Colby and Dan to discuss business.

Once back at home she went into the drawing room, sat down at the piano and very softly played the first movement of the Chopin étude. Then she sat, with her eyes blinded by tears, thinking of all her experiences with René; of his charm, his eager, poetic intelligence, his ardor, and then, the kiss! She wept for him. She wept for herself. Then at last she rose and spoke softly, aloud. "Incident closed," she said.

And the February snows ended and March began. Dan was coming home later, it seemed, every day, but although the press of affairs was heavy upon him, he had now about him the air of a victor. All the threads were being gathered safely together for the merger. The stockholders' meeting was set forth the fifteenth and he now allowed himself in the evenings to detail more fully to Liza what the future would mean. With the two large companies united there would be a new power to reckon with in the coal industry. He described to her the extent of the coke ovens then, which because of their relation to steel were his especial interest. There would be the question later of whether to start their own steel company, an idea he had delayed bringing up to Hadley, or to "buy into" a large, going one, like Premium. Dan rather favored the latter, seeing himself finally on the board, as he laughingly told Liza. At all events he was cheerfully sure of the immediate outcome of the plans.

Liza made a request one evening. "You know the Child Welfare Agency I work for, Dan?"

"Yes, what about it?"

"I would like for us to make a gift to it. They need money terribly."

"Give anything you want," he said.

"Will you write the check?"

"No. I'll let you attend to it."

"I would like to make it a generous one. Anything," she added softly, "connected with *children* means so much to me."

He changed the subject at once.

"If I get on the board of a Steel Company someday, you'll see me stand a little higher in my shoes," he said. "I suppose most men have a big dream in the back of their heads. Well, this is mine, and this is where the merger comes in. First."

Then one afternoon he came home earlier than usual and as Liza saw his face she was terrified. It was stone white and drawn.

"Dan, are you sick?" she cried as she rushed toward him.

"No, I'm not sick." He went over to a chair in the library, next to the fire, and sank down in it. "But I've had a blow and I'm pretty well shot."

"Oh, what is it?" But even as she asked he was drawing from his inside pocket a square envelope and handing it to her. When she opened it she saw Mrs. Moreland's crested stationery.

> DEAR DAN: [it read, in her less than firm handwriting]
> I should have told you this some time ago, I suppose, but I put it off. I am not too well and have been trying this winter (as the Bible says) to put my house in order. One of my large assets, as you know, is the Morgan Company stock. I

have no legal heir, no living relative, but Paula, as you also know, is like my daughter. So I am transferring this stock to her. My real reason for doing it is the joy of being able to give her this gift now when I am alive. She is very happy over it. As to how she will eventually vote it as a shareholder I do not know. But I hope you will understand my motives. It is hard to be old and without family. Paula is all I have.

With affectionate good wishes,

ELIZABETH MORELAND

For a minute Liza could not speak. She could only look at Dan's stricken face.

"Have you been in touch with Paula?" she said at last.

"I called her as soon as I got the letter. I explained about the voting of the stock." He swallowed with difficulty. "I really had to tell her how much the assent of all the shareholders will mean to me. I *loathed* doing this, but I had to."

"What did she say?"

"She was insolent. She said—oh, Liza, I can't repeat this to you."

"You know you can tell me anything. Please go on, Dan."

"Well, she said she had always wished she had a lever in addition to her *charms*—that's the word she used—and now she had one and I might as well know she intended to use it. And she added that she had a friend or two who, she thought, would vote the way she did."

"Not *Dunmore*," Liza breathed.

"That's what I'm afraid of. And his father has some shares. The three of them could block me. I can't bring myself to talk to Dunmore about it until the last ditch. I told Paula how the merger would affect her own interests and said we must all think only of the business advantages and nothing else. I said I'd call her in another week or two and we'd talk about it again. That I *wanted* to talk to her."

"Oh, Dan, my heart aches for you. Maybe she'll come around. We can hope. But you mustn't look so despairing. Even if the merger falls through it won't be the end of the world."

"It will be the end of a lot of things to me," he said.

He was silent that evening and Liza, in her misery for him,

could make no conversation. The next night was little better and she forbore to ask questions. The following week, however, Dan told her he had been in touch with Paula. She had explained that she would talk to him but at her own apartment. She would be out to dinner the next evening but would be home by eleven and would expect him then.

"Did you tell her you would go?"

"Yes, I did. However, if I feel differently tomorrow morning I'll call it off. I have a lot of paper work to do tonight, Liza. I think I'll go up to my office as soon as I've had dinner. But I really must try to talk to her," he added. "There's just a chance I can. But . . . I . . . feel . . . like . . . the . . . devil."

When Dan came down to breakfast the next day he looked as though he had not slept at all. The lines upon his face seemed to have been cut more deeply as though graven there. His lips were tight and grim. Liza watched him anxiously but said nothing since he himself did not speak. After a second cup of coffee he stood up, refusing the other food.

"I'm sticking to my decision," he said. "I'm going to go to see Paula tonight as she has asked me to do. There's nothing else for it. In all my career I've never been in such a tight spot."

Liza had risen, too, and was looking at him steadily.

"Dan, did she give you an ultimatum?"

"She did."

"What do you intend to do about that?"

His face looked even more grim. "I do *not* intend to ruin my merger chances if it can be avoided."

"I see." Her face whitened. "I believe," she added slowly, "that I'll drive up to Aunt Sarah's this morning, and stay for a few days. If you don't mind." She felt the slight sarcasm creep into her voice on the last words but he apparently did not detect it.

"You want to? Well, of course it's all right. How long will you be staying?"

"I'm not sure," she said. "I haven't been up for a while."

"That's true. Just call me when you're back. I'll stay in at the apartment while you're gone. You have the phone number there in case you need it in between."

"I don't expect to," she replied icily. But once again he seemed unaware of her tone.

"I'd better take a few things with me then," he said. He turned abruptly, went upstairs and came down with his bag. Liza had not moved.

"Tell Aunt Sarah I'd like to see her too. And drive carefully. Would you want John to take you up and go for you?"

"No thanks. I like to drive."

"Well, good-bye," he said.

"Good-bye, Dan."

He turned at the door and looked back at her as though he intended to say something more, then in a moment he was gone.

Liza sank down again at the table with her face in her hands, her own food untasted. In all the conflicting emotions she had experienced during the months of her marriage, there had been nothing like this. This was utter disillusionment. This was utter desolation. She had conditioned herself to Dan's casual friendliness, to his meager responses, to his lack of warmth. But always she had felt that underneath all this, he was true as steel. This confidence had supported her as a woman. No matter what lack in him saddened her at times, she was sure she would never know the racking jealousy that tore at some wives' hearts. If she was less than content, she was at least secure. So she had always thought. But now . . .

She felt the hot tears running down her cheeks and a sob amazed her by choking her throat. When Horace came in with hot coffee, even his imperturbable face was broken up with inquiry.

"Mrs. Morgan . . . you're not well . . . is there anything . . ."

Liza controlled herself, and with a great effort, smiled.

"I'm very foolish, Horace. I think I've been a little homesick without knowing it. Mr. Morgan and I have just arranged that I'll drive up to my aunt's today. He'll stay in at the apartment while I'm gone. I feel very silly but the thought of seeing her . . . she's not young now, you know . . ."

It was rather lame but the best she could do. Horace fell in with it at once. "Of course, ma'am. It's natural an' her your only mother, you might say. A little time up there will do you good. Have some hot coffee now an' eat a bit too. You'll need it. Can Maggie help with your packing?"

"No, thanks, Horace. I can manage nicely."

"Will you be staying long, ma'am?"

"Just a few days, I think."

"Very good, ma'am. Maggie an' me will look after things here. I'll tell John to check your car now for you an' bring it around. I do hope you'll have a good trip. I may say Maggie an' me will be pleased to see you back again when you come."

"Thank you, Horace. You are both a great comfort to me and to Mr. Morgan, too."

Here, she thought, was a little human warmth if it did come from the butler. It had become increasingly apparent that Horace and Maggie had given up the idea of retiring, at least for the present. And while she knew they liked and respected Dan, she also knew that their feeling for her had colored their decision. She was genuinely fond of them, and their constant solicitude for her helped ease the dull ache in her heart which she thought sometimes they half suspected.

She got up from the table now after choking down a roll and draining her coffee cup, and went into the Garden Hall where her engagement book lay beside the phone. She must clear that before she took her sudden departure. Fortunately the rest of the week had only two notations: one a sherry party at the Warrens' down the road which would not demand regrets, although she was sorry to miss it; the other was dinner Thursday evening at Matt's. Here she did feel compunction as well as disappointment, but she had to go ahead. When she got Matt at last on the phone to explain, that lady was angry.

"Liza, you can't just throw over a dinner engagement like that, I don't care what kind of a business meeting Dan has on. You've got to assert yourself, Liza! I think you just let him . . ."

"Listen, Matt. This isn't Dan's doing at all. It's me . . . I. I feel I've got to go up today to Aunt Sarah's."

"Is she sick?"

Liza trod warily among her phrases. "No . . . no, not sick. But I get suddenly anxious about her sometimes. She's not getting any younger. I just have a sort of 'thing' that I've got to go up today. I do hope you'll forgive me, for I'm truly disappointed about the dinner."

"Well," Matt said slowly, "if it's anything to do with Aunt Sarah I suppose I can't be mad at you. I'm crazy about her, myself. How long will you be gone?"

"I can't tell until I get there. I imagine I'll be home the last of the week."

"Then, give me a call and we'll make a new date. And listen, Liza . . ."

"Yes?"

"I never know whether I should repeat things to you or not."

"Oh, I guess you should. What is it now?"

"Dan looks simply terrible. What's wrong with him?"

"Oh, business, you might know. Was that what you wanted to tell me?"

"N . . . no," Matt said. "We were out last night at a party and Paula Ruston was there looking like a cat that had swallowed the canary. I heard one fellah ask her how she was and she said, 'Wonderful, and hope soon to be still better.' Now what would she mean by that?"

"Heaven knows," Liza felt her lips stiff on the reply. "Maybe she's leaving for a trip."

"Yes," Matt agreed. "I thought of that too, for she usually does go off somewhere about this time. But she's a snake of the first water, Liza, so keep your eyes open! And Dan's too," she added. "Well, give my love to Aunt Sarah. Good-bye."

Liza packed quickly. If anything could have given her heart an extra pang it was the words that Matt had just quoted from Paula. It was all arranged then. Paula knew, Dan knew. He was going to pay her price. And after that, what?

The day was fine and a little of her tension eased as she drove along. Spring was breaking, although it was only the beginning of March. Along the roadside a blush was rising in the stems of the sumac and a delicate tremor of something less than green but more verdant than winter's brown seemed to be moving in all the boughs of the trees. That night, Liza knew, as she lay in bed there would be heard a few first pipings of the little new frogs in the village pond. If only there could be spring in her heart, with its gentle healing, instead of the deadly weight of mordancy which lay upon it!

She drove as fast as she dared for she knew every curve of the road. It was only four o'clock when she turned into the familiar drive and saw the spreading old white house with a feeling of relief mixed with dismay. She was glad, *glad* to be here in her only haven, but what could she tell Aunt Sarah, whose piercing eyes penetrated anybody's inner armor, most surely of all that of her beloved child. Perhaps, Liza thought, as she parked the car and took out her bag, it will be *given me* what to say, as the Bible puts it.

She went over the back porch and into the kitchen. At once an atmosphere of homely serenity enveloped her. There was a rich smell of baking rolls from the oven and Mrs. Phinney was paring turnips in leisurely fashion at the sink, letting the long purple and white curls fall from her hand.

"Well, *Liza!*" she exclaimed. "This is a surprise. Why didn't you let us know? You'll get a pretty plain supper, I'm afraid."

"That will suit me. Oh, I just took a sudden notion to come up. Where's Aunt Sarah?"

"In the sitting room, workin' on a rug."

"I'll go right in."

When Aunt Sarah looked up from her work, astonishment in her eyes, Liza knew that her self control had left her and the tears were again running down her cheeks.

"Well, well," Aunt Sarah said, as her niece kissed her. "You did give me a jolt. What brought you? Any trouble? Looks like it," she added.

As there was no answer she went on. "Go and hang up your things and then come here to the fire and warm yourself. Your hands are cold. And tell me whatever you want to. Is Dan all right?"

"Yes," Liza managed.

"Have you had a quarrel?"

"No."

"Does he know you're here?"

"Oh, yes."

"Well, that clears the air a little. We can go on from there."

As Liza was hanging her coat and hat on the old-fashioned

tree in the hall she suddenly knew what she could, in all honesty, tell Aunt Sarah.

"Well, sit down, child, and get settled and if you want to,
tell me what brought you up here all of a sudden with your
eyes runnin' like a rain spout."

Liza smiled in spite of herself. Aunt Sarah's comments were
always tonic in themselves.

"I'll tell you," she said. "I just suddenly found out that
Dan's business means more to him than I do. And it hit me
pretty hard."

"So you ran off."

"Not exactly. Dan was willing for me to come."

"But you didn't tell him why?"

"No."

"Uhm . . . uhm. Well, I could have told you what you're
worrying about now, or something like it. The business, I
mean. You know Dan and I had a pretty long talk the time
you brought him up when you got engaged."

"What did he say then about me, Aunt Sarah? Oh, please
tell me everything."

"How can I remember everything? He said a lot about
you, naturally. But one thing did strike me. He said he wasn't
just a youth but he'd never wanted to marry a girl before
until now he wanted to marry you. That ought to be enough
for you. But about the business . . ."

"Yes?" Liza prompted eagerly.

"He told me the whole story. He's fought his way up from
the time he was fourteen, as I guess you know. Of *course* the
business means a lot to him. I don't think you should be so
childish about it. Now I'll tell you just what to do."

"Yes?" faintly.

"You stay up here a few days and relax and forget about
this. You look tired out to me. Been pretty busy with social
things?"

"I've done a good deal this winter."

"I thought so. Anything else working you? A baby for instance?"

"No."

"Well, there ought to be by this time, but that's none of
my business. I think after a little visit you'll go back with
your mind cleared and know just where you stand."

"I think I will."

"Good. And I may add I'm glad you came. I've been in the dumps myself."

"Have you been sick?"

"Rheumatism in my fingers. I hope to finish this rug but I doubt if I can do another. And then what will I keep busy at? This one is for either you or Dan. Bathroom, I thought."

"It's beautiful," Liza said, going over to examine it. "I think Dan would love it. He said to tell you he'd like to see you."

"Well, he knows where I live. I'd like to see him, too. We're just having spare ribs and turnips for supper, Liza. You'll have to take pot luck."

"Nothing could be better." She leaned back in the old-fashioned rocker and drew a long breath. "It's good to be here. Now, tell me all the town news."

As usual there was plenty. On her part Aunt Sarah wanted to hear about all the parties and insisted that no details be omitted. Before it seemed possible that evening the big clock in the corner struck nine and Aunt Sarah began checking doors and windows, putting out lights and finally setting the cat out the back door.

"Sleep," she said to her niece, "is the very best thing for you. So get to bed and tomorrow everything will look brighter."

Liza made no demur but selected a book from the table and went slowly up the stairs, said good night and found herself in her old girlhood room. But sleep, she knew, was the last thing possible for her. She read until eleven, then paced the floor until midnight. When she finally got into bed it was only to toss until two when she fell into a sort of troubled unconsciousness.

Dan had reached the office early that morning, tired, harassed, and angry, but with his mind made up about the course he would pursue with Paula. He knew all too well her general and unsavory traits as a woman, but he had learned, partly from Mrs. Moreland, of a somewhat masculine quality which she possessed to a remarkable degree. She loved money. For its own sake, and still more for what it would give her. She was extravagant, she demanded luxury, she indulged herself recklessly. Dan had been at some pains to find out in various devious ways, about what her assets were. She had inherited a little money from her family and had received a large settlement from her ex-husband. But even all of this plus the value of the stock Mrs. Moreland had turned over to her was not enough, he felt, to make her indifferent to a larger fortune. So, he had decided to go to her tonight and offer to buy the stock at *twice its value*. This would serve a dual purpose. It would get rid, he hoped, of her troublesome pursuit of him (in fact he would make this a condition) and it would give him control of this large block of Morgan stock which in his own voting power would make the merger sure.

One nagging anxiety had haunted him day and night since the news of Mrs. Moreland's gift had reached him. This was Dunmore's reaction. When Dan had told him of the transfer, for one split second there had been on Dunmore's face a look of satisfaction, of pleasure, even. Then it was gone and he had discussed all the implications of the gift seriously with Dan. But that fleeting look had been *there*. Why, why, Dan kept asking himself, had this been so? There had, indeed, been a shadow of disappointment in connection with the new business relationship, as far as Dan himself had been concerned. Over the years of his association with Dunmore, the latter had been easy to work with, always pleasantly deferent, keen of insight and sound in his business judgments. Now during these intervening months the younger man had shown a slight tendency to aggressiveness, an occasional attitude of "I, too, am in the driver's seat." While he had never been as enthusiastic about the steel business as Dan had been, he had recognized the advantage and discussed the whole problem with an intelligent compliance. Until lately. Now he had seemed to be dragging his feet in respect to the merger which would provide more coal to make coke to make possible the manufacture of steel.

Dan had worked his way to the top practically alone as far as dependence on outside advice went. He had felt himself an almost infallible judge of men when it came to hiring them as workers in their various fields. Could he, *could* he have been mistaken in Dunmore? Could Liza conceivably have been right in her strange "hunch" about him? This was to him a bitterly impossible idea, and he thrust it from him. He not only trusted Dunmore implicitly but he was actually fond of him. Through the lonely years Dunmore had been very close. So, he still would be. Dan decided now, however, that he would not confess his plan about the stock, for the money he intended to use as a lever would be taken not from company funds, but at a severe cost from his own private fortune. He merely mentioned to Dunmore that he intended to go to Paula's that night for a conference about the business.

"Tonight?" Dunmore asked with quick raised eyebrow. "Why not this afternoon?"

Dan was surprised at the question but gave the explanation at once. Paula had set the time. She was very busy all this week and even tonight was going to a dinner party. She would be home, however, by eleven and would expect him then. It was the only hour convenient to see him.

"And I hope," Dan added, looking at his desk, "that by *some* means I can win her over."

Dunmore turned and to Dan's amazement walked out of the office without saying a word.

"That was funny," he muttered to himself, as he pressed the buzzer for Miss Ross. "That was *damned* funny of Dunmore. What can be eating him?"

That evening Dan dressed carefully, ate sparingly of his dinner, went over again the papers he was taking with him and watched the slow passage of the clock hands nervously as the hours passed. He thought of Liza. She and Aunt Sarah would be in the sitting room talking before the fire, while Mrs. Phinney rattled the dishes in the kitchen. Liza would be asking about the affairs of the village. Suddenly he jumped up and went to the phone. He would call her and make sure she had gotten there safely. Then he stopped. That would make him appear fussy and Liza mightn't like it. She was a very self-contained person and this quality suited him down to the ground. He hadn't dared to expect such restraint, such a calm lack of emotion. Just like his own. He wondered sometimes about her. Was her cool acceptance of what he had offered and given her the result of her New England blood and upbringing? Or could it be possible that she had once known a real but disappointing love and because of this was able to agree to his bargain and demand no more than what amounted to general friendliness? He had wondered about this more in recent months. When sitting across from her at dinner with the candlelight falling on her soft coils of golden brown hair and white throat he was conscious that she was a very beautiful woman. In the old office days he had considered her merely a pleasant, neat-looking secretary.

As to his own heart he knew exactly when it had turned to stone. He realized also, now more clearly than ever before, that through the ensuing years, he had deliberately killed any slightest warmth of feeling that showed signs of rising within him. The business had been his only love and to it he had given his very blood. To take the place of normal emotional outlets there had been the fierce and unrelenting mastery of his ambition. His body had been driven every day to the point of exhaustion. He wondered sometimes whether had he known the normal satisfactions of love and a home he could have achieved what he had done.

He looked at the clock. It was ten-thirty. Allowing for traffic it might be best to start now. He was nervous. He hated this interview, but he felt withal a certain confidence. Money was power and he had it.

The night had turned wet and chill. He shivered as he went into the street and hailed a taxi. He had decided against his own car since there might be parking problems. The address was on East Seventieth, a new and very fashionable apartment building where Mrs. Moreland now lived adjoining Paula. He and Liza had been there once to dinner when it seemed impossible to refuse. Mrs. Moreland, who was there too, he thought, was badly showing her years.

The cab stopped at last, he walked under the elegant awning and spoke briefly to the doorman, who was pleasantly communicative.

"Good evening, sir. A bad night it's turned out."

"Yes, the fog's settling fast."

"Good night for a murder, as we used to say in Old England."

"That's right," Dan agreed and moved over the marble floor to the elevator. The operator was elderly and also spoke pleasantly.

"Floor, sir?"

For a second Dan was not sure. How could he have slipped up on this?

"I believe the tenth. Mrs. Ruston's apartment."

"Tenth it is, sir. When you get out, walk to your right, and it's the last one at the end."

"Thank you," Dan said, aware of a certain knowing male look in the man's eye. Well, let him surmise what he likes, Dan thought.

He walked the length of the hall, the carpet lush under his feet, and pressed the bell at the last apartment, his heart in spite of him beating fast. A young woman in a maid's uniform opened the door.

"Mr. Morgan?"

"Yes. Mrs. Ruston is expecting me."

"She told me to show you right in. Just come this way, sir."

It was a very large apartment and they passed the living room, a smaller library and then the dining room without any sign of the maid's stopping. She finally paused before a door, tapped lightly, opened it and said, "Mr. Morgan, ma'am," then stood aside to let him enter and closed the door behind him.

Dan had seldom known fear. He knew it now. The room in which he stood was as nearly a bedroom as made no difference. The wide couch had satin sheets upon which, propped up with pillows, Paula gracefully reclined in a filmy black negligee. The lights were soft, the air perfumed.

"Hello, Dan," she said, as though this was a natural setting for his call. "So, here you are! I thought my ultimatum would bring you."

"You're wrong," he said sharply. "I'm here to talk business. I am going to make you an offer which I'm sure you won't refuse. I am . . ."

"Oh, relax, Dan. Here we are alone for the first time. Can't you let your guards down at last and be human? You surely know by this time that I love you. I know you *don't* love Liza, so doesn't that make things pretty clear between us? Give me a light, will you?"

Dan felt speechless with anger. He lighted her cigarette automatically and she took the lighter into her own hand, examining it with a smile.

"A pretty thing," she said.

"Beautiful! Mrs. Moreland gave it to me," he answered stiffly.

"That's what *you* think. I selected this with great care, had it engraved, paid for it and just let Ma Moreland present it to you for fear you wouldn't take it otherwise. So you've been using a very expensive gift from me all this time."

"You can keep it!"

"With your name on it? Well, maybe I will at that. Oh, Dan, try to be normal. Don't look like a storm cloud. I'm not in the habit of begging for love. Au contraire!" She laughed as she said it.

"And I am not interested in love. I came to tell you that I will buy your Morgan stock for twice its value and give you a check for it!" He stood straighter as he said it, with something like triumph in his tone.

Paula slowly put aside the satin sheet and stood up, facing him.

"And I will tell you," she said in a caressing voice, "that I don't give a damn about the money or the stock either. If you act like a man instead of a robot I'll vote my shares the way you want. If you stay stubborn . . . but somehow I know you won't."

She crossed over to him and put her arms swiftly around his neck, raising her face close to his. For a long minute he stood as though paralyzed, watching the seductive beauty of her, the shining black hair, the smooth curve of her cheeks, the hot, red, sensuous mouth. And as he looked he was seeing another with just such hair, just such lips, a girl who had lain in his arms in the back bedroom of the Patch house while he had poured out his first young, physical love. And suddenly in one great psychological flash at the memory this feeling which he had thought never again to know, this *capability* for love, came surging tempestuously over him, even as great waters freed from restraint rush in headlong flood.

He flung Paula from him with difficulty and all but ran to the door and on down the inner hallway, with his pursuer alternately pleading and cursing behind him. He gained the outer hall and rushed toward the elevator, his breath coming almost in gasps, so strong were the emotions within him.

"Down, sir?"

"To the lobby. As fast as you can," Dan heard himself saying. His one thought was to escape, to get back to his apartment and consider this incredible thing that had happened to him. In the lobby he hurried across the floor.

"May I call you a taxi, sir?" the doorman asked.

"No, no," Dan said shortly. "I'll get one myself," and he rushed out to the sidewalk. As he looked left and right for a cab he could see the doorman, now out under the awning, watching him curiously.

At the next corner he finally caught a cab, gave the address and relaxed in the seat. That is, if he could be said to relax, for his whole being seemed to be on fire. With some attempt at logical analysis he knew that the sudden acute realization of his own normal, warm-blooded youth which Paula's face so near to his own had brought to him more vividly than mere memory's recall, had made the stone in his breast turn to flesh again, warm, palpitating flesh. But though Paula had caused this upleap of his heart his one impulse had been to get away from her. For as the Bible he had been nurtured on would put it, "his desire was not toward her." His desire, this new and undreamed of desire was toward his wife, his own, his beloved whom he had not until now realized *was* his beloved. Liza! Liza! Oh, the stark, stubborn ignorance of his own proud and implacable heart! Coldly setting forth his *bargain*, with no real thought of her! Could she ever forgive him? Could he woo her to the same passion he now, himself, felt? All undeserving as he was, would she yet accept him as lover and true husband? He would call her up now, tonight. It must be twelve o'clock but he could not wait. This tremendous change in himself must somehow be imparted to her at once.

He paid the taxi driver with a tip so generous the fellow kept sputtering his thanks. Dan let himself in to the apartment and went at once to the phone. But there he stopped. What could he say that would give Liza any idea of his own feelings? Voice would be borne to voice by the mystery of the wire, but unrelenting distance would still separate heart from heart. No, when he told her of the miracle wrought in him it must be when he held her in his arms, when he pressed his cheek against the braids of hair she had not cut for his sake, when he kissed her lips as he had never done before. He would start early in the morning and drive up as fast as he could. And before he left, as soon as he felt she would be awake, he would call her then to say, "I'm coming to you today. I have to see you." Then he would add, *"Darling."* A word he had never used in his life. That would surely tell her something. That would in some measure prepare her for what was to come.

He went out to the kitchen and wrote a note for Wing, his house-man, who had still stayed on in the apartment.

Please call me at seven promptly and have a good big breakfast ready for half past. I'm leaving for Vermont at eight.

He smiled as he propped the paper against the coffee-pot, then, still smiling, he went to his room and prepared for bed. Just before he fell asleep he suddenly sat bolt upright. He had just realized that up till that moment he had never thought of the stock, the voting, or the merger!

"And, the queer thing is, it doesn't seem too important," he muttered as he lay down again.

He was awake the next morning before Wing tapped on his door. He had never felt better. He whistled as he dressed; he hummed a tune as he packed his bag. When, he wondered, had he ever hummed a tune before? Not for a long time. He suddenly thought of the problem of the two cars, but he could have John go up later to bring Liza's car down. He would of course bring her back in his own. He could call John from Vermont, and the office, too, if he decided to stay a few days.

He went out to the dining room, seated himself and half absently picked up the morning paper which Wing always laid, folded by his plate. He opened it and then sat as though frozen. Under his eyes ran the heavy black letters.

BEAUTIFUL YOUNG
SOCIALITE MURDERED

Mrs. Paula Ruston, former wife of Fred Ruston, famous polo player, found dead in her apartment by her maid shortly after midnight. Death apparently due to strangulation. Police are working already upon certain clues . . .

For a minute he could not speak but sat staring unbelievingly at the page before him. Then, "My God! My *God!*" he kept repeating in an anguished voice. "Paula! Murdered! Why, it can't be! I was there myself until nearly midnight."

Even as he said the words his face blanched. The hand that held the paper shook. He did not hear the doorbell, nor voices in the hall. He knew nothing until Wing stood beside him.

"Two gentlemen to see you Mr. Morgan. In the libely. I told them you were at blekfast but they say matter velly important."

CHAPTER VIII

When Dan reached the library he found two men standing there. One was youngish, blond and thin with keen wintry blue eyes. The other was older, heavier and swarthy with black eyes, sharp too, but with laughter wrinkles around them.

"Good morning, gentlemen," Dan tried to say pleasantly, even though his lips felt stiff. "This is a very early call. What may I do for you? Will you sit down."

They remained standing. The older man spoke. "I'm Lieutenant Hickley and this is Sergeant Jamison. We're from the homicide squad and we would like to ask you a few questions. You are Daniel Morgan?"

"I am."

"Have you by any chance seen a morning paper?"

"I had just read the headlines when you came in. I feel"—he searched for a word—"stunned."

"Yes, quite so. I should tell you at once, Mr. Morgan—though you no doubt know about questioning of this nature—that anything you say could be held as evidence against you."

"I know of nothing that could be 'held against me' as you put it."

"May I ask where you were between eleven and twelve o'clock last night?"

"Certainly, and I'm glad to tell you." He tried to sound calm but in spite of himself he found his knees shaking beneath him. "I went to Mrs. Ruston's apartment at eleven at her request. She said she would be out until then. There was a business matter I had to talk over with her."

Jamison's cold eyes seemed to hold a nasty surmise and Dan's anger rose within him along with his fear.

"Just when did you leave Mrs. Ruston's apartment?"

"I can't tell you exactly, but I got back here at a quarter past twelve."

"How are you so certain of that time?"

"Because I looked at the clock as I came in. I had intended to call my wife. She's in Vermont. When I found it was as late as that I decided against it."

"I see. Then from that can you approximate the time you left Mrs. Ruston's apartment?"

"I would say it took me perhaps ten to fifteen minutes to get out on the street and find a cab. It was a very bad night. From then I would guess it was about twenty minutes until I was back here."

"Which you say was at twelve-fifteen."

"It was."

"Thirty-five minutes then before that time would mean you left the apartment at about twenty minutes to twelve?"

"I should think about that. As I say I can't be more definite."

"The doctor who examined the body said death was apparently due to strangulation which could have taken place within the hour. The Medical Examiner will of course give his report later."

Dan felt his hair prickling his scalp. He looked dumbly at the men before him, remembering something he had recently read that anyone suddenly accused of a crime, even though innocent, might react as though he were guilty.

The black-eyed Hickley went on. "Since you have confessed to being . . ."

Dan stopped him shortly. "I have 'confessed,' as you put it, to nothing, Lieutenant, because I have nothing to confess. I have told you honestly what you have asked me."

Hickley cleared his throat. "What I was about to say, Mr. Morgan, was that if you had not seen fit to tell us you were with the decedent last night, we have evidence of it anyway. You left some of your property there. Your cigarette lighter, plainly marked with your name."

Dan automatically slapped his pocket. "Good Lord," he said. "That's right."

"In view of all this I'm afraid we'll have to ask you, Mr. Morgan, to be good enough to come with us down to the

Precinct Detective Squad room. The Captain, there, wants to ask you a few questions."

"Certainly," said Dan. "I have nothing to hide. But I've had no breakfast. Won't you come out to the dining room and have a cup of coffee with me? You can then keep your eyes on me while I eat."

There was no answering smile to his intended witticism, which frightened him more than anything else had done up to the moment.

"I believe we will not wait for that. You will have something later," Hickey said.

He was wondering about calling Liza. What could he say? Paula Ruston was murdered last night and since I was certainly there near the time at least I am under suspicion by the police? He *couldn't* say that to her just yet and at this hour. She would not see a New York paper. Aunt Sarah wouldn't have one in the house. She said they were too disturbing. Even so! He agreed. He would wait until he had satisfied the police, then he would call. He hoped to heaven no one here in the city—Matt for instance—would do it first. It would be just like her, as soon as she read the news.

Dan summoned Wing and gave him directions. If the office called he was merely to say Mr. Morgan was not in. Nothing further.

"All right, gentlemen. I'm ready."

He saw the two exchange glances. Hickley started to say, "Perhaps you'd better . . ." and then stopped. "We'll be on our way, then. We have our car here."

During the ride to the precinct office Dan's abortive efforts at conversation soon ceased from lack of response, and he was left to pursue his own thoughts in silence. It was all fantastic, incredible, but yet he was a man inured over the years to facing hard facts and drawing logical conclusions. Until the real murderer was discovered and apprehended he could understand the dark suspicion that would rest upon him. He pictured the office as it would be this morning. The girls' wild, excited repetition of the news, the men's less vocal consternation. They all knew of Paula. And what about Dunmore? He must get in touch with him as soon as he could. By the following morning it was to be hoped he would have satisfied the law and be back at work. He must then say something. The whole thing was too grim, too tragic to allow a light jest about his own predicament, which might then be known. No, he decided, he would have Dunmore, Miss Ross and a few others in to his office and explain frankly his reason for going to Paula's at that hour, and that upon her refusal to sell her stock he had left immediately. The great, blinding trouble was that the whole thing, no matter how he phrased its telling, looked black against him. But surely innocence could always be proved.

"Well, here we are," Hickley said as the cab stopped before what Dan thought was a sinister looking building with barred windows. They entered, went up in an elevator to the third floor, and stopped before a door lettered PRECINCT HEADQUARTERS.

Inside, an elderly man with iron-gray, thinning hair and an inscrutable face sat behind a high desk.

"This is Daniel Morgan," Hickley intoned, adding, "Detective O'Brien."

The man behind the desk was courteous. "I'm sorry we have to trouble you so early, Mr. Morgan. Murder is never a pleasant business, but we are obliged to find out all you know about this particular one."

"I know nothing about it," Dan said.

"Your full name?" O'Brien asked calmly.

"Daniel McAllister Morgan."

"Residence?"

"Barmoor House, near Greenwich, Connecticut, and an apartment here in the city at . . ."

"Yes, we have that. Occupation?"

"President and director of the Morgan Coal Company."

"Yes. Now will you tell me just where you were between eleven and twelve last night?"

"I've already gone over all that with the officers here. I was in Mrs. Ruston's apartment from eleven until about eleven-thirty or so. I can't tell exactly when I left. I saw the clock when I got back to my apartment and it stood at a quarter past midnight. I had to wait for a taxi uptown and then it was a foggy night as you recall and the traffic was slow so it took longer than it usually would to come from Seventieth down."

The detective took another tack.

"Would you recognize Mrs. Ruston's maid?"

"I think so. Yes, I'm sure I would. I've seen her before. She let me in last night and named me," he added.

"Did you see her as you left?"

"No, I didn't."

"Well, she saw you. She was at the other end of the corridor where she had been visiting with another maid in someone else's apartment. She, the elevator operator and the doorman have already told us that you seemed upset, agitated and in a great hurry as you left. Can you explain this?"

To Dan's horror he felt a hot color rising to the very roots of his hair. O'Brien was watching him closely.

"Can you explain this, Mr. Morgan?"

"N . . . no," Dan stammered, "except that I was under strong emotion. Personal," he added.

"Would you care to tell me just why you went to see Mrs. Ruston at that hour?"

"I'll be glad to explain *that*," Dan hurried to answer. "She set the time because of her many social engagements. She had been out to dinner that evening. I went to talk business with her about some stock she owns in my company."

"Proceed."

"She had recently been given this stock by an old lady who is fond of her. I am hoping for a merger with another coal company and the stockholders will have their say. I was not sure how Mrs. Ruston would vote so I went to see her to make a proposition. I was willing to buy her stock at more than its value."

"You felt she would agree to this?"

"I hoped so. Yes, I felt sure she would."

"And did she?"

"No, she refused."

"This, I presume was upsetting to you?"

"Yes, very. Though I haven't thought much about it since." He added this wonderingly as though to himself alone.

Another man entered the room, and Dan's instinctive feeling as he looked at him was that his presence boded no good for his own problem. The stranger was introduced as District Attorney Brown, and from that point on with a clarity which amazed and terrified Dan the scenes of the night before were gone over in detail, the questioning sharper than before. It

was all spread out now as on a page. Dan had been with
Paula from eleven until about eleven-thirty. The point was
stressed that he had been seen by three different people leaving in haste and under great emotional stress. The maid who
was one of these witnesses had gone straight into the Ruston
apartment and the door locked automatically behind her.
This was the only entrance and no one else had come in.

At midnight, knowing that Mrs. Ruston was then alone,
she had gone as usual to see if her mistress needed anything
further and had found her dead on the bed which showed
signs of a struggle, with Dan's cigarette lighter (engraved, it
was repeated) beside her. The maid had called a doctor; he
had called the police. Almost at once the radio cars had arrived with detectives and a sergeant, photo and lab units, and
the newsmen close upon their heels. Dan had spoken then.

"All this, *so fast?*" he said.

"In our business we have to work fast, Mr. Morgan," the
District Attorney answered crisply.

The fingerprint tests showed Dan's in a number of places,
even on the bed post.

"But I can explain that," Dan said eagerly. "Mrs. Ruston
was sort of reclining there and she asked for a light. I had to
lean over slightly and I steadied myself by putting one hand
on the post. She held on to the lighter," he added. "That's
how it came to be there."

It all sounded lame to Dan, himself, who alone knew it to
be the truth. The questioning continued and while the voices
were coolly courteous, the eyes, to him, looked hostile. His
face under their gaze turned pale as the statement came that
the body of the deceased was now in Bellevue Morgue, waiting the Medical Examiner. It seemed pretty certain, however,
Brown said, that death had been due to strangulation.

Dan's head felt dazed and heavy. In spite of his control he
stammered at times on his answers. He felt like a man who
had been walking strongly and securely along a familiar road
when he suddenly stepped into quicksand. There was in the
very air a certain pressure, the swift, sure turning of the
wheels of an alien business, the concerted movement of men
who knew the law as he knew coal.

At last he heard the incredible statement that he was being
booked on a charge of homicide. He roused then!

"You mean I'm *arrested!* But this is fantastic! This is pre-posterous! I'm as innocent of that murder as any of you are. You haven't a shred of real evidence against me. It's all purely circumstantial and that doesn't count!"

"I'm afraid it does, Mr. Morgan," Brown said. "In a great many trials that is all the prosecution has to go on. In your case, unfortunately, everything checks so far. I am afraid we must hold you for further routine procedures."

Dan's face was white. "I can't believe that this could happen to an innocent man in a free country. I must see a law-yer at once, and I suppose I can make some phone calls?" There was bitterness in his voice.

"You may make three calls. And you should arrange to have counsel immediately." He signed to Jamison.

"Will you see that Mr. Morgan is as comfortable as possi-ble at the police station and send someone to pick up what-ever personal things he wishes brought, his shaving gear and so on. He will make his phone calls there."

"Very good," Jamison said and motioned for Dan to come with him.

"This is the final ignominy," Dan said as he got into the patrol car.

"We can hope so, sir," Jamison responded mildly.

Dan had been correct in his surmise that another call to Vermont might precede his own. Liza was examining some old quilts which Aunt Sarah had brought down after break-fast to the living room when the phone rang. It was Matt. At the sound of her voice Liza laughed.

"Now, Matt, I really can't turn right around and get back for your dinner party no matter how much I love you."

But Matt's voice sounded strange. "Do you see a New York paper there, Liza?"

"Never."

"I thought not. Well, there's news in it this morning I felt you should know. Something terrible has happened to Paula Ruston."

"What?"

"She was murdered last night about eleven-thirty, accord-ing to the doctor."

Liza sank back weakly in her chair, and her voice failed her.

"Liza? Did you hear me?"

"Yes," she managed. "I'm just too shocked to speak. Are there . . . are there any suspects?"

"It's too soon I suppose for the police to know. The afternoon papers may have some more facts. Of course Dan will be calling you soon but after the way I've hounded you about watching out for her I couldn't resist calling to tell you she is no longer a menace. Of course it's simply too utterly *ghastly* but I don't know a soul who will be grief-stricken over it except poor old Mrs. Moreland. This will just about finish her."

"Yes," Liza said faintly, "I'm afraid it will."

"Well, good-bye. Hope you aren't too upset, but I just had to tell you. I feel awfully queer myself. She was at a dinner party with us only two nights ago as I told you, and now, *murdered*. It doesn't seem . . ."

But Liza had hung up the phone. It was only a few minutes until Dan called.

"Liza?"

"Yes, Dan. Matt just told me"

"The devil she did. I was expecting that. Well, I'm in a bind if ever there was one. I suppose I needn't tell you that I did *not* kill Paula."

"No," Liza said simply, "you certainly don't have to tell me that."

"But the trouble is, that according to the timing it looks bad for me. I'm really under suspicion. I'm . . . I'm actually being *held* here at headquarters."

"Oh, Dan! I'm coming right home. I'll start at once."

"No! No! Stay there until things are cleared up."

"I can't. You'll need a lawyer at once."

"I must have one as soon as possible."

"Matt's husband, Tom, is a good one. Maybe not for this kind of a case but he knows everybody. I'll get in touch right away with him. Dan, don't worry. When you're innocent that's all that matters."

"That's the way I feel. Well, it's good to talk to you. If they let me I'll call you tonight and make sure you're safely home. I guess I'm glad after all you're coming."

She called Tom's office immediately and told him the situation, praying that her voice would hold steady.

"This is a horrible business, Tom, but Dan of course is innocent. He was there, though, on business at Paula's request last night and now, as I say, he's been arrested. He has just talked to me. He may already be in touch with his own law firm, but they're corporation lawyers. Could you help?"

Tom's voice was grave.

"I needn't tell you I'll do everything in my power for him, but I'm not a criminal lawyer. A friend of mine, though, Mark Harrison, is one of the best in the city. I'll get on to him right away, if you say so. And I'll see Dan myself as soon as it's possible."

"Oh, that's such a relief. The whole thing is so fantastic, I keep telling myself it can't be happening. You do believe he's completely innocent, don't you, Tom?"

Tom replied slowly. "Yes, I do. I've seen men fall into these circumstantial nets before. There's something about Dan that just doesn't seem to fit in with murder, to my mind."

"That's a load off my heart, to hear you say that. Could you see him tonight?"

"I will if they let me. Try not to worry too much, Liza. Harrison is tops in his field, and I'm sure I can get him. When I see Dan, have you a message?"

"Yes. Tell him I'll be right there, at home, and will be in to see him as soon as it's allowed."

"Right. Now, take it easy. There's no use denying this is a bad business, but when Dan is innocent there's also no use in being pessimistic. How did the police know where to find him?"

"I imagine from Paula's maid. She would recognize him, I think, and Paula, I'm sure, would have both the house here and Dan's apartment in her address book. I know she got hold of his city telephone number even though it's unlisted."

"Yes," Tom agreed. "She would. Well, let's see how fast we can work. Call me any time, Liza."

When Liza told Aunt Sarah the facts that intrepid lady's face at once turned pale. At sight of it, Liza felt the fear she had been trying to master overwhelming her.

"I've got to go back at once, Aunt Sarah. I've got to be near, though I'm sure he won't be . . . detained long. When he's innocent, they couldn't . . . I mean nothing could . . . Oh, Aunt Sarah, I'm so *scared*."

"Well now," Aunt Sarah said, though her face was still white, "just keep hold of yourself, but I think, too, you should go back right away. Did you know he was going to see that woman last night?"

"Yes, I did."

"That was what brought you up here?"

"Yes. Of course his going was all tied up with the business. She's got stock in the company. But I've never liked her."

"Um-hm. Well, I'll tell you something. I may not be the world's greatest judge of character but if I were the wife of Dan Morgan I'd trust him through hell and high water. Now get off as soon as you can. And Liza, watch your driving. Keep your mind on the road."

It was early dusk when she drove up to the house, which somehow looked to her more beautiful than ever. She had only reached the front door when Horace opened it, his face stricken.

"I've been on the look-out for you, madam. I felt sure you'd come as soon as you heard."

"Have an evening paper, Horace?"

"Yes, but I hate to show it to you. They name him right out. It's all a mistake, surely."

Liza's tone was angry. "Of course, it's a mistake. He's as innocent as I am, but he was at Mrs. Ruston's apartment last night on business and until the police find the guilty person, they will probably hold Mr. Morgan. It's all dreadful, but it will be cleared up. Have there been any calls?"

"A good many, but some didn't leave their names. Have you had dinner, Ma'am?"

"No. I drove right through. I guess I could do with some. I'll make some calls myself, first."

"Very good, Ma'am. We have something all ready for you as soon as you let us know."

"And please get me the paper right away, Horace."

He seemed reluctant but brought it from the kitchen. The details were on the front page. Gruesome enough. Daniel Morgan, coal magnate, was being held for the murder of

Paula Ruston, popular socialite. The evidence already in the hands of the police was considered extremely damaging. The article went on with its ghastly repetitious details. Liza's hand went involuntarily to her heart as she laid the paper down.

She ate some dinner for she felt faint, and then called Dunmore's apartment with a strange tremor in her heart. From the first news she had wondered about him. If Aunt Sarah's surmise was correct and he had been in love with Paula, could he, blind with anger as a harshly rejected suitor, have committed the crime? It did not seem likely. And yet, *"All men kill the things they love."* The words were in her mind as she made the call.

When Dunmore answered and she gave her name, his tone was sharp and bitter. "I'm too upset to talk to you, Liza. I don't know why you're calling *me*. You'd better concentrate on your husband."

"Why, Dunmore, you surely don't believe that Dan is *guilty?*" Her voice shook on the words.

"Well, what would anyone think who has read the papers? The police aren't fools. I'm sorry for you, Liza, but I can't talk about it any more." and he hung up.

Then he *had* been in love with her, she thought to herself, and now he is hurt beyond healing and if he believes Dan is guilty he'll hate him with a terrible hatred and do all he can against him. And the business? Would it be safe until Dan was back again at his desk? And, oh, when would that be? Tom's remark that he had seen other men caught in nets of circumstantial evidence was somehow far from comforting as she recalled it. Deep in her heart she knew now that Dan was in ghastly trouble; that it was not a matter of the inconvenience and embarrassment of a few days' time. The mills of the law like those of the gods ground slowly.

She walked through the beautiful house, trying to calm her terrifying thoughts, then she went to the kitchen and sat down, for comfort, with Horace and Maggie, whose faces reflected the horror of her own.

Tom called her the next morning. He had moved fast, had managed to see Dan, was completely convinced of his innocence and had arranged with Mark Harrison to take the case. The latter was already on the job. She, Liza, had better wait another day before trying to see Dan. When asked how he looked, Tom hesitated a second. "Well, what he's up against is not calculated to make him look too *good* but he's well enough, I'm sure."

"But, Tom, won't he soon be out *on bail?*"

"Liza, dear, I hate to tell you but the chances are slim for that, I'm afraid. When a man's booked for homicide, there is very, very little likelihood of bail. Once in a great while it happens, but we can't count on it."

"And he'll have to stay in *jail?*"

"I'm afraid so. You see, there's what we call an arraignment first before the police officers when the charges are read out. Then the D.A. presents the case to the Grand Jury, and they decide whether there's enough evidence for a trial. That's the way it works. I'll keep you posted, and you can call me at any time. I'll see that you meet Harrison too. He's as clever as the devil, so keep up a good heart."

Over her solitary lunch Liza made a decision. She first wrote a brief note to Dan, making it as cheerful as possible and signing it simply, *Liza.* Then she got John to take her to New York. It seemed odd to be going to the office again after all the intervening months, but in a sense it was a relief. It was a resumption of an old pattern, and it was *doing* something when agonizing idly at home was more than she could bear.

She went in the familiar door, up in the same elevator where the old operator smiled nervously at her, and tried to make conversation, and finally reached the office where Miss Ross and the two other girls sat at their typewriters. When they saw her they first froze in their places and then with one accord rose and came up to her.

"Hello, girls," Liza said trying to sound normal. "I wanted to come and explain some things you must be wondering about."

Lila Ross spoke first. "Liza, it's all too unbelievable. We've hardly been able to work at all since we read about it."

"Now listen," Liza said. "This is how the whole terrible business—as far as Dan is concerned—came about. He wanted to talk to Mrs. Ruston about the stock she holds in the company. He hoped to convince her to vote the right way on this merger business. She said she was busy for days ahead with luncheons and dinners but she would be home by eleven on Wednesday evening and he could come then. He explained all this to me that morning. Apparently just after he left her that night someone went in and . . . well, you know what happened. The fact that Dan had been there near the time of course made the police suspicious and he's being . . . held. You remember Matt Harvey? *You* do, Lila. Her husband, Tom, is a lawyer and he told me he'd seen other innocent men who had got caught just this way in a web of circumstantial evidence. Well, that's the story and it's hard enough to bear, but I'm sure the real criminal will soon be found."

Miss Ross drew a long breath. "Thank God you came, Liza. Maybe we can settle down a bit now." She lowered her voice. "Have you seen Dunmore yet?"

"No, but I intend to now if he's in."

Miss Ross looked around her carefully. "He's been acting very strange. We've all felt scared. He was drinking yesterday and ugly to everybody. Once in a while he shouted out some awful things."

"Such as what?"

"Well, you know a drunk man will say anything."

"Just what did he say?" Liza persisted.

"He said if the law didn't take care of Morgan, he would himself."

"You see," Liza explained to the white-faced girls, "he knew Mrs. Ruston very well. He often dated her, so of course he is sort of in a state of shock. But that shouldn't make him distrust his friend. He'll calm down soon, I hope. Just now I'd like to go into Dan's office. There may be some things I can attend to myself and I can make a list of matters he should know about."

"Come on," said Lila Ross, "and thank goodness again you're here. I don't think Dunmore's been in today at all and it's bad to let letters go even for several days."

They went into the familiar office and something caught in Liza's throat. She remembered just how Dan had looked when he asked her to marry him. She remembered how she had all but stopped breathing in amazement and joy as she heard his words. She thought again of his manner of severe and intensive honesty as he had tried to make clear to her what the limitations of the marriage would be. It had been her own heart that had not been honest with him then or since. But how could she help that?

She sat down at his desk with Miss Ross in her own old place opposite.

"This does seem queer, Lila, to be on the other side of the fence," Liza said with a smile.

"You've a good right to be there. Just go ahead."

With her experienced eye Liza ran over the mail, dictated a number of letters, and made a note of such matters as she could discuss with Dan when she saw him. Then she picked up a small blue slip tucked in the side of the blotter. She remembered such memorandums well. It had been Dan's habit at the end of the afternoon to list the most important matters coming up the next day. She ran down the items now. At the end she read: *Discuss with Dunmore the situation with P.R.* This, she thought bitterly, was now not necessary.

"I believe," she said slowly, "that it might be a good idea if a few of the men would come in here. I could tell them what I told you girls. What do you think?"

"I'll go and round them up right away. Which ones?"

"Well, David Colby, and the others I'll leave to your judgment. There are one or two new ones, I believe."

In a few minutes five men entered the office. Liza had come from behind the desk and stood now before it. Colby shook hands and they all spoke. There was no smile on any face.

"I felt," Liza began, "that it was due you to explain certain facts about this dreadful situation." She went on, then, to tell them what she knew: *why* he had gone to Paula's at that hour; *why* he had gone at all (she could honestly say again that the visit was connected with the stock now in Mrs. Ruston's possession); *why* suspicion had lighted upon him because of his being there near the time the murder was committed, though, she need not add, he was entirely innocent, of course.

When she had finished she watched them closely. There was in their eyes a certain male awareness of the terrible provocations of sex. There was, in fact, writ large upon their faces a doubt, a disbelief.

"I believe Mr. Dunmore has not been in today."

"He's pretty well shot, Liza," Colby said. "Of course he knew Paula very well."

"I understand that. The shock is frightening for us all. Will you take care of his desk until he's back, David? I'll plan to be here every day for a few hours and do what I can. I know you'll all carry on until this thing is straightened out."

They were courteous, of course, expressed sympathy (in the case of Colby) for her, but when they were gone she realized that not one of them had sent any message to Dan! She told the girls her sudden decision about returning each day and left them in a measure cheered and eagerly compliant. But all the way home, during dinner and that night in her sleepless bed she knew that what she had told the office people was true as far as it went, but in her own mind she did not know whether or not Dan had paid Paula's price before the tragedy.

In the days that followed Tom and Matt Harvey were both a means of comfort and distress to her. Tom was inherently honest and Matt completely untactful. Between them she found out all the evidence against Dan and her heart was chilled. Two things sustained her: her nightly calls to Aunt Sarah, who for once did not chide her for the expense of them, and of course most of all, her visits with Dan himself. The first time she saw him in his jail surroundings, and through the glass screen, she knew a sudden and terrible sickness. When she had mastered the feeling enough to talk she tried to make a joke of it, though Dan would not smile. He was different, she found. While, as usual, he had no words of affection, his voice was gentler. He kept watching her with a sort of anguished gaze that went to her heart.

"To think I've gotten you involved in this unspeakable mess, Liza! Does it seem possible to you?"

"It seems to me ridiculous," Liza said stoutly. "Over the years we'll laugh about it. Even if we can't just now," she added as Dan remained sober. "What do you think of Mark Harrison?"

"I think he's great. A man after my own heart. Goes straight to the point and a devilish hard worker. I think he'll come up with something."

"Has he checked on Fred Ruston? There could have been old enmity between him and Paula."

"The police went after him right away. He's been out in
California for two months playing polo. His alibi is iron-
bound. Besides, it seems he was as willing for the divorce as
Paula. I can understand that. So he hadn't a motive in the
world. At the moment I hate to say it but I'm very impressed
with the police. They go after the least possible clue like a
dog after a bone. The trouble as far as I'm concerned is that
none of the other clues have led to anything so far."

"But they will, Dan. They're bound to. Have you heard
anything about Mrs. Moreland? This will kill her."

"It almost has, according to Harrison. He's been up and he
says she's in a bad way. The police didn't bother her that
night because she was asleep, but they questioned her next
morning for all they were worth. She told them everything
they asked and then collapsed. Harrison says she's pathetic.
Of course she was the only person I think who really loved
Paula. I have a feeling she'll stick to me now, but I don't
know."

"Should I go up or write her, do you think? I've done
nothing yet and I feel I should."

"Maybe writing would be best. Harrison says she's pretty
shaky. Have you seen Dunmore?" he added suddenly.

Liza had known this question must come and had dreaded
it. She told him then as carefully as she could what the situation was, beginning with Aunt Sarah's shrewd surmise the
day of the party last fall. Dan was dumfounded.

"In love with Paula? I can't believe it. Good God, if he
was, he must be pretty shot now. But surely he doesn't think
. . ." He eyed her shrewdly.

"I've taken quite a lot," he said, "so I can take more. Tell
me all you know, Liza."

She soon saw that Dunmore's attitude had hit him very
hard. It was a blow to the business and to him personally.
His face looked even more drawn than before. He set about
at once, however, planning a replacement if Dunmore should
continue to shirk his office duties. It was decided between
them that Colby would look after Dunmore's work and that
Liza would go each day according to her plan and take care
of his own desk, bringing all possible material back to discuss
with him, as she had done today. They went over it now as

she outlined it, Liza taking dictation as she had done so often before.

"It's like old times," she said, smiling.

He looked up. "There's something I want to tell you. I've been in rough spots before this one in my life, and I've survived. I'm tough."

"Stout fellow!" Liza said and had the satisfaction of an answering smile.

After the arraignment and the heavy blow of the Grand Jury's decision that Dan must stand trial, the weeks fell strangely, incredibly into a regular pattern. The District Attorney evidently felt he had his case, but Harrison wanted more time. So, out at Barmoor House spring came on and then summer. The daffodils bloomed and were gone, then the roses and after the warm, mixed glory of the garden beds. In the gray streets surrounding the police building men went upon their grubby and erratic ways, all unaware, of course, of the interned lives so near to them. Indeed, Liza thought sometimes as the weeks passed, that Dan seemed to have been removed from the earthly scene as completely as Paula herself had been. The newspapers now were silent upon the tragedy, having constantly new ones to make headlines.

It was only while she was making her calls upon Dan, taking with her anything her mind could conceive for his comfort, that his vitality still made itself felt. The greatest help to him in her visits, she knew, were the business papers she brought with her. With his old vigor he dictated letters and outlined messages to the other men. Harrison had asked the District Attorney if Dan and Liza could meet in a small private room for these sessions and the request had been granted. Dan could tell that Liza was bringing its usual smooth efficiency to the office, but he had mentioned Dunmore only once.

"You may have been right about him," he said slowly one day. "After this I'll listen to your advice."

As a matter of fact Dunmore was still unpredictable in his comings and goings, but he had, after the first weeks, begun to handle certain phases of the Pittsburgh business which he knew better than any of the others. He had even made sev-

eral trips out there. The merger, of course, now lay dormant.
Liza had tried to present the tragic situation in as reasonable
a light as possible to the men still closely connected with the
company as purchasers or associates. Dan, too, had written
them on business matters as though he were still at his desk.

One day Liza ran into Dunmore in the hall. "Wait," she
called as he was rushing off. "I want to talk to you."

He half turned. "I've told you I have nothing to say to
you."

"But, Dunmore, you've been his closest friend for years.
How can you possibly believe this dreadful thing? Suppose
you were called as a character witness. You *couldn't* say anything against him, could you?"

There was something almost like a sneer on the man's face.
"I should certainly not obstruct *justice,*" he said, and was
gone.

As against this enigmatic remark (over which Liza agonized often) there was the kindly letter from Mr. Hadley. He
could never connect Dan Morgan with a crime and would be
available at any time to do anything he could for him. There
had been one or two more letters of this nature but, sadly
enough, not many. Dan's nature had not been the kind to
draw others to him in personal friendship. Men had respected
his ability and his business integrity but there had not, Lisa
realized, been any sort of affection. She knew only too well
the cold, hard wall he had built up between himself and human
warmth. One business fact was in his favor. He had been accustomed to dealing with men who knew their job and could
be depended upon to carry a project to successful completion.
So he frequently showed to Liza a certain optimism about his
own case.

"I've faced all the facts squarely. I know I'm in plenty of
trouble, damn it. But I also know that Harrison is one of the
best criminal lawyers in the country, and I'm going to put
some faith in his skill. Also," he added, "I happen to be innocent."

When August approached Liza knew that if Dan was holding up, she herself was breaking. She asked Harrison and
Tom to come out one evening to the house. She had to have
some idea of what was going on if it killed her. She made no

pretense at casual amenities—when they were seated, she went straight to the point.

"Mr. Harrison, I want to know how you think things are going. In Dan's case," she added.

He lighted a cigarette and remained silent for a moment. He was a man in his late fifties, tall and spare with the craggy features of a Scot.

"I wish, Mrs. Morgan," he said at last, "that I could tell you I have now built up an impregnable defense for him. The truth is I am not yet satisfied. With his innocence, yes. But I've never before run into such a lot of evidence so simple and yet so damning. We've not been able to uncover another plausible suspect. We wind up every time in a blind alley or I should say an unassailable alibi. Take this young Dunmore, for instance."

"Yes?" Liza prompted quickly.

"He had been a great deal with Mrs. Ruston, we found. There could easily have been a violent quarrel. The police checked him right away. I did myself. The night of the murder he had three men to dinner in his apartment and they played poker until two o'clock. The other men are reputable people and they can all swear that outside of perhaps five minutes Dunmore wasn't out of their sight all that time. That's just an example of the way it's gone with everyone I have hoped to pin down."

"And fingerprints?" Liza asked.

"No good. There were none about the body, except on the cigarette lighter. She was wearing a chiffon negligee with a ruffle round the neck. There were no clear ones in the room except your husband's, the maid's, and her own."

"But you don't think . . ." Liza's voice was anguished.

"No. No. I don't think it's hopeless. It's simply a difficult case, but I've had them before. There's one thing . . ."

He hesitated and then went on. "Mr. Morgan has been as open as a book with me except in one particular. He was seen by several people rushing out of that apartment. He looked half dazed and was evidently in a highly emotional state. He refuses to go into that. Your husband is a very reserved man, as you know. He merely says he was upset because Mrs. Ruston would not accede to his business offer and he wanted to get away as soon as possible, which seems to me hardly enough explanation. The District Attorney is going to make a lot of this. Do you think, Mrs. Morgan, you could prevail upon him to clarify this any further?"

Liza felt all the blood rushing to her head. "I don't think so. He must be the one to decide about that."

Tom came to her rescue. "You mustn't feel despairing, Liza. Dan's in good hands with Harrison, here. Just take it easy."

"When do you think the trial will be?" she asked.

"Soon, I imagine," Harrison answered. "I have my plans pretty well in hand now. As I say, it's a hard case but that just presents a good challenge and while it would not be wise to give away all my procedure to you, let me just say that there are some things working for us which I couldn't go into. The D.A. has been ready for some time. I should say the date will be fixed in a week or so, for the first term of September Court."

"I can be there, can't I? In court?"

"If you wish."

"Matt says she'll go with you any time you want. And I'll be in and out as I can. Get the doctor to give you some tranquilizers, Liza. They might be good to have around. How is Dan these days?" Tom asked.

"Amazingly calm. He works away at business things, and Mr. Harrison, he has the greatest faith in you."

"Well, I'll do my best. I can assure you, to justify it."

When the men had gone Liza sat very still. From the conversation she had deduced two things. One was that Harrison would fight to the end for his client, and the other was that he didn't have too much with which to fight. She decided, as Tom had advised, to see a doctor and get something to calm her nerves and help give her some sleep. If possible she would need it now more than ever, for she felt only too sure that *she* and she alone knew the truth as to why Dan had rushed from Paula's apartment on that tragic night. And in spite of all her rationalization the ache in her heart, even with the doctor's good offices, would keep her, she feared, wide-eyed and weeping through the still hours.

She could not know of course that Dan too lay wakeful night after night going over a decision which he regularly made and unmade. As he watched Liza on her visits to him he knew how terribly he loved her. He wanted now to touch her, to hold her in his arms, to kiss her like a lover. He longed to tell her of this strange thing that had happened to him that night when Paula had tried to cling to him. How the black hair, the red lips, the seductive beauty had brought back to him the young passion that had lain dead for so many years. But there were two reasons why he was always dissuaded from this confession: one was that his whole soul revolted from the first declaration of his love in these present surroundings. Not *in jail* with its ugly and intolerable lack of privacy even in their business sessions. Oh, he couldn't tell her here.

The other reason was that he knew she had enough to bear without any additional shock or anxiety. As far as he had been able to discover Liza had accepted the bargain as willingly as he, himself, had made it. Never at any time had she given the slightest evidence of emotion in connection with him. What her reaction would be to his avowal when he made it, he had no idea. He could only *hope* that he could somehow win her true love. In the dead of night sometimes a great darkness of the spirit also settled upon him. Suppose the worst. Suppose in spite of his innocence and Harrison's skill, the jury remained unconvinced? What then? He shuddered. Could he possibly tell her then, when perhaps permanent separation would close in upon them?

But in the mornings something like hope returned to him, along with his decision to keep his secret in his breast and betray nothing to Liza which might startle or upset her.

And then the news came. The trial had been set for September the fifteenth.

CHAPTER IX

They had a long visit together the day before the trial. Dan looked more haggard, Liza thought, and still watched her with a strange intentness, but was cheerful.

"Isn't it the damnedest, most incredible thing that this is happening?" he asked. "You'd think by this time I'd be used to the idea but I'm not at all."

"Neither am I. Could we possibly both be dreaming it?"

"Afraid not. Well, anyway, I'll get to see what goes on in a courtroom. I've never been in one, have you?"

"Never."

"Harrison's a good lawyer. He's working like a dog. He's tracked down every man that's ever taken Paula out or who seemed to have a yen for her. He's gone through her diary. Of course the police did that right away. He's investigated the other families in the apartment. I suggested she might have been having an affair with one of the men there and a jealous wife did the deed. But he's uncovered nothing so far. Paula certainly didn't lead a nun's life, I'm sure, but she covered all her tracks. What was that remark she made once to Matt? I needn't tell you it's not vanity that makes me ask."

Liza swallowed painfully. "She said there was just one man in whom she was really interested and she meant to get him . . ." the last words she couldn't say.

"You see, that doesn't help much. Oh, well, let's forget her now. Everything's *got* to come out right some way. Your hair looks pretty today, Liza."

She felt herself coloring. "Why, Dan, what a nice thing for you to say."

"Do you still want to have it cut?"

"No, I never even think of it now."

"That day you asked me . . . I mean making that a *condition*, you could have knocked me over with a feather."

"The real trouble was," Liza said with a laugh, "you were surprised I made any conditions at all."

"That's right. Pretty cocky, wasn't I? Well, the time's long up about the hair. Why don't you have it cut now? A good time. Give you something new to take up your mind."

"And have you look back at me and think, 'Who's that strange woman with Tom Harvey?' You know he's going to be with me part of every day and Matt will be there a lot too."

"I wish you wouldn't go at all. Why don't you promise me you'll stay home and let Tom report to you. I really ask this."

"No good, sir, marriage vows to the contrary. I'm going to be right there. And now it looks as though it's time for me to be leaving."

They looked long into each others' eyes then he waved and managed a feeble grin.

"See you in court, then."

She smiled back. "See you in court."

But when she reached the door that led to the outer steps she had to lean for support against the wall. She could not see for the tears and, besides, her whole body was trembling. A young officer came up to her.

"Can I help you, miss?"

"If you would. My car is just a little way along the street, but I feel a bit shaky."

"I'll go with you. You're Mrs. Morgan, aren't you?"

"Yes."

"Well, just take it easy," he kept saying as they walked to the car. "Take it easy. You're all right to drive?"

"I'm fine now. Thank you so much."

His eyes looked sympathetic. She heard one more "Take it easy" as she started. It was all he could find to say, she supposed.

Tom called for her next morning and cheered her with a gallant whistle when she stepped out. She had really taken pains with her outfit. It must be in a sense sober, but she wanted intensely to look well for Dan's sake. So she had finally settled on a navy linen of exquisite cut with a matching hat faced with white which flared above her braids. Tom chatted agreeably about nothing in particular as they drove along, with unusual restraint, she thought. She realized later that he had planned it, that they would not be in the court-room too early.

She had a chance to look around for a few minutes, how-ever, after they entered from the gray, grim-looking hall. It was a large room with long rows of benchlike oak seats. The front ones, Tom explained, were for the Press and were al-ready filled, as indeed, were most of the others. What, Liza wondered, could have brought all these people who could surely have no interest in Dan's trial? But she answered her own question. The papers had announced it, and the great vulture, *Curiosity,* had spread its morbid wings and led them here.

In front of the press ran a little railing and in front of that again were several tables and chairs just below the Bench where of course the judge would preside. Would he be wise? Oh, would he be kind? Would he be humanly sympathetic to Dan as one man might be to another in danger? Would he read the innocence in Dan's eyes? Could a judge ever have *feelings* like other mortals, or was his heart as dry, as cold, as immutably fixed as his own books of law?

At the left of the Bench and somewhat below was a small square platform with a sturdy, uncompromising-looking chair upon it. This would be the witness stand and beyond it, but near, were the rows of empty jury seats. All this she could deduce without Tom's help. But she felt him nudge her arm now.

"Here we go!" he said, and just after, a loud and remark-ably clear voice rang through the courtroom.

"His Honor! His Honor the court! Rise, please." There was the rustle of everyone rising at once.

"Who's that who called out?" Liza whispered.

"The court crier. Listen. He always uses the old form."

"Hear ye! Hear ye! Hear ye! All those having business with this honorable court draw near, give your attention and you shall be heard."

The Judge in his black robes entered, tall, graying, his manner judicial, his face inscrutable, and stood in his place behind the Bench, as the crier went on with Liza catching only part of it. "The State of New York, the county . . . the Honorable Judge Carter presiding. Be seated, please."

"But where's Dan?" Liza whispered again, indicating where her thoughts had been.

"He'll come through that door to the left of the Judge. There he is now."

The door opened and Dan walked in, head erect, face set. He crossed to the table beside which stood Harrison, and they both sat down. Dan searched the room with his eyes and when he saw Liza and Tom he half smiled and inclined his head, then looked quickly away.

The Judge rapped with his gavel.

"Now," whispered Tom, "they pick the jury and I should have warned you this can take a long time. But I guess you'll want to sit it out, won't you? Even if it's the rest of the week?"

"I'm going to sit everything out," she answered, trying to smile.

And it took the rest of the week. Liza grew accustomed, day after day, to the alternate questioning of Brown and Harrison, the repetition, the monotony, as the possible jurors were either dismissed—as in most cases—or accepted and sent to the jury box.

"Do you believe in capital punishment?"

"Has any member of your family ever been the victim of a crime?"

"Do you think you could fairly judge testimony in a murder trial?"

Once when a Mrs. Wilson was called Harrison was at once on his feet.

"I challenge for cause, your Honor!"

"State the cause."

"The victim of this crime was a woman. The person accused of it is a man."

"You feel this might prejudice a woman's judgment?"

"I do, your Honor."

"I'm afraid I can't agree with you on this, Counselor."

"Then, your Honor, I will take a peremptory."

"Granted," said the Judge.

It was one o'clock on Friday that the tale of the jury was at last completed. Twelve men: a garage owner, a stock broker, a druggist, a teacher, an engineer, a chef . . . There they sat, with fixed or stolid expressions. "The judgment of his peers!" The words rang in Liza's brain. That was what Dan was awaiting. *The judgment of his peers.* But were they? And even so, what measure of mercy, of capability, of understanding lay behind those inscrutable faces?

The Judge's deep voice suddenly sounded in the silence.

"Gentlemen of the jury, you will now be given the usual charge that you are not to discuss this case among yourselves during the trial nor permit anyone outside your own body to discuss it with you. You will keep your minds open until the defendant has had his side of the case heard. Also you are to decide finally only *upon the law,* which is the last thing you will hear from this court. Until then you will suspend judgment. Court is now adjourned until two o'clock."

When they were back once more after lunch, a great and respectful silence fell, as the District Attorney rose and with a measured step approached the Bench and bowed to the box.

"May it please your Honor," he began in a firm, resonant voice. There was in his manner and tone an assurance that communicated itself to the whole courtroom. He was a handsome man, too, as opposed to Harrison's rangy form and irregular features.

"Oh, Tom, I hate him," Liza whispered. "He terrifies me."

"Shhh," he whispered back. "That's part of his act."

"On the night of March twenty-fifth about six months ago, there was committed in this city a crime so brutal, so shocking, so *unbelievable* that everyone who read of it must have shuddered. It was the murder of a very beautiful young woman whose portrait even now hangs in one of our important art galleries; a young woman prominent in the social life of this city, who in her own bedroom, *in her own bed* apparently, was strangled to death. The state will prove to you that the defendant, Daniel Morgan, went to see her that evening at eleven o'clock where she awaited him, vibrant with health and beauty, and that he left her, at about eleven-thirty or a few minutes thereafter—dead, *murdered.* We will prove that Mrs. Ruston was in her apartment at that hour, that the defendant, by his own admission, was with her at that time, and according to our investigation, was the *only* other person there. Other evidence will be brought out by the various witnesses."

"I call first the Medical Examiner."

His testimony was brief and definite, as was that of the Police Sergeant. Harrison questioned neither.

"I call to the stand next, Miss Marie Duval."

It crossed Liza's mind now that of course Paula would have a *French* maid.

"Do you recognize her?" Tom whispered.

"Yes. We were at Paula's for dinner one night."

"You are Marie Duval?" the District Attorney was asking.

"I am." The voice was small but clear and her whole appearance pleasing: dark suit with white blouse and gloves, and small black hat. Smart but restrained. She sat decorously with knees well together, a very small, very decorative figure on the solid wooden chair.

"Where were you born, Miss Duval?"

"In France. Paris." There was a quite noticeable and alluring accent. The men in the jury box seemed to lean forward.

"How long have you been in this country?"

"Five years, this spring."

"Will you state carefully now your relationship with the decedent, Mrs. Paula Ruston?"

Miss Duval swallowed noticeably.

"Three years ago I came to her as maid. Since she was alone she employed besides me only a cook, who came in for the day and did the cleaning also. I acted as personal maid and waited on table and also prepared the meals on the cook's days off. The duties were not heavy and the pay was good."

"Quite so. Now, will you please try to give us an accurate picture of the apartment, beginning with the front door?"

"It was on the tenth floor and there was just the one entrance, at the end of the outside corridor. When you went in the door there was a long hall which connected with the back of the apartment. The first door from the hall opened on the right into the drawing room and you could go through it to the library, then to the dining room, though there was an entrance to it also from the hall. Behind the dining room was Mrs. Ruston's bedroom, which she also used as a sort of sitting room. Her desk was there and easy chairs and the radio.

The kitchen and my room were at the other side of the hall toward the back."

"I see. One point I wish you to make clear again. There was only one outside entrance to the apartment?"

"That is correct, sir."

"Now, Miss Duval, will you tell us again in your own words just what happened on the night of March twenty-fifth?"

Miss Duval seemed at this point very nervous, and in the courtroom you could have heard a pin drop. Even the gentlemen of the press sat in an attitude of silent and eager attention. It had been evident to Liza in her hasty glance at the members of the Fourth Estate that they were all eyeing Miss Duval with approval.

She began again slowly. "Mrs. Ruston had been out to dinner but told me she would return by ten-thirty as she expected a guest at eleven. When she came in she said she wished to change to something more comfortable, and I assisted her to do so." At this point a slow color crept into Miss Duval's cheeks.

"Could you," the District Attorney pursued gently, "tell us just what she was wearing then?"

"She put on a black chiffon negligee, very lovely, with knife pleating and lace . . ."

"It will not be necessary to describe it further. Could you tell us please what she was wearing *underneath* the negligee?"

Miss Duval's color rose still higher. "Her night dress," she said softly but distinctly.

There was a little wave just short of a murmur through the courtroom, enough to cause Judge Carter to rap smartly with his gavel. Liza, her own cheeks crimson, looked at Dan, but his face was hidden by that of Harrison, who was leaning toward him.

"Will you proceed, Miss Duval. Did the decedent ask you to do anything else?"

"Yes. She asked me to turn off the main light and to spray a little of her favorite perfume about the room. I told her I wished to go down the hall to see one of the maids there and she said as soon as I answered the door I could leave."

"Anything else?" pursued the D.A.

Miss Duval had the grace to look embarrassed. Oddly enough it seemed becoming to her.

"Yes," she said softly.

"Will you tell us what it was?"

"She said she would not need me again until later. *Much* later," she said.

Another hum in the courtroom, and another blow from the Judge's gavel.

"Mr. Brown," he said, "court is adjourned until ten tomorrow morning. You may continue with this witness at that time."

The newsmen hurried out first and then the others followed. Liza and Tom made their way out to the hot, gray street, Liza forcing back the tears that insisted on rising. Tom hailed a cab.

"We'll go to this restaurant where we had lunch. Matt's going to join us for a little refreshment. I may have to go to the office first in the morning, but I'll be with you as soon as I can. I've warned Matt that we are not going to talk about the trial now. You are going to forget it for an hour and get a bit of food and Italian wine into you. Agreed?"

"Thanks, Tom. But you mustn't have me so on your mind and Matt mustn't either. John is driving me in every day and staying so he'll be with me. For support," she added with a wry smile.

"Nonsense. My work won't suffer. I've got a good partner. Besides, don't you suppose I'm interested in the case? I don't think Harrison and his staff will miss a trick, but I'll be watching too, like a hawk. That will make another of us. Here we are. It's sort of a dive but it's close at hand. And there's Matt!"

"Tom," Liza said suddenly, "why was the D.A. so anxious for Marie Duval to tell just . . . just what Paula had on that night?"

"I'm wondering myself, but he must have something in his craw. Don't let that part throw you, Liza."

As they sat together Liza was amused in spite of herself at the skillful way in which Tom firmly held Matt to safe topics of conversation while it was obvious she was fairly bristling with questions. Also, Liza realized that she was very hungry and the hot tidbits and good wine were sending through her a comfortable glow. She must force herself to eat a proper breakfast tomorrow, she decided.

The next morning when Miss Duval was once more on the stand the District Attorney's voice was even more assured than before. He smiled at his witness and encompassed the jurors with the final trace of it.

"You will remember, Miss Duval," the Judge said, "that you are still under oath."

"I do, sir."

"Very well. Proceed, Mr. Brown."

"Before adjournment, Miss Duval, you had testified as to the preparations the decedent had asked you to make before she received her guest. Would you say she was feeling happy at this time?"

"Objection," came from Mr. Harrison, rising quickly to his feet. "The question calls for a conclusion on the part of the witness."

"Sustained," said the Judge.

"I will rephrase it," the D.A. went on imperturbably. "Did the decedent *appear* to you to be happy at this time?"

"Oh, yes," Miss Duval answered. "She seemed very happy. Indeed, when I left the room to answer the bell, she was singing."

"*Singing,*" the D.A. echoed as though he had received more than he had bargained for.

"Well, maybe—how do you say—*humming?* It was that song about my love, my love!"

A small ripple went through the room but ceased as the Judge's stern eye swept it.

"You answered the bell, then, Miss Duval. When you opened the door, who stood there?"

"Mr. Daniel Morgan."

"How did you recognize him?"

"He had been to the apartment once to dinner and I heard his name then."

"Do you see him in this courtroom?"

"I do. Over there," she said, "at that table."

"The witness has just indicated the defendant," the D.A. said to the jury. "Now what did you do next, Miss Duval?"

"I showed Mr. Morgan into Mrs. Ruston's room, then I left and went down the corridor to see my friend."

"At what time was this?"

"Just eleven, by Mrs. Ruston's clock."

"How long did you visit your friend?"

"Just till eleven-thirty, for her mistress wanted to retire then."

"Now, Miss Duval, will you answer carefully. Much depends upon this coming testimony. As you emerged from the door at the opposite end of the corridor where you had been, whom, if anyone, did you see?"

"I saw Mr. Morgan coming out of Mrs. Ruston's apartment."

"You could see him clearly?"

"But of course. I was as close to him as to that door there," pointing to the door into the courtroom.

"Could you describe his movements and appearance?"

"He was hurrying very fast. His face was red and he looked as though he hardly saw where he was going. He pressed the bell for the elevator over and over. John, that's the operator, was there in a minute. He must have been just on the floor below. He opened the cage and I heard Mr. Morgan say, 'First floor, as fast as you can.'"

"What did you do then, Miss Duval?"

"I was surprised. I went on into the apartment and locked the door behind me and then went to my own room."

"A question here. You say you locked the door. In what way?"

"Well, Mrs. Ruston was timid. She had a double lock put on the door and a bolt, for nights especially. I locked them all."

"Could anyone possibly have entered the apartment after you did this?"

"No, sir. Not possibly."

"How long did you remain in your room?"

"Until midnight. Knowing Mr. Morgan was gone I thought it strange I hadn't been called. So I went to the bedroom. The door was closed. I knocked and there was no answer, so I went in." The witness's face was now white and she was visibly shaken.

"I realize this is hard for you, Miss Duval, but your testimony at this point is vitally important. Will you describe just what you saw?"

"I . . . I saw Mrs. Ruston on the bed, not straight on it but a little across it. And," here Miss Duval swallowed several times, "I saw that her eyes were open. I went closer and I was sure then she was . . ."

"Dead?" inquired the District Attorney.

"Yes, sir."

"Did you notice anything beside the body on the bed?"

"Yes, sir. I saw a silver cigarette lighter."

"Did you touch it?"

"No, sir."

The prosecutor turned to the table behind him and picked up a small object.

"Was this the lighter?"

"Objection!" snapped Harrison.

"Sustained," said the Judge.

"I will reframe the question. Does this *look* like the lighter you saw on the bed?"

"Yes, sir. Exactly."

Brown cast a malevolent look at Harrison as he handed Miss Duval the lighter.

"Will you be kind enough to read for the court and the jury what is engraved upon this."

"It says, *Daniel M. Morgan. Christmas 1933.*"

"The prosecution wishes to offer this lighter as evidence and have it so marked."

"Any objection, Mr. Harrison?"

"None," he answered.

"What did you do next after your sight of what was on the bed?" the District Attorney proceeded.

"I called Dr. Lewis, who lives in the apartment, and he came at once, and then he called the police."

"Thank you, Miss Duval. Your witness, Counselor."

It was when court readjourned at two that Harrison rose deliberately and inclined his head courteously.

"Your Honor, it is the purpose of the defense to prove that Daniel Morgan had nothing whatever to do with this murder, but has been caught in a web of purely circumstantial evidence. Now, Miss Duval," his voice sharpened. Somehow by the very tone he produced the impression that the witness was not to be trusted. "You say you have been in this country for five years?"

"Yes, sir."

"And you were employed by Mrs. Ruston for three?"

"That is so."

"May I ask if you had another position before that time?"

"Yes."

"Will you tell us, please, what it was?"

Miss Duval looked embarrassed.

"As lady's maid."

"In what home?"

"I . . . I would rather not say."

Harrison looked to the Judge, who leaned forward on his desk.

"You must answer the question, Miss Duval."

"It was in the home of Mrs. George Whitmore."

"I see," went on Harrison. "Your mistress was kind?"

"Oh, very."

"Your salary good?"

"Very."

"Your room pleasant?"

A faint nostalgic smile flitted across the features of Miss Duval.

"It was lovely."

"And yet you left this most desirable position. *Why?*" The word rang out like a shot.

"Good old Harrison! He's dug up something," Tom said under his breath.

The witness looked to right and left and then fastened her eyes piteously on the Judge.

"Must I answer that, your Honor?"

"Yes, Miss Duval."

"Mrs. Whitmore accused me of lying."

Another faint ripple in the courtroom.

"And what was the nature of these accusations?" Now Harrison looked assured and the D.A. anxious.

"Well, it was like this. Mr. Whitmore was beginning to make—how do you say—advances to me, and I thought perhaps if I told Mrs. Whitmore—in a nice way—she could speak to him perhaps . . . But she said I was lying and dis-

missed me. And," added Miss Duval with her chin up and
her eyes flashing, "I do not lie. What I told her was the
truth."

Tom drew in his breath sharply. "Was that bad?" Liza
asked.

"She's spiked his guns," Tom whispered back. "He was
trying to discredit her reliability."

There was, indeed, in the courtroom a subtle, indefinable
response on the part of the spectators, favorable to Marie
Duval. It was as though in the silence a corporate voice
spoke saying, "That girl can be trusted."

Although Mr. Harrison had evidently lost a point upon
which he had greatly counted, he went on calmly with his
cross examination, checking over each answer, upon none of
which the witness could be shaken.

"You say you were with Mrs. Ruston in the capacity you
have described, for three years?"

"Yes, sir."

"Were you fond of her?"

"Fond?" The witness seemed to consider.

"Well, no, not fond perhaps."

"Did she ever use sharp words to you?"

"S . . . sometimes."

"Did she ever accuse you of a crime?"

"Well, once she could not find a piece of jewelry and she
blamed me and then she found it just where she herself had
put it and she apologized."

"But you were angry at the time?"

"But naturally."

"You had lately been looking for a new position?"

"Yes."

"Why? When the work was light and the wages good?"

"Because," Miss Duval answered slowly, "Mrs. Ruston was
at times a little . . . difficult."

"You mean that occasionally she made you angry?"

"Yes, sir," the witness answered with perfect candor.

"Now, Miss Duval, you have said that after Mr. Morgan
left the apartment you went in and locked the door behind
you."

"I did."

"You have said that no one after that could have entered."

"That is so."

"But between the time Mr. Morgan left until the doctor arrived there was someone besides Mrs. Ruston in the apartment."

"What do you mean?"

"I mean that you, yourself, where there, were you not?"

"Why . . . why of course."

"Then I submit that it would have been perfectly possible, I say *possible* for you to have murdered your mistress."

"Me?" The exclamation was one of pure shock as the girl's face turned white.

"That was dirty," Tom whispered, "but I suppose he had to do it."

"That is all," Harrison said.

The prosecutor was on his feet in an instant. "Your Honor, may I have permission to reexamine?"

"Granted."

"We have heard the Medical Examiner testify that death in this case was due to strangulation. Miss Duval, will you please remove your gloves?"

The girl did so, still looking frightened.

"Now, will you raise both hands where the court and the jury can see them?"

Miss Duval raised two tiny, birdlike members.

"That will be all, Miss Duval. Thank you."

"You may step down," said the Judge kindly, and then added; "Since it is now after three, court will stand adjourned until tomorrow at ten."

He rapped with his gavel, made his decorous exit and the crowd began to pass out. Liza waited tensely for Dan to look again toward her, but he did not. He was talking to Harrison. When she, with Matt and Tom, reached the outer steps that afternoon, Tom halted.

"Look up there, Liza," he said, pointing to the left, where letters were cut deeply in the rising curve of stone above them: *Why should there not be a patient confidence in the ultimate justice of the people.*

He read the words slowly aloud and Liza stood still, repeating them to herself. "I'll remember those when I'm trying to get to sleep tonight," she said. "But, Tom, how do you think it went today?"

"Well," Tom answered honestly, "I think when Harrison dug up the fact that the Duval had been accused on her last job of lying, he felt pretty smug about discrediting her testimony. But the thing backfired. However, he *did* succeed in suggesting to the jury that she, herself, might have done the deed."

"Do you suppose they will believe that?"

"I hardly think so, but the important thing is, he has put the idea in their heads. He has planted one *reasonable doubt*. So, I should say the day hasn't gone too badly. Keep your chin up, Liza."

John was waiting in the car. Matt kissed her and, to her surprise, so did Tom. The caresses, light as they were, fell like balm upon her lonely and repressed heart. And that night before she slept she stood out on her little balcony breathing in the late-summer fragrance from the garden and thought of Paris, of her honeymoon, such as it had been, and felt again as she had then, the passionate fervor of Héloïse and Abelard. Strange that she, born and bred to New England self-restraint, should crave these raptures. Oh, the sweet vocables of love! If, when she visited Dan he would even say one tender word to her, she would have something upon which her heart could feed. But he did not. Although his eyes looked into hers with a new and peculiar intensity and his voice was now always gentle, his attitude was the same as it had ever been.

She looked toward her bed, almost dreading to lie down upon it, for it seemed to her then an incubus was there in wait for her. When she did put out her light at last she repeated again the words on the outer wall of the Police Court: *Why should there not be a patient confidence in the ultimate justice of the people.* She would hang on to that.

The next morning, by the very virtue of repetition of scene and technique, Liza suffered a little less than the day before. John, the elevator operator, the first witness called, was nervously anxious to do what was expected of him. He identified the defendant, testified that he had seen him go toward Mrs. Ruston's apartment at about eleven o'clock on the evening in question and that he had seemed "red-faced and upset," and asked to get down fast to the lobby a little later. Harrison's cross-examination was brief.

"Have you ever seen other men enter the elevator, 'red-faced and upset'?" he asked.

"Oh, yes, sir," John smiled.

"Have you ever been asked by other men to get them down to the lobby as fast as possible?"

"Yes, sir, many a time."

"No further questions."

It was Michael Moore, the doorman, who afforded the semi-comedy of the morning. He was tall, broad, ruddy, and apparently highly pleased over his performance as a witness. He identified Dan, then waited complacently for more questions.

"Now, Mr. Moore," said the District Attorney, "when the defendant entered the lobby on the night of March twenty-fifth, can you tell us what, if any, conversation took place between you?"

"Yes, sir, I can say that. I says to him, 'It's dirty weather, this, sir,' an' he says, 'Yes, the fog's risin',' an' I said, 'As we say in old England, 'A good night for a murder, sir.' But mind I'd never have said it if I'd known he was goin' to . . .'"

Harrison was on his feet with a roar, while a wave of mixed sound passed over the courtroom. The Judge pounded his gavel. "Silence!" he called. "Silence! That last answer will be stricken in its entirety from the record."

Moore looked around like a hurt child. "I just done what you asked me," he said to the District Attorney.

"Yes, yes," the latter said, "but you'll please stick to facts." It could not be said, however, that he appeared too disturbed by his witness's remark.

"Now, Mr. Moore," he went on, "when the defendant came down again into the lobby, could you very briefly describe his actions then."

"Well, he got out of the elevator an' he went toward the door like a bat out of hell, as the sayin' goes."

"What did you, if anything, say to him?"

"I says, 'Will I get you a cab, sir?' an' he never looked at me. He just said, 'No, I'll get one myself,' an' he was out the door like a shot."

"Did you look after him?"

"Yes, sir, I did that, for he acted so queer, like. I went

under the markey an' watched him to the next corner an'
that's the last I seen of him an' that's God's truth."

"Your witness, Counselor."

"No questions," Harrison snapped.

Tom joined Liza and Matt at lunch and heard the news of
the morning. He gave a short laugh over Moore's testimony.
"I doubt if that would do much harm."

"But neither would it do Dan any good," Liza said. "It's
like what you said about putting a suggestion in the minds of
the jury as Harrison did about Marie Duval."

"There's one difference," Tom said gently. "The idea of
Dan's implication is already in the minds of the jury. But
now here is something Harrison is counting heavily upon. I
talked to him last night. There is in this case no witness to
the murder of course, there is no murder weapon, but most
important of all *there is no apparent motive.* Harrison doesn't
think they can get around that."

Liza drew a long breath. "I've never thought of that. There
almost *has* to be one, hasn't there?"

But that very afternoon, a possible motive was uncovered.

The first witness after lunch was Mrs. Healy, the cook,
whose testimony was highly loquacious, impossible to stem
and negligible in content.

"You were employed by the decedent?" the District Attorney asked.

"If you mean Mrs. Ruston why don't you say so? It's awful
callin' the poor woman that name like killin' her all over
every time you say it . . ."

"Mrs. Healy, please answer my questions with *yes* or *no,*
without elaboration."

"I ain't elaboratin'. I'm tellin' the straight truth, so help
me, God."

"Yes. Do you recognize the defendant, Mr. Morgan?"

"Sure, I do. He an' his wife was at a dinner party we give
early last spring. There's a little glass in the door I can look
through to tell when to have the courses ready. An' old Mrs.
Moreland was there that night too, as happy as you please
an' you ought to see her now. She has neither chick nor child
'n' that's why she moved into the next apartment. She was like
a mother to Mrs. Ruston, she was, an' ever since the you-
know-what she's been prostrate an' no wonder from the

shock, poor soul. I took her in some broth the other day for I've no brew of that cook of hers an' it's my opinion," she faced the judge and then the jury solemnly, *"that she's not going to last long!"*

"Your witness," the District Attorney said with evident relief.

"Mrs. Healy," Harrison began, "did your employer often have dinner parties?"

"Yes, sir, she did, an' if I do say it . . ."

"Quite so. Did she ever to your knowledge entertain one gentleman alone at dinner?"

"No, sir, if it was just one gentleman she went out to dinner with him, an' as to how she entertained him when they got back I wouldn't know an' I wouldn't say if I did," she added belligerently, as the courtroom howled with laughter.

The Judge pounded his desk. "One more outbreak like that and I'll have the courtroom cleared. Are you finished with the witness, Counselor?"

"I certainly am."

"Then you may step down, Mrs. Healy."

The next witness was quite another matter. He was faultlessly dressed, dignified in manner, with a keen, good-featured, middle-aged face.

"Your name?" asked the District Attorney.

"John Clement Bentley." He spoke very slowly.

"Your profession?"

"I am a lawyer."

"Were you acquainted with the decedent?"

"I was."

"In what respect? Social or professional?"

"I was her attorney."

"When was the last occasion in which you acted for her in that capacity?"

"Last January the twenty-eighth, when I drew up her will."

You could feel the sharp intake of many breaths and the tenseness of the gentlemen of the press, who always caught the scent miles ahead of the pack.

"You have seen this will since the decedent's death?"

"I have. It was left in my possession."

"Without, of course, making any inquiry about the estate as a whole, I would like to ask one question. Was there not in the assets of the decedent a considerable block of the Morgan Coal Company stock?"

"There was."

"What disposition was made of this stock in the will?"

"Upon the death of Mrs. Ruston it was to go to Mr. Daniel Morgan."

There was no noise in the courtroom following this statement. It would have been easier to bear, Liza thought, if there had been. Instead there was a complete and deadly silence. Only Tom's whispered, "Oh, my God!" came to her ear. She looked at Dan. He was sitting staring at the lawyer with stunned, graven face, which did not move even as Harrison leaned over to speak to him.

"Your witness, Counselor," the Prosecutor said with what under pleasant circumstances might have been an almost jaunty air.

Harrison rose slowly. "Your Honor," he said, "before I cross-examine this witness upon what is new evidence I would like an opportunity to consult with my client. May I reserve the right to call this witness later on to the stand if I feel that is essential?"

"You may, Mr. Harrison. Do you expect the testimony of your next witness to consume considerable time, Mr. Brown?"

"I do."

"Then court will adjourn now until ten-thirty tomorrow morning."

As the newsmen hurried past, Liza caught one sentence. "Well, I guess that tears it!"

Matt had insisted upon stopping for her that morning so now the three of them drove back together and at Liza's urgent request Matt and Tom stayed for dinner.

"I don't believe I could swallow tonight if I were alone," she said, and then added, "You know, Tom, I've mentally lived through so much that you needn't try to spare me anything. This today about the will is about the worst that has happened, isn't it?"

"For the build-up in the minds of the jury, yes, I would say so. Of course if they have any logic they will realize that most people never know of bequests in their favor until *after* the death of the testator. Do you think Dan knew of this?"

"I've no idea," Liza said. "But if he did, I'm sure he would have paid no attention whatever to it."

"Yes, that is exactly what I think myself. But under cross-examination . . ."

"He'll tell the absolute truth."

"Right again."

"There's one thing that keeps worrying me all the time," Liza went on. "It's Dunmore. As I've told you he was evidently in love with Paula and now he's beside himself with shock and rage. I know he thinks Dan is guilty, and I'm perfectly sure he's working hand and glove with the D.A. It's just possible that if Dan himself knew anything about that will, Dunmore knew it too. The idea would have meant so little to Dan he could even have made a joke of it to him. I don't know what more harm he can do, but *I don't trust Dunmore.* I'm sure Dan doesn't now himself after the way he's acted all through these last months."

"It's so strange," Matt said reflectively, "so unlike a regular murder mystery for us. We know now that Dan is innocent, so theoretically there should be no *suspense* for us at all."

"Ah," Liza said slowly, her face white, "the suspense lies in the fact that the *jury* doesn't know he is innocent and they are the ones who hold his life in their hands."

CHAPTER X

The next morning as Tom met her, his face, to Liza, showed more concern than he had permitted before.

"What is it, Tom?" she asked quickly.

"I had a long talk with Harrison last night. He has found out in some devious way that Brown is bringing a surprise witness to the stand, and he's, of course, uneasy about new evidence. But he told me he is going to put Dan on his own defense at the last and that ought to turn the tide. Now, keep a stiff upper lip, Liza. By the way, do you know anything in connection with Dan's life that you have not told Harrison?"

"Nothing!"

"Harrison feels Dan may be a bit secretive about himself and that's no help to a lawyer. If there's anything you can do . . . Well, we'd better get to our seats."

After the preliminaries to which Liza had grown accustomed, the District Attorney rose and bowed to the Judge and the jury. While his face always wore a certain smugness, this was now intensified by an expression of assurance.

"Your Honor, the prosecution has proved to you that on the night the decedent was murdered the defendant was in her bedroom with her at or near the time of the crime, and that no one else could possibly have been there. The testimony of the decedent's lawyer points to a possible motive. We will now prove to you that the defendant is a man of violent passion capable of anger sufficient to cause him to inflict bodily injury upon another."

"Objection," Harrison barked. "I object to the District Attorney's *testifying!*"

"Overruled. Proceed with your witness, Mr. Brown."

"I call to the stand Mrs. Donna Galucci."

Liza looked at Dan and saw his face turn ashen. He turned

at once to Harrison, who began to scribble furiously on the paper before him, looking both disturbed and annoyed as he apparently plied Dan with quick questions. She turned her gaze then to the woman who was walking on teetering heels, too high to support her over-ripe body, up to the witness chair. She took the oath with a sort of swagger, then sat down and scanned the court with her long-lashed black eyes until they finally came to rest upon Dan, when her chin went up higher, and a small sardonic smile touched her mouth. Her hair was glossy black, her cheeks pink, her full lips red, but there was in spite of these elements of beauty a certain coarseness of countenance for which her over-weight condition was not wholly responsible.

"Please state your name," the D.A. asked almost with tenderness.

"Donna Galucci."

"You are a resident of New York State at the present?"

"Yes, sir, I am."

"Do you recognize the defendant in this case, Mr. Daniel Morgan?"

"I certainly do," she snapped.

"What at any time was your relationship with the man?"

"I was his wife."

There was a sound like the buzzing of bees in the courtroom, and the Judge rapped smartly for order. Tom quietly took Liza's hand and held it tightly in his own. She was watching Dan, who was still whispering to Harrison as though in desperation. Her own heart seemed to have stopped beating.

"Ah, yes," Brown was repeating unctuously, "his wife. Now, Mrs. Galucci, will you tell us whether this marriage to Mr. Morgan was in every way a happy one?"

"It certainly was not. Not to me, anyhow."

"You say you were once his wife. How did this marriage terminate, *end,*" he added.

"It ended in divorce, but mind you . . ."

"Now, Mrs. Galucci, will you state what your feelings were after this divorce had been granted?"

"Well, I was sorry. I wanted to go back to him and get married over again and let bygones be bygones."

"Did you go back?"

"Yes, sir, I did."

"Where was he living then?"

"In the same house in the Patch where we had lived before."

"Just what do you mean by the Patch?"

"It's the houses round the mines."

"This was in what place?"

"Hardingville, Pennsylvania."

"Now, Mrs. Galucci, when you returned to this house, did you find the defendant there?"

"He was there all right."

"What did you do?"

"Why, I went in an' told him I was sorry I'd left him, but mind you he'd paid no attention to me after he started that coal mine of his an' I said I'd like to come back to him an' we could be married over. I said I was sorry for everything."

"And what did he say?"

"His face got red an' he said, 'I think I could kill you,' an' he took me by the shoulders an' threw me out the door. You can see he's strong an' I fell down the steps, they were awful steep to that house, an' hit my head an' laid there unconscious till the men come from work an' picked me up an' took me down to my mother's house."

"Did you suffer other injuries from this fall?"

"I'll say I did. I was in the family way an' I lost it an' near to died."

"Did you receive any compensation for this injury caused by the defendant?"

"From Dan? Well, not much. The doctor for the works got round me an' got me to sign a paper that I'd never ask for any more damages if I took this hundred dollars. I needed the money so I took it. But it wasn't enough. You can see that."

"When you had recovered sufficiently what did you do then?"

"I had to go to work. I got a job in a factory in Pittsburgh till I married Galucci. It was an awful hard job too."

"One more question. After you had been thrown down those steps did the defendant come in any way to your assistance?"

"Well, if he come out he didn't do nothing for me. I just laid there till the men came from work."

"Thank you, Mrs. Galucci. Your witness, Counselor."

Harrison rose slowly, his little sheaf of notes in his hand. He approached the chair and looked steadily at the witness until she finally lowered her eyes.

"Mrs. Galucci, you say you were once married to the defendant, Daniel Morgan?"

"I certainly was."

"How old were you at the time of this marriage?"

"I guess about sixteen."

"And his age then?"

"Well, he'd be eighteen, I 'spose."

"You have spoken of leaving him. How long did you live with him from your marriage until you left him?"

She looked disturbed. "Well, we was married in August an' I left in November a year."

"I see. Then you lived with him just about fifteen months. Is that correct?"

"I guess so."

"Now, Mrs. Galucci, when you left your husband, did you go alone?"

She glanced anxiously at Brown.

"Well, as I told you for weeks an' weeks he'd hardly paid any attention to me. He'd opened up this coal bank on a farm an' he'd go off in the morning to it an' come home at night and throw himself down on the bed an' go to sleep an' never . . . He *neglected* me, an' this Tony had been after me for a long time so he said how did I stand it an' if I'd go off with him he'd pay some attention to me . . ."

"Quite so. Then you ran away with another man."

The witness still kept eyeing the District Attorney as though asking for help.

"Well, I 'spose you could say that. But mind if Dan had acted like a husband I'd never . . ."

"It was Mr. Morgan then who secured the divorce?"

"Sure. *I* wasn't goin' to divorce him."

"Were you still living with this Tony when you decided to try to return to your former husband?"

"No, he had just gone. He wasn't no good, Tony wasn't."

"I see. When you reached the defendant's house and told him of your desire for re-marriage, do you remember exactly what he said at first?"

"I sure do. He yelled at me. He said, 'Get out!' He was ugly about it, I'm tellin' you."

"Did he ask you more than once to leave?"

"He sure did. He kept yellin' it, over an' over. 'Get away from my house,' he says an' then he says, 'I could kill you,' he says, an' then's when he threw me out."

"So he had asked you several times to leave and you refused to go, before he put you out forcibly. Is that correct?"

The witness seemed flustered.

"Well, yes, but here I was talkin' nice to him an' he . . ."

"Yes, Mrs. Galucci. One more point. It was brought out in direct testimony that the defendant gave you one hundred dollars after your . . . your fall."

"Yes, sir, an' I was a fool to sign that paper lettin' him off that easy. I should ought to have *sued*, an' got more. It was old Doc just got round me."

"This was over twenty years ago. Has the defendant ever given you any money since that time?"

The witness turned red to the roots of her black hair and looked appealingly at the District Attorney. It was evident this point had not been covered between them. As she remained silent the Judge spoke firmly.

"Answer the question, Mrs. Galucci."

"Well, yes, he's sent me some through his lawyer. An' why wouldn't he? Rich like he is an' I was his wife once an' look what he done to me an' all."

"You have asked him for money?"

Her head went up. "Of course I have. I had a right."

"Hardly. He was no longer your husband. In all these years has he ever refused your requests?"

"Yes," she said with bitterness. "The last time I wrote him just a few months ago."

"Was this money for any special purpose?"

"Yes, it was. Galucci's brother, he got him this job in New York State but we couldn't afford to bring up our things so I wanted to buy new furniture. An' you should have seen the letter Dan's lawyer wrote me. It was so nasty I couldn't hardly believe it. An' why would Dan refuse me this time when . . ."

"When he never had before through all the years?"

"That's right an' him a millionaire. Why would he?"

"Why, indeed," Harrison echoed sarcastically. "Thank you, Mrs. Galucci, that will be all. Your Honor, in view of the disclosures of the last witness I would like to have a chance to confer further with my client. I would therefore respectfully ask for an adjournment until tomorrow morning."

"Any objection, Mr. Brown?"

"No objection."

"I agree to your request, Counselor. Anything more on redirect, Mr. Brown?"

"There is, your Honor." The District Attorney, still with an air of assurance, went toward the witness stand.

"Our learned Counselor," he said with the faintest possible sneer, "has brought out, as the jury will note, a number of facts wholly irrelevant to this case . . ."

The Judge interrupted sharply.

"Mr. Brown, I believe all of the Counselor's questions were based upon material opened up by direct testimony."

"I beg your Honor's pardon. The thought in mind was that much of the information elicited had no bearing upon what the Prosecution is trying to prove. Therefore, Mrs. Galucci, I would like to repeat one or two questions."

"Yes, sir." It was quite evident that the witness was willing to be interrogated as long as possible.

"When you returned to your husband, willing, eager to beg for a resumption of your former relations and a re-marriage, will you state again what his attitude was?"

"Why, he was fit to be tied, he was so mad. He got red in the face an' shook his fists an' yelled at me something terrible."

"And what did he say just before he caught hold of you to throw you out?"

"He said, 'I think I could kill you!' "

"And as a result of his violent handling of you, you did, indeed, nearly die?"

"I sure did."

"Thank you, Mrs. Galucci, that will be all. Your Honor, the state rests its case."

"You may step down, Mrs. Galucci," said the Judge. "Court is adjourned until ten-thirty tomorrow morning."

Liza was not even aware that Tom's arm was around her, supporting her, as they left the courtroom. Her eyes seemed to see no one as they went down in the elevator, crossed the stone lobby and reached the waiting cars.

"I'm driving you home, Liza. I'll tell John to go on."

As they went over the familiar road Liza still could not speak, and Tom respected her silence. Just before they turned into the Barmoor drive, Tom said gently, "You knew of this early marriage, Liza?"

"Just the bare fact. Dan said he never wanted to talk about it."

"One thing now, you must remember. All this happened nearly twenty-five years ago. Hang on to that. But how do you suppose Brown ever dug it all up?"

"Dunmore," Liza answered bitterly. "He could have heard all the old story from somebody back at the mines. He hates Dan. He thinks he's guilty. He would track this woman down. Oh, Tom, what effect will this have . . ."

They were going up the drive and another car stood before them. Henry West got out and came over to them. He helped Liza to the walk and then began to speak.

"Now, I'm no lawyer like Mr. Harvey here, but I was in court this afternoon . . ."

"You were?" Liza echoed in surprise.

"Yes, I dropped in and I want to tell you just as an average man who *could* have been a juror that I don't think that woman's testimony will do Dan much harm. She's a hussy from the word go and to quote anything said twenty-five years ago is ridiculous. What do you think, Mr. Harvey?"

"Well," Tom answered with his quiet honesty, "we certainly wouldn't have chosen to have that woman on the witness stand, but when the jurors think it over I don't believe they'll swallow all she said without some questions. Besides, I think the whole story hasn't come out yet. You see, Brown would be so elated to get her at all and quite evidently satisfied with what he felt were the salient points for the prosecution that he maybe didn't dig too deep. When Dan gets on the stand he may add some more facts."

"He won't say anything about his youth," Liza's tone was despairing, "not even about his mother. *His mother,*" she repeated, looking strangely at Tom. "There may, as you say, be more to the story than we've heard."

"That's right, so bear up, Liza. You're the bravest girl I know. See you tomorrow."

He got into his car and drove off. West lingered. "Would you care to come down and have dinner with us? Helen would be pleased."

"Thanks, Henry. You've both been so wonderful to me, but tonight I believe I would rather stay at home. I am a bit shaken."

"No wonder, but don't let that dame throw you. Any man would know by one look that she's no good. It's just as well there are all men on the panel. Well, I'll be getting along. Maybe Helen will be up later if it's all right."

"Oh, yes. She always helps me somehow. And you've cheered me, Henry, really."

From the time the ugly news of the murder and Dan's arrest had first appeared in the newspapers up to and during the days of the trial Liza had been enveloped in a tender solicitude on the part of her friends and neighbors. Whether they believed in Dan's guilt or innocence they had rallied to her own support. Much of the time she had accepted this comfort without comment, almost without awareness since her need was too deep for words. Sometimes, as on this evening, she was overborne by the kindness, for more than at any other time callers kept coming. Helen West, with her gentle affection, the Carstairs who often dropped in to talk interestingly of many things that might divert her mind; the Gibbses, the Darlings, and finally when the rest had all left, David Colby and Anne Scott. They came with shining eyes to tell her a secret.

"You introduced us, Liza, so we wanted to see you first of all," Colby began. "Anne has agreed to marry me and I'm pretty happy, I can tell you!"

"And what about me?" Anne said. "I've never known what real happiness was before this. Maybe we shouldn't be boasting of it to you just now . . ."

"You certainly should. If ever I needed to hear good news, it's tonight. Sit down. We've got to celebrate a little. By the way, you couldn't possibly be hungry, could you?"

They looked at each other and laughed. "You're psychic," Colby said. "As a matter of fact we were so excited we didn't eat much, and we're going to hunt something up now when we leave."

"That makes it perfect. I couldn't manage my dinner either and now with company . . . I'll go tell Horace and Maggie. This will cheer them up too."

So it came about that they had supper together with champagne at the end, and Liza's heart was for a short time lifted from the abyss. As the guests left at last Colby said quietly, "I'll be in court tomorrow morning, Liza. Harrison's called me as a character witness and I'm certainly glad to serve. I've admired Dan for a good many years and now I'll have a chance to show it."

"And I'll tell you something, though I don't think you two need anything to make you happier tonight. Dan has you slated, David, for a big increase in position and salary, taking Dunmore's place, as soon as . . . I mean if he . . ."

"When he is back," Colby said calmly. "Why that's wonderful news. Dunmore's a dog. I think it would please me terribly to step into his shoes. I've been doing his work now for three months. I think he's intending to leave the company, anyway."

"Do you know who the other character witnesses are?" Liza asked eagerly.

"No, I don't. Harrison wanted to get Mrs. Moreland, but she's in no shape to come. I hear she's in a bad way, poor old soul."

"I know she is. No wonder. But what about other men Dan's known in business?"

"That's the trouble. There are plenty who could testify to his ability and his honesty and all that, but they don't really *know* him personally. When you come right down to it, he had hardly any close friends."

"I realize that," Liza admitted sadly. "Well, I'm glad you're going to stand up for him, David."

"And I must add one word to you before we leave. Like most young men I've fancied myself in love more than once. I know now that for the first time I feel the real thing. You understand?"

"Of course I do, and I'm so happy for you both. This has

been one of my worst evenings to live through and you've no idea how your coming has helped me. Come in often and tell me all your plans."

When they had gone Liza sat down in the library, with Horace bringing more coffee and hovering over her.

"I seen the night's paper, Ma'am, an' I'd just say this. Mr. Morgan was only eighteen when he married that first time an' you must mind that a boy that age is awful easy taken in. It's not like as if he'd been a man grown. I can't think any ill of Mr. Morgan. An' as for what he said about wantin' to kill her that don't mean a thing. I'll tell you what Maggie an' me heard just last week if you'll believe it. We was visitin' the butler an' his wife on down the road. You don't know the people. An' the boy, about seventeen an' his father was havin' an awful set-to in the dining room an' the sounds come out to us. The boy wanted one of these fast sports cars an' his father said he wouldn't buy it for him an' the boy got so mad he yelled, 'I hate you for bein' so mean,' he says. 'I could a'most kill you.' An' the father says, 'The feelin's mutual at the moment but we don't neither of us mean a word of it so you go on up to your room an' think it over.' An' then it got quiet but you see how people say awful-like things that are just words an' nothin' more."

"I hope the jury will realize that."

"There ought to be a few of them with some sense. I'm bringing you a hot toddy now, Ma'am. Champagne's a light thing when what you need is something with authority to it."

Liza rested her head against the chair and closed her eyes. Through all the trial she had never felt as sharp a hurt in her heart as on this day. The disclosures of that unspeakable woman had cut deeply into her life with Dan. That he could have kept from her such vital facts of his early years; had even, apparently, since their marriage been sending money to *his first wife,* this caused a bitterness to rise within her that she could not control. She sipped the hot drink gratefully when it came and tried first by a great effort of will to erase from her memory the events of the day; then, when that proved hopeless, to concentrate upon Dan's personality, which had been capable of this deception.

As she thought of this she suddenly remembered what he had said as he saw her to the door of the office on that first incredible morning when he had asked her to marry him. "I must add for what it is worth, that I *respect* you, Miss Hanford. I respect you deeply." At the time this had seemed cold comfort, so far removed from the words a lover would have spoken. But now, in the light of the day's testimony she realized the profound significance of them. Dan had been offering her from a bruised and disillusioned heart the one choice gift in his power to give her. Respect. It meant that through his man's life, touched as it had apparently been in his most impressionable years by ugliness, he had still retained certain ideals of womanhood and tried, in his restrained way, to tell her so. She mused upon this—upon the deep reticences of his nature which had, indeed, built a wall between them. She thought too, on the other hand, of his kindness to her, his generosity and the strength of his character which she had constantly felt. How then, in the face of all this, could he have fallen a victim to Paula's ultimatum? For try as she could to disbelieve this, the evidence still rose to haunt her. If what she feared had not happened, why would he have rushed precipitously from her apartment that awful night as though in shame, in revulsion, in hatred of himself?

But with all her thinking the soreness of her heart gave place at last to the greatest fear of all and that was the jeopardy in which Dan stood, which threatened his very life.

The next day's trial opened as usual except that now Harrison's turn had come for the defense. To Liza's surprise Mr. Hadley and a Mr. Thornton from Pittsburgh had come on to testify as character witnesses. The questioning in each case was brief. Had they known Mr. Morgan over a period of years? They had. Could they testify as to his integrity? They could. Had they ever known him to tell an untruth? Never. Had they ever seen him in anger? They had not.

The District Attorney's cross-examination was also brief. Were their own business interests in any way involved with those of Mr. Morgan? Well, yes, they were.

"No further questions," he said smugly, allowing the implication to sink into the minds of the jury. With Colby, however, he was more detailed.

"Now, Mr. Colby, you have given the defendant a wonderful recommendation, have you not?"

"I was glad to tell the truth about him."

"Ah, yes. Mr. Morgan is your employer?"

"He is."

"You have a good position?"

"Yes, you could say that."

"If your employer wished he could fire you."

"Certainly."

"It is to your advantage, then, to keep his good will?"

"I would not say to my advantage, rather to my satisfaction."

"Oh, you would not be disturbed then if you lost this good position?"

"Personally, yes, but not for business reasons."

"Will you explain what you mean by 'not for business reasons'?"

"Because as far as the job goes I could get another just as good without any trouble."

"You seem very sure of yourself, indeed."

"I am only sure of my own capabilities in the coal business."

"No further questions," Brown snapped. "You may step down."

Harrison came forward and paused, eyeing the Judge and the jury. He even allowed his eyes, as if for further suspense, to sweep the courtroom.

"I call to the stand the defendant, Daniel Morgan."

Dan rose, pale and grim, took the oath and seated himself. For one second his eyes sought for Liza and then looked stonily at Harrison.

"Your name?"

"Daniel Morgan."

"Your position?"

"President of the Morgan Coal Company of Pittsburgh, Pennsylvania, with sales offices here in New York."

"Now yesterday, Mr. Morgan, along with us you heard the testimony of Mrs. Donna Galucci."

"I did."

"Will you please tell the court what led up to your marriage with her?"

"She begged me to save her from an old man her father had been determined to marry her to."

"After your marriage where did you live?"

"With my mother. My father had just been killed in the mine a short time before."

"Was your mother kind to this girl?"

"Very."

"Was there any . . . ah . . . issue from this union?"

"There was a child."

Liza caught her breath as though it strangled her.

"What was your wife's attitude toward this child?"

"She didn't pay too much attention to it. My mother took most of its care."

"Now, Mr. Morgan, will you please tell in your own words exactly what happened just before and on the day your wife left?"

Dan swallowed hard. "Well, it was a cold, wet week. My mother had a cough and so had . . . the child. Donna said it was only a cold with both of them, it was foolish to make a fuss about it. The night before . . . that day . . . I had been up a good many times with the coughing . . ."

"You mean your wife did not get up?"

"No, sir. She slept very soundly. I was sure my mother was really sick and the . . . the baby did not seem right to me, though I didn't know much about . . . those things."

He swallowed again painfully.

"The next morning I got up early as I always did and made up the fires. Those Patch houses were just shells and hard to heat. Just little coal stoves. I woke Donna and told her I was sure my mother was sick . . ."

"And what did she say?"

"She said she would be up fast enough when she smelled coffee and it was just a cold with both of them. I begged her to keep the fires up and look after them and I'd come home early and go for the doctor if they were no better."

"When did you return?"

"I guess it was a little after two. I found the house stone cold and Donna gone. I made up the fires and then hurried down to her mother's to get her to come up and see what she could do while I went for the doctor. She told me Donna had gone off with Tony."

"You got the doctor?"

"As fast as I could, but it was too late. They both . . . died. Pneumonia."

"Your feeling, then, was that this was due in large part, at least, to your wife's carelessness?"

"That was my belief."

"How long was it until you obtained your divorce?"

"About six months."

"How long then from the time she left until she came back?"

"Nearly a year, I should say."

"You had not seen her in the meantime?"

"Never."

"When she returned that day, could you describe in your own words what happened?"

"I had stopped work a little early so I was home. When she opened the door and walked in all that had happened just rose up in my mind. I shouted to her to get out, that I never wanted to see her again. I told her three or four times to get out and she wouldn't go, then I caught her by the shoulders and pushed her out the door and shut it."

"You did not, then, throw her down the steps?"

"I did not. I pushed her out onto the little platform. She must have lost her footing and fallen down the steps. They were high," he added.

"Did you have any idea she was lying there at the foot of the steps, unconscious?"

"I did not."

"If you had known so would you have gone to her aid?"

"Yes. If I'd thought she was really hurt I'd have taken her down to where her mother and brother lived."

"But after all that happened, after she left you for another man, after she was in part at least responsible for the death of your mother and child—after all this, you have still sent her money through the years?"

"Yes."

"Why?"

"Well," Dan said, as though considering, "for one reason as time went on I *had* the money, and then I realized how young we both had been."

"You mean you forgave her?"

"No, sir, I don't mean that. But I did perhaps feel a little less bitterness than I had at first."

"Mr. Morgan, my next question deals with your acquaintance with the decedent. When did you first meet her?"

"About five years ago."

"Under what circumstances?"

"I was introduced to her by Mrs. Moreland at a dinner party given at her home."

"What was your relationship with Mrs. Moreland?"

"Her husband and I had had business dealings and I was very fond of him. Since his death Mrs. Moreland has continued her kindness to me, having me at her house, introducing me to her friends, and so on."

"At the time you met the decedent, was she married?"

"She was. To Fred Ruston, the polo player."

"Have you any idea when this marriage was terminated?"

"I heard of it through Mrs. Moreland about three years ago."

"Since then have you seen the decedent frequently?"

"I wouldn't say frequently but I have met her, of course, occasionally at various social events."

"You are married, Mr. Morgan?"

"I am."

"Have you and your wife ever entertained the decedent at your own home?"

"Twice," said Dan. "Once at a large Open House party and once at a rather large dinner."

"Were you ever at her apartment?"

"Once to dinner."

"With your wife?"

"Certainly with my wife, and also Mrs. Moreland."

"Could you say, then, that your relations with the decedent had been purely casual social ones?"

"They had definitely been casual."

"Very good. Now, Mr. Morgan, I want you to tell the court and the jury in your own words what led up to your call upon the decedent the night of the twenty-fifth of March and what happened during that call."

Dan straightened, and his face if possible grew more grim. The members of the Fourth Estate strained forward, notebooks poised, and the rest of the occupants of the courtroom seemed to have ceased breathing, tense, waiting, listening.

"For some time," Dan began quietly, "a matter of a year, perhaps, I have been trying to arrange a merger between my own company and the Hadley Coal Company of Pittsburgh. To do this it is necessary at the last to have the consent of the stockholders. They have to vote. Mr. Hadley had his affairs well in order and I thought I had mine until last March I received a letter from Mrs. Moreland. She had inherited from her husband a considerable block of stock of my company. She told me in this letter that she regarded Mrs. Ruston as a daughter and since she had no living relatives and wished to relieve her estate of as much taxes as was legal she had turned over all her Morgan stock to Mrs. Ruston."

Dan paused and Harrison came to his rescue with a question.

"This disturbed you?"

"Very much indeed. I got in touch with Mrs. Ruston and explained all the advantages of the merger, but she still was completely evasive as to how she would vote. I told her the time was growing short and said I would like to talk it all over in person. I asked her to come to my office and she refused. She said she would see me only at her own apartment and due to her social commitments it would have to be Thursday the twenty-fifth when she got home from a dinner party, at eleven o'clock. As you all know," he added, "I went at that time."

"Yes, Mr. Morgan. Did you have any definite plan in mind when you went to see her?"

"I did. She was, I felt, rather well off but she lived very extravagantly. I thought money would appeal to her. So I had decided to offer to buy that stock for twice its value, even at a sacrifice to myself. I felt in the long run it would be worth it." For one moment his eyes swept the jury. "I never for a moment thought she would refuse," he added.

"When you reached the decedent's apartment, will you tell us what happened?"

"Well, I was surprised, for the maid took me on past the living room, the library and dining room and into a sort of boudoir."

"Where was the decedent when you entered the room?"

Dan looked painfully embarrassed. "She was sort of half lying against big pillows on the bed."

"Now," said Harrison, "there has been offered in evidence your cigarette lighter engraved with your name, which was found on this bed. Can you explain its position there?"

"I can, indeed. I was hardly in the room until Mrs. Ruston took a cigarette and asked me for a light. I gave it to her and she took the lighter in her hands and admired it. She didn't give it back to me and that's how it came to be . . . in the bed."

"You presented your plan to her?"

"I did."

"How soon after entering the boudoir?"

"At once. After I'd lighted her cigarette."

"What was her reaction?"

"She refused absolutely."

"Had you any idea at this point that she had left this stock to you in her will?"

Something almost like a smile crossed Dan's grim face.

"I certainly had *not*," he said.

"Have you any idea why she would have done this?"

"Yes," Dan said thoughtfully. "I think I have. You see, Mrs. Moreland is quite a friend of mine, as her husband was. She would feel, perhaps, that if I should outlive Mrs. Ruston I was the one who should have the stock. So she might have made the bequest a condition when she gave the stock. Knowing her, I can imagine this. I would have no other explanation."

"Good!" Tom whispered. "I'll bet you Brown sort of smelled this and won't touch the will at all."

"Now, Mr. Morgan, when the decedent refused this very considerable amount of money which you have testified you stood ready to give her in double payment for this stock, you were upset?"

"Yes," he brought the answer out slowly.

"What reason did she give for declining?"

Dan flushed then, until his whole face was red, and said nothing. The Judge looked at him gravely, curiously even.

"Answer the question, Mr. Morgan. Put it again, Counselor."

"Did the decedent tell you why she declined this very generous offer?"

"Yes," Dan said.

"Please give us the reason she stated."

There was a breathless quiet in the courtroom, so Dan's low voice penetrated to the farthest corner. His extreme embarrassment was manifest.

"She said she would rather have . . . me . . . than the money." Soft buzz and movement in the courtroom.

"I see," said Harrison. "And when her wishes had been made quite clear to you, what did you do?"

"I got out."

"In haste?"

"Yes."

"Then we may say that your distraught appearance in the corridors as you were leaving, described by several witnesses, was due to the emotional effects of the decedent's demands upon you?"

"Yes, sir."

"One more question. Where was the decedent when you left her room?"

For one very bad moment during which Liza could feel Tom breathing deeply, Dan hesitated. Then he said slowly, "She was following me. I think she was right behind me at the door."

"Not on the bed?"

"No, no."

"Then, Mr. Morgan, when you left that room you were fleeing like Joseph of old from the designs of a woman, were you not?"

"Dan's eyes looked off over the courtroom as though he saw no one in it.

"That, I think, would be true."

"Cross-examine," said Harrison.

Mr. Brown came forward with his usual small enigmatic smile.

"Now, Mr. Morgan, when certain unfortunate things happened during your first marriage you were working at a country coal bank, is that right?"

"It is."

"Whose bank was it?"

"My own."

"Could you give us an idea of the pattern of your days? Your routine of work?"

"Yes," Dan said slowly. "I'd just gone into debt to buy this bank. I couldn't right then afford any help, so I shored it up and did the digging for the farmers myself. It was heavy work. I left the house in the mornings usually before six and worked until dark."

"And when you got home?"

"I ate some supper my mother always had ready and then I guess I fell asleep. I was pretty well exhausted."

"Your wife then was how old?"

"Seventeen."

"Pretty?"

Dan flushed. "Yes. I think you would say so."

"Lively?"

"Yes."

"Then this life you have pictured was not very pleasant for her, was it?"

"She had a child and I had explained to her that I was working this way to get a start in the coal business."

"But for the most part during this period, you neglected her?"

"I beg your pardon?"

"I think you are familiar with that expression. Let me put it this way. When you returned each night in this exhausted condition you probably did not talk to her, caress her or play the part of a husband in general, did you?"

"No, I suppose not."

"You suppose?"

"This was all twenty-five years ago, sir. My memory is not too clear."

"Let us now," Brown hastened on, "proceed to the day she returned, begging your forgiveness. You were surprised to see her?"

"Completely."

"You were angry?"

"Very."

"Now you say that you heard nothing as the men from the mine found your former wife unconscious and carried her down to her mother's. How could this be?"

"Very easily," said Dan. "The front door was shut and I was back in the kitchen. There was always talking as the men came home from work so I had no way of knowing there was anything unusual about it then."

"An important question, Mr. Morgan. You have yourself testified that you were angry when your former wife returned. Would you say you were *very* angry?"

"Yes, I would say that."

"She has testified that before you laid violent hands upon her to thrust her from the door you said, 'I think I could kill you.' Do you admit saying this?"

Dan drew his brows and considered. "As I have reminded you, this all happened long ago but as to these words,"—he hesitated—"while I can't remember exactly, I would think it highly probable that I said something like that."

Tom said, "Good Lord," under his breath, and Liza moved closer to him.

The Judge looked keenly at the witness.

"Did you know your former wife lay at the point of death because of this accident?"

"I didn't know until she was better. The doctor told me then."

"Was it his suggestion you pay her the one hundred dollars and have her sign a release?"

"It was."

"Did it not occur to you then that this was a small amount, considering what had happened?"

Dan smiled. "No, it didn't. I was just twenty years old at that time and this seemed a good deal of money."

"But you have sent more over the years to atone, shall we say, for this arrangement?"

"Not in the slightest to atone, as you say. I have already given my reasons for sending the money."

"Mrs. Galucci has testified that you refused her last request for financial help. Can you tell why?"

"Certainly. I suddenly felt I had done it long enough and that was the last straw."

"Now, turning from this, Mr. Morgan, I wish to reexamine the scene in the decedent's boudoir on the night of March twenty-fifth in a little more realistic manner than it has been portrayed to us. When you entered that room, Mr. Morgan, did you notice the light was very soft, almost dim?"

"Yes, I did."

"Were you conscious that the air was perfumed?"

"I don't believe I thought much about that."

"We have heard testimoney that it was. Perfume often steals upon the senses unnoticed and affects them sensuously. You saw the decedent reclining upon the bed?"

"I did."

"You heard the maid testify that she was wearing at that time only a night dress and a chiffon negligee. Is that your recollection?"

"I believe so."

"You have doubtless also heard that the decedent was considered one of the most beautiful young women in the city?"

"I have heard so."

"As you lighted her cigarette you had to lean over her?"

"Slightly, because of her own position."

"Just so. Was she smiling up at you?"

"I believe so."

"Did her attitude seem to you to be one of eager expectancy, shall we say?"

Dan hesitated. "Well, I hadn't thought of it like that, but I suppose it was."

"Did she make her desire perfectly plain to you at this time?"

"Perfectly."

"Did you leave at once after she had stated her wishes?"

"Not just at once," said Dan, his face coloring.

"Mr. Morgan, do you expect us to believe that in the face of this overwhelming beauty and seductiveness and desire, you, a mere mortal and a man, were unaffected by it?"

"I can't help what you believe," Dan said curtly.

"Yes, unfortunately for you, that is true."

"Objection!" said Harrison.

"Sustained," said the Judge. "Mr. Brown, I have allowed you some latitude in the matter of comments pertinent to the testimoney, but personal remarks we will not have. Strike that last from the record, and please be careful in future."

"I apologize, your Honor. I was just carried away by my own thinking."

"The dog," Tom murmured. "He got it across all right."

"Now, Mr. Morgan, I would ask you to consider my next

question very carefully as it is important to you as well as to the prosecution in the matter of timing. How long after the decedent's wishes had been fulfilled did you . . ."

"Objection!" Harrison yelled.

"Sustained," said the Judge sharply. "Mr. Brown, you based that question upon a wholly unwarranted assumption. It will be stricken from the record, and of course the witness . . ."

Here Dan's voice broke in. "Your Honor!" And a great silence fell upon the courtroom. "I would like the privilege of answering that question, or at least the implication in it as I understand it. May I do so?"

The Judge looked at him in surprise but nodded his head. "This is somewhat irregular but since the question was partly phrased you may respond if you wish."

"I would like to state unequivocally that I did not make love to Paula Ruston on that night or at any other time in my life."

The dropping of the proverbial pin would have made quite a clatter. One young woman sat with the tears flowing unheeded down her cheeks while her body, all at once relaxed, drooped against the seat as though life had gone out of her. There was, however a smile of singular sweetness upon her lips. The young woman was Liza, and Tom, beside her, had the sensitiveness not to touch her or to speak.

The Dictrict Attorney now drew a little nearer to the witness stand with a confidential air. His face showed no discomfiture. It even looked as though Dan's last statement had been quite to his liking.

"Mr. Morgan, you are doubtless aware that there is one emotion, one passion stronger than love. Will you name it, please?"

Dan looked thoughtful and then replied slowly. "Hate, I suppose."

"You are quite right. May we assume from your last statement that you had no feeling of love for the decedent?"

"That is correct."

"But you did feel hate?"

"Hardly that."

"Dislike?"

"Yes."

"Intense dislike?"

Dan considered. "You could say that."

"I wish with the permission of your Honor to make an observation to the jury in connection with the testimony. And that is that there is a very thin line between deadly anger and intense dislike. Now, Mr. Morgan, you say the decedent was standing in the room as you left it?"

"I do."

"When she found her advances unavailing did she try to exert any physical pressure upon you?"

"She did."

"Because of this was there anything like a struggle between you?"

Dan hesitated over this. "Well, in a way," he said slowly.

"O God!" Tom muttered. "I hope the jury recognizes an honest man when they see him."

The District Attorney's voice had an air of triumph in it.

"*That* will be all, Mr. Morgan."

"Anything on re-direct, Counselor?"

Harrison rose. His face was haggard with the look of defeat upon it.

"Mr. Morgan, will you please describe in detail just what this so-called *struggle* was."

"Well, Mrs. Ruston had . . . this is rather distasteful to me to tell . . ."

"I realize that, but it is necessary."

"She had put both arms around my neck, and I had to loose them in order to get away."

"That was the extent of the struggle?"

"It was."

"Now, I am going to ask you only one more question. *Did you murder Paula Ruston?*"

"I did not." Dan's voice was clear and emphatic.

"That will be all. The defense rests, your Honor."

"Very well, Counselor. You may step down, Mr. Morgan. Court will now adjourn until tomorrow morning at ten at which time you, Mr. Brown, may present your summation."

There was the usual rush of the Press for the door and Liza, straining her ears to catch a remark from them as they passed, heard one. "I think he's a gone duck, myself," a young man said with certainty to another.

CHAPTER XI

When Tom left her that afternoon after once again driving her home, he looked at her anxiously. "I'm going to try to see Dan for a minute tonight by grace of Brown. I wish it were possible for you to come along."

She shook her head. "I couldn't anyway, Tom. I haven't got the strength. I'm so afraid I can't hold up till . . . till the end."

"Yes, you can," he said. "There's practically no limit to what a brave person can bear. And you're surely that. Have you any special message to send to Dan? Just your love, I suppose?"

"No, not that, please. We'll assume that. Tell him I send him my heart's admiration and respect. Can you remember that? *Only* that," she added.

Tom looked at her for a moment without speaking. "I can certainly remember. It's not the usual message from a wife to a husband but I think it's the most beautiful I've ever heard. Do you keep checking with your doctor, Liza?"

She smiled. "Oh yes. I have ever conceivable kind of pill. But the thing the medical profession doesn't seem able to dispense is 'balm of Gilead.' Ever hear of that?"

"Many times." Tom smiled too. "Hold steady," he said. "That might come yet."

"I can never half express my thanks to you, Tom, for what you've done for me during these unspeakable days. The girls have all been so kind taking turns to be with me when you couldn't. But you've been my tower of strength. Dan has always looked back and when he's seen you beside me—I don't think I imagined this—his face seemed to relax a little. You have been wonderful."

"You're the wonderful one. I've never known a girl like

you. If I'd met you during college days who knows what might have happened!"

"Not a thing," Lida said promptly. "Matt's perfect for you and you know it."

"Of course I do. I was only joking. But I can at least be fond of you, can't I?"

"Please do. I need everybody's affection right now. And by the way, I return it."

"It's a bargain!" Tom said, and then suddenly caught her arm. "What is it? Do you feel faint? Just all at once you turned white. I'll take you into the house."

He didn't leave until Horace and Maggie had taken full charge. Added to her own reassurances Horace kept repeating, "It's all right. We'll take care of her, sir. When she's had a bit o' rest an' some dinner she'll feel better. It's been a bad time this, an' no mistake."

She went to her room early, giving orders that if anyone called she was not to be disturbed.

"They'll understand, Ma'am, that you're off to an early sleep," Horace assured her.

"*Sleep!*" she thought to herself, as she lay in bed, watching through the open French doors as the evening shadows fell. Even a recumbent position was rest at least after the hard bench of the day. But *sleep!* She wondered what it would feel like once again to drift off at once into a peaceful unconsciousness. There would be tomorrow, according to Tom, the summations of Harrison and of Brown, then the charge to the jury and then . . . the utter agony of the wait for the verdict. Could she live through this? Could she endure the suspense without breaking? She had to, for Dan's sake. And oh, surely, *surely* innocence must prevail. Would those twelve men not see that in his complete honesty Dan had even made certain admissions prejudicial to his own case?

And yet. Slowly, steadily as the District Attorney himself had done, she built up statement upon statement, evidence upon evidence, that could, her logical mind had to admit, seem to be proof of Dan's guilt. Harrison and his staff doing their capable best, had had so little to go on to refute this. Then as she lay there, tense and anguished, a warmth stole strangely through her veins. In the face of all temptation Dan

had never wavered. He had been faithful. He had been true
to her and to the best in himself.

For a long time she held this fact close to her heart as
though it were a living thing. She saw him again on the witness stand, a strong man with the marks of the long years'
struggle upon his face, accentuated now by the threat, all undeserved, of a new and utter disaster. She went over again in
her mind the testimony of the woman Donna, and Dan's restrained explanation of it. She felt now no more anger at his
secrecy with her, only an understanding of his refusal to
bring up the buried tragedy of the past; and her very soul
ached with pity for him. His mother! He must have loved her
deeply, *and there had been a child*.

The hours passed. The crickets in the garden sang their
threnody of summer from the warm September grasses. She
could hear car after car coming into the drive, voices at the
door and then silence as the callers went away, at Horace's
behest. It had to be so now, for she could not have spoken
with anyone tonight without breaking down. The doctor had
told her she might take two of the capsules . . .

When even the crickets were still and no more sounds
came from the road, Liza suddenly sat up in bed overtaken
by a new thought. From the first moment when she had
heard of the murder, through all the damaging deadly testimony of the trial, even with the knowledge she felt she alone
possessed, she had never for one single instant doubted Dan's
innocence of the crime. It was only now—and when she most
needed solace—that she realized this was in itself an unusual
situation. *Any* wife, no matter how completely devoted,
might have been excused in the face of the circumstances for
one terror stricken moment in which she asked herself, *Could
it be? Could he be guilty?* Even though once suppressed
and forgotten, the fleeting question might have passed
through her mind. Indeed it would seem almost inevitable
that such would be the case. But it had not been so with her.
Just as Dan had been faithful in his actions so she had been
in her very thoughts.

She sank back on the pillows exhausted, but curiously relaxed. For the first time since the trial began, she fell at once
to sleep.

In court next morning there was a new undercurrent of excitement. It could be felt in the members of the Press—like hounds at last in sight of the fox, Liza thought bitterly. And yet they had their job to do. The strange muffled wave of half sound and half silence seemed to lap about the room, now crowded to capacity.

Tom came in and sat beside her. "I got to see Dan by special arrangement for a few minutes last night. I gave him your message and he said to please give the same back to you."

"Thank you. How did he seem?"

"He's a stout fellow," Tom said, his voice husky. "You know, Liza, if things should—by any chance—go against him Harrison will *appeal* at once. You know that, don't you?"

The Sergeant at Arms was calling upon them to rise. Judge Carter entered, looking taller than usual in his black robe, and stood before them. Did a Judge sleep well at night? Liza wondered. The crier went through his usual phrases, Dan entered, the lawyers were in their places, they all sat down and the Judge rapped his gavel.

When Harrison rose to give his summation, Liza's head felt light and heavy by turns. The hours of unaccustomed sleep had evidently drugged her mind instead of refreshing it. She forced herself to concentrate upon Harrison's words, but sometimes they escaped her. She knew, however, that his voice had been strong and full and assured as he began.

"Your Honor, gentlemen of the jury, there now lies upon me the heaviest responsibility that a man can assume: that of saving an innocent life. As you know the defense does not need to *prove* the innocence of the defendant who sits here before you. The burden lies entirely upon the state to prove his guilt. And gentlemen, this is what the state has *not done* as I will proceed to show you."

Slowly then, with an eloquence which Liza would never have suspected, Harrison began to describe first Dan himself, his standing in the world of business, his integrity, his veracity, as brought out by witness and by his own straightforward testimony.

The room was hot and Liza felt her head swimming as Harrison's voice went on and on. He was deliberate, he was forceful. It seemed to her no jury could listen to him and not believe everything he said. He pictured poignantly before them the unfortunate young marriage and its tragic results, resolving, unrelentingly, the testimony of the woman, Donna, until nothing was left of the whole relationship but her greedy acceptance of Dan's undeserved generosity over the years.

He dealt then with Paula Ruston, of her annoying pursuit of a man who cared nothing for her; of the business facts which led up to the defendant's call upon her on the fateful night; of his definite purpose in going, his utter confidence in her acceptance of his proposal for the purchase of the stock; and then, with tremendous dramatic effect, he pictured her scorn of the proposal and her seductive attempts to use all her beauty as allure to attain her own evil ends. He pictured vividly and with a poignance that seemed to Liza irresistible the defendant's flight from the scene of temptation, leaving the decedent alive behind him, following him to the door, his precipitous exit from the building, using again with every word delicately sharpened to a sword's point, the classic illustration of Joseph and the wife of Potiphar. There was scarcely the sound of breathing in the courtroom. The jurors sat with tense, grave faces, and even among the members of the Fourth Estate there was no movement.

"Gentlemen of the Jury," Harrison finally concluded, "I have told you the truth, which is what you are here to discover. The *truth,* which is mightier than all fallible assumptions, mightier than all circumstantial evidence which sometimes, as you well know, accidentally touches a good, noble and innocent man. The unshakable truth, I have given you. On your part I expect you as twelve honest and intelligent men to return the only verdict possible. *Not guilty."*

The sweat was running down Harrison's cheeks as he sank into his chair. The Judge broke the almost unbearable silence. "Since it is now well past twelve, court will adjourn until two o'clock this afternoon."

As soon as they were in the little restaurant where she always had lunch with Tom if he was there, Liza began quickly, "I missed a lot of what he said for my head felt so swimmy, but oh, Tom, wasn't Harrison marvelous?"

"He was superb," Tom said. "I told you he's the best there is and I've never heard him do better than he did today."

"Then"—Liza looked appealingly at him—"then you think . . . it . . . will be . . . all right?"

"I think he made a very fine impression on the jury. But my dear girl, I must prepare you for one thing. Brown is good too, devilish good, or he wouldn't be where he is. And he has the last word. I've often thought this is unfair but it's the law and we have to stick with it. The thing about Brown is that while Harrison slowly and eloquently builds up his case, Brown's style is just the opposite, which gives him the advantage of contrast. He sums up in quick, staccato sentences, puncturing all that's gone before with what he claims are *facts,* hitting the jury with them like bullets. I just felt I had to warn you. So far, so good, Liza, but remember there is more to come, and we must just hope and hold steady."

He urged her to eat, with a sternness in his voice she had never heard before, so she forced down the food he ordered, drank the wine and then the strong black coffee at the end. She admitted then that her head had cleared and she now was in full possession of herself. "I think I'm ready to take whatever comes," she said with a brave attempt at a smile as they rose to go back.

The courtroom had never settled so quickly and so quietly to order as it did that afternoon. Strange, Liza thought, how the faces of the merely curious, brought here by the drama as the newspapers unfolded it day by day, should now look tense and even anxious. Could it be that they *cared,* these strangers? Or was it to them merely the suspense of the final act of the play?

All was deathly quiet as the District Attorney rose and bowed to the Judge. "Your Honor." Then he faced about. "And gentlemen of the jury. If it were possible for me to accept the pleasing, flattering, touching description of the defendant which the learned Counsel for the defense has just this morning given you; if it were possible for me to believe that all he has told of the circumstances concerning that dreadful night of March twenty-fifth, is *the truth,* no one would be happier than I."

"Liar!" Tom muttered under his breath.

"But I cannot do that. Because, gentlemen, the *truth* is not a matter of a man's moving eloquence. The truth is shown only in the light of the *facts* which support it. And gentlemen, the state will prove to you now that the facts in this case point to one conclusion and one only, that the defendant, Daniel Morgan, is guilty of this crime.

"Now, let us begin with the crime itself. It is only natural that your thoughts should have been so centered upon the defendant that at times you may have forgotten the victim, Paula Ruston. A woman, young, beautiful, vivid, filled with eager life, who on the night we speak of was killed, gentlemen, by cruel and relentless hands, almost with a song on her lips, according to testimony given. She was *murdered*. She is now dead. That bright life is ended. These, gentlemen, are the first facts with which we have to deal. Facts which no one, even the defense,"—he glanced over his shoulder—"can deny. Now, with these firmly fixed in your minds, let us go on . . ."

It was as Tom had told her. Brown was more than merely *good* in his part, he was diabolically clever and compelling. Not only every word, every action, but every tiny suggestion, innuendo and possibility, were somehow turned by him into the *facts* which he needed and boasted of producing. There was a terrible assurance in every cadence of his voice, sometimes rising to unexpected harshness and then sinking again to its steady, deadly aim at the twelve men in front of him. After the first hour Liza felt all hope leave her heart. Glancing at Tom she saw, even on his controlled countenance, the mirror of her own despair. And on the faces of the jury there was a certain look of intentness, of acceptance, as though each was thinking, *This, then, must be the truth.*

It was three o'clock when there could be heard a stir at the outer door of the courtroom. There was a break in the attention of the crowd and a turning of heads as the muffled sounds changed to a voice and there could be seen coming slowly up the aisle an old woman supported on the one side by a liveried chauffeur and on the other by a Sergeant of the court. The voice became clearer.

"I have to speak to the Judge."

Liza, who had sat stunned clutched Tom's arm. *"It's Mrs. Moreland,"* she whispered.

"Your Honor, I have testimony. I have evidence I have to give at once before it's too late." She was now nearing the front of the room.

Brown turned about in righteous anger. "Your Honor, I protest this most unseemly interruption. I respectfully request that . . ."

The Judge motioned Brown to be quiet.

"In view of the seriousness of this case, I cannot refuse to hear any testimony offered. Will you approach the Bench, Madam, and give us your name."

She seemed to sag for a moment, but the men held her up.

"I am Elizabeth Moreland and as soon as I knew I hadn't long to live I came as fast as I could to clear Dan . . . Mr. Morgan. He is completely innocent. I . . . I was the one who did it . . . who . . . who killed Paula." Her voice broke in a sob.

It was as though a wind had swept violently through the courtroom. The Judge rapped hard with his gavel.

"Silence!" he ordered. "And no one will leave this room until Court is adjourned." His eyes were on the Press, half of whom were already on their feet.

"Madam," he said gently, "are you able to go up to the witness stand and be sworn? You may be seated, Mr. Brown."

Mrs. Moreland reached the stand and took the oath, her hand shaking violently as it lay on the Bible. "Could I have some water?" she asked faintly. The matron brought it at once and supported her as she drank.

"Now, Mrs. Moreland, could you tell us in your own words just what happened on the night of the . . . the night with which we are concerned," the Judge said, his voice still strangely gentle.

Mrs. Moreland tried to straighten. Strands of her usually carefully coiffed gray hair were loose about her face, her hat was awry and the small fur had slipped from her shoulders.

"The doctor saw me just about an hour ago," she began, "and told me my heart . . . I haven't been well . . . he said I might go any hour, any minute so I came as fast as I could to clear Dan—Mr. Morgan. You see I had thought if the jury would find him innocent I would never need to . . . confess."

"But now, Mrs. Moreland," the Judge prompted quietly, "it is necessary that you should tell us everything. In your own way," he added.

She sat for a moment as though deciding how to start and then began again.

"I have no relatives in the world. I always thought of Paula—Mrs. Ruston—as a daughter. I gave her so much, I poured out my love on her and I always thought . . ." She stopped and wiped her eyes.

"Last winter," she went on, "I took the apartment adjoining hers so I would be near her. The closets in our bedrooms backed up on each other and I suggested we have a little narrow door cut through so that if I got sick in the night she could get to me quickly. She didn't like the idea too well. She said it invaded her privacy but I insisted. She didn't want anyone to know so the carpenter did the work on the maid's days off and put in this little panel door. Nobody would ever guess it was there. She said it was *only* to be used in emergency. Before I knew how strongly she felt about it I think I mentioned once to Mr. and Mrs. Morgan or maybe it was to Mr. Dunmore, that we would have a door cut through, but if I did they probably never thought of it again. Even if they had, even if the police had found it, no one would ever have suspected that I . . . You see I loved her so much."

Her voice faltered and she took another sip of the water.

"That night, I had gone to bed when I heard voices in Paula's bedroom. I was sure one was Dan's—Mr. Morgan's—but of course I couldn't hear what was said. After a while the outer door slammed and I knew he was gone. Then I heard Paula crying and sobbing sort of hysterically and . . . and cursing. It was odd. *Those* words came through. I thought maybe I could do something for her. I was anxious, for I'd never known her to cry before. So I decided this *was* an emergency and for the first time I went through the little door in the closet."

She stopped again and looked pathetically at the Judge. "I'm not sure I can go on," she said.

"Please try, Mrs. Moreland. What comes next is extremely important."

"Well, she was angry that I had come in and she turned on me. She said everything was my fault. That Dan would have nothing to do with her and he was the only man she ever wanted, and that I had introduced them and tried to make a

match between them—and that was true only Dan married
someone else—and that I was always meddling in her affairs
and she only put up with it because of the money I gave her
and that she . . . she *hated* me."

Mrs. Moreland breathed heavily. She looked piteously at
the Judge but he only nodded, gravely.

"Then," she went on, her voice breaking, "She caught me
by the shoulders and shook me. Like a dog would shake a
rat. Your Honor, none of us knows what we would do if we
were attacked. She kept on. My hands were free and they've
always been strong." She held them up. They were indeed,
not the slender fingertips of the usual lady of leisure, but
miller's hands, artist's hands, with thick, blunt fingers. "I
managed to get them to her throat and I pressed as hard as I
could. I didn't really know what I was doing. I only knew
that her grip on my shoulders was relaxing a little. She tried
to reach my hands but I only pressed harder and harder. I
was clear beyond myself then. I pushed her back till she fell
across the bed and even then I still kept pressing until I saw
. . . I saw . . ."

Mrs. Moreland's head fell upon her breast. Through the
dead silence of the room her voice, hardly more than a whisper, could be heard the length of it..

"Oh, to think she . . . she *hated* me."

Harrison was suddenly on his feet. His own voice was unsteady.

"Your Honor, in view of the confession we have just
heard, I move to dismiss the indictment."

"Mr. Brown?" the Judge questioned.

The District Attorney rose slowly. "This is most unusual
procedure but I will certainly not oppose the motion."

"Motion granted," said the Judge. "The Jury is excused,
with our thanks. Before adjournment I wish to ask . . ."

Liza caught Tom's arm. "I have to go, Tom. I don't feel
well, but I'll be all right. John will take me home. You just
stay and see Dan." And, keeping close to the seats, like a slim
wraith, she managed to slip to the door and go out.

John was waiting. He had made an excuse not to go into
the courtroom that day. She told him the news that Mr. Morgan was free, was cleared, that she now wanted to get home
as fast as possible. Mr. Morgan would no doubt be detained

for quite a while before he could leave. John's relief and delight were pathetically voluble. He couldn't say enough. "But who done it?" he asked. When she told him he could hardly speak for astonishment. Then when Liza sank into the back seat and closed her eyes, he concentrated upon the road before him and kept silent.

As they reached home she asked him to check her own car and bring it to the front of the house. He looked startled but assented. When she went inside she moved slowly, slowly, through the rooms, looking at each as though for the last time. She went on out to the kitchen, told the news to Horace and Maggie, who were beside themselves with relief and amazement.

"I'm going on up to my room, Horace. Could you bring me a tray there? Just something simple . . ."

"You're clean done out an' no wonder. I'll have something up to you in no time an' then you can rest till Mr. Morgan comes. He'll have to stay on talkin' to people an' mebbe to do something for poor Mrs. Moreland. You did right to come on home. Ah, a strange Providence, this, but it's ended right for us all, anyway."

Liza went up to her room, got out her largest suitcase and almost blindly began filling it with clothes. She ate quickly the sandwiches and tea Horace brought, staving off as best she could the flood of his excited conversation. Then she sat down at the precious little escritoire and drew paper toward her, wondering now that it had come to the end, what she could find to say. For as in a blinding flash, during Mrs. Moreland's testimony she had seen what she must do. During all the anguished days of the trial she had never once thought of what it would be like if Dan was acquitted and came home, where they would meet alone, face to face, man and wife, standing close together, safe from the yawning hell that had threatened them . . . She knew then. She knew.

She put the pen slowly to the paper, pondering each word as she wrote.

DEAR DAN:

Thank God, oh, *thank God* you are safe and free. There are no words strong enough in the language to tell you the relief in my heart. You will understand this. But, Dan, I will not see you when you come home, for I am leaving. I hope you can forgive me. You see, I have deceived you from the very first. I have not been honest with you, for I loved you for years before you ever asked me to marry you. Then when you offered me the strange bargain I accepted at once for I would have married you under any circumstances whatsoever. I *hoped,* of course—but I soon learned you meant exactly what you said: that our union would be a sort of business relationship, and that you would dislike, even *hate* any show of emotion from me. You have told me that more than once. So I have kept on, trying to fulfill your conditions. But I can do this no longer, for in all the years, I have never loved you so deeply, so passionately, as I have during these last terrible days. If I were to see you now, even touch your hand, I would give myself away completely and, to you, I know this would be the last insufferable, unnerving straw after all you have gone through. My restraint is all used up. My control is gone, so I must go, myself.

Later on you can get in touch with me, of course, at Aunt Sarah's. I will do anything you wish, but I cannot go on living with you as we have been doing. After hearing some of the testimony at the trial I think I can better understand your own feelings. Please try to understand mine and forgive me. God bless you always.

LIZA

She sealed the envelope, addressed it, picked up her suitcase and went softly down the stairs. She could hear Horace and Maggie still talking animatedly in the kitchen. She propped the envelope in front of Dan's place at the table already laid for dinner, then she went out the front door, unseen, got into the car and drove away.

It was nearly midnight when she reached Waverly. The big white house on the outskirts was unlighted except for the rays of the full moon which now bathed it even as they had shone on the road she had just gone over. There were no clouds, so a brightness like day picked out the windows as though candles were burning behind them. Liza parked the car and, carrying her suitcase with an effort, made her way to the back door. It would be better to rouse Mrs. Phinney at this hour than Aunt Sarah. She knocked and then called softly. But it was Aunt Sarah who had been lying wakeful. She heard and came hurrying down the back stairs, her gray hair in a twist on the top of her head, her wrapper flying about her.

"*Liza!*" she said in a breaking voice, "what's the verdict?"

"He's free, Aunt Sarah, completely cleared."

Then Liza did what she had never done before in her life. Very slowly and quietly as though she had practiced it for the stage, she sank down in a small inert heap on the kitchen floor.

When she came to, at last, she found herself on the old lounge against the wall with the two frightened faces leaning over her. Aunt Sarah had a glass in her hand.

"Now drink this right down. It'll warm you up. It'll put new life in you. You weren't in too good shape to drive by yourself, that's certain, but you did right to come on ahead of Dan. He'll likely have to wait to clear some loose ends up. We'll take care of you. This is where you ought to be at a time like this. Do you feel better?"

"I'm really all right now. What a shame to give you such a scare. I'll go right up to bed and you can get back to yours. I'll tell you everything tomorrow. Tonight I'm just too tired to talk."

"An' *overdone,* that's what it is an' I'd say no wonder! The miracle is you held up as long as you did. Well, we've got the big news, anyway, an' the rest will keep. Dan can fill in the details from his side when he gets here."

Liza did not reply, but she ate the hot soup and crackers Mrs. Phinney brought to her. Then they helped her up to her old room, where Mrs. Phinney partly unpacked the suitcase and Aunt Sarah put her to bed as if she were a child.

"I'll leave your door open," she said, "so if you want anything, just call. I've a feeling by tomorrow you'll be like a new woman. Well, at least tonight I can ease up a little on my prayers!"

When she was alone, Liza lay very still as though all energy had been drained out of her. She could not even consider whether or not she had done right to leave the letter and to go away. That and all the incredible events of the day moved in a strange kaleidoscope through her mind, which had no power of its own to pass upon them. So she lay, supine, suspended it seemed between waking and sleeping, almost between life and death, even as the old town around her lay in the hush of the night.

The big clock in the hall below had struck two when she heard, at first vaguely, a car hard driven along the quiet street. She sat up as it turned into the driveway, as its door slammed, as steps came along the walk and across the porch. She heard the front door open. Oh, Aunt Sarah, then, had left it unlocked! Liza was on her feet now as quick steps came up the stairs, as Dan himself entered through her open door and into the room. They stood there, then, facing each other in the moonlight, Liza a slim, white shape with her braids which no one had thought to undo, hanging down at each side of her face; Dan, haggard, disheveled, his breath coming heavily as though he and not the car had physically traversed the miles between them. And all about them the air was throbbing as with winged heartbeats.

"Liza," he began, "it took me so long to see to everything —and to Mrs. Moreland—but I started as soon as I read your note and I've driven here as fast as I dared. I must tell you, and you *have* to believe me, that I was planning if I was acquitted and got home tonight, to explain to you all that had happened to change me, to beg you to let me make a new bargain, to begin all over again, to . . ."

Then he stopped. "Why am I waiting to say all this? What I want to tell you is that I can't live without you! Darling, I love you! *I love you!*"

And he swept her into his arms.